THE BRAY HOUSE

Eilís Ní Dhuibhne

Attic Press
Dublin

First published in 1990 by
Attic Press
44 East Essex Street
Dublin 2

British Library Cataloguing in Publication Data
Ni Dhuibhne, Eilis
        The Bray house.
        I. Title
        823'.914 [F]

        ISBN 0-946211-96-5

Cover Design: Paula Nolan
Origination: Attic Press
Made and printed in Great Britain by
The Guernsey Press Co. Ltd., Guernsey, Channel Islands.

The publishers acknowledge the assistance of The Arts Council/An Chomhairle Ealaíon who grant aided this book. The author was assisted by the "Authors Royalty Scheme Loan" of The Arts Council/An Chomhairle Ealaíon.

To my mother and father

Chapter One

We embarked at Gothenburg just before dawn on 28 April.
The sea was black, dappled in places with milky blobs of
light, reflections from the port authority lamps. At regular
intervals the beam from the lighthouse swept like a silver
scythe around the harbour, illuminating slices of vessels at
anchor in the shelter of the port: ships, yachts, hovercraft, sat
still and silent on the dark gloss of water. Red lights glowed
like brilliant rubies on the pilot boats and behind us, in the
eastern sky, the morning star shone serenely. Although it
was almost five o'clock, a vast silence enveloped everything,
and we had the impression that the whole harbour and even
the whole city still slept, and we were the only active people
in the world, as we began our long westward journey into
the unknown.

I was affected by strong feelings of heroism, loneliness
and exhilaration, as I left the embracing arms of the harbour,
and crossed the bar to the open sea. And I felt certain that all
my crew shared my emotions. Only the virtually dead could
have been impervious to the powerful sentimental energy

ignited by this most elemental and traditional of humanity's pursuits: setting out on a voyage of exploration.

Most of all, of course, what moved us was a sense of novelty: a clean slate, a new leaf, an open road, were what we possessed for the moment, and in the fresh and springy atmosphere hatchets were buried and goodwill blossomed. The tensions which had inevitably developed during the long period of preparation for the voyage, as we tussled with packets and vitamin pills and quarrelled about protective clothing, vanished. We loved one another for the first, and, frankly, for the last time.

A few days later, this state of affairs no longer prevailed. Already we had seen and suffered too much. That is to say, we had seen absolutely nothing, apart from grey empty water which looked dismally dead but was certainly vibrant with radioactivity. This obliged us to remain encased in our comfortable but somewhat restrictive suits. Hence the suffering.

We had made them as attractive as possible, having had them dyed in colours of our own choice: Karen had a brilliant pink and deep purple set, Jenny one blue-green and one, rather gloomy, brown. Karl had selected a red and a blue, quite predictably, since men, simple souls, invariably favour blue and red above all other colours. I had chosen a black for practicality and a yellow for days when I was bored with black. But, although we looked like a group of joggers or an aerobics class, we did not feel it. The cloth of which the suits were fashioned was, of necessity, closely woven, and did not allow the skin to breathe.

"If only we could sunbathe on deck or something!" Karen, my principal assistant, moaned, in a childish manner which I knew, all too well, to be typical of her. Karen tended to whinge. The rest of us nodded grimly. We shared her sentiment - at least I did - although sunbathing has been discouraged in Sweden for several years, with good reason. But we were less than thankful to hear complaints of any kind at this early stage in the project. Worse discomforts would certainly come our way, and what is the point of grumbling about the inevitable? As I observed Karen's thin white face, with its gash of red lipstick smeared like a skinless snake from cheek to cheek and its dry, chemically coloured hair encircling it like a cloud of acid rain, I began to feel my subdued dislike of her pushing to the surface of my consciousness. It was with the greatest effort that I pushed it into the nether regions where it must, for the time being, remain buried. I had not made a mistake in selecting Karen. I had not.

I rarely, if ever, make mistakes.

Certainly it had been no easy task to persuade Karen to join the crew of the *Saint Patrick*. I recalled vividly the scene in my office, on a day six months prior to our departure, when I had set my final trap for her, having been unsuccessfully dropping persuasive hints, flattering promises, for a month or more. My bait on the occasion in question had been a pound of real coffee, which a colleague of mine had presented me with recently in return for a small favour (a glowing review of a book which had little to recommend it, apart from that store of coffee which its writer had secreted for years in her freezer in anticipation of a rainy day).

"Others will come too, Karen," I pointed out, as I poured the dark delicious liquid into a china mug and sniffed ecstatically. "It's going to be quite a large project."

"Oh, yes, I know all that," she said, extending her long brownish fingers, tipped with crimson talons. How somebody who is one of the world's most skilful diggers can preserve hands in a state comparable to those of a Chinese empress has always been a mystery to me. But Karen, a silly but essentially efficient woman, could. Modern technology played its part, no doubt, in the shaping of her hands and other aspects of her feminine image. But it took more than technology to maintain that perfectly-balanced combination of traditional femininity, albeit in its less worthy manifestations, and brilliant employability. One aspect of her personality, a major one, warned that she would be altogether too individualistic, too concerned with personal and domestic affairs, too interested in freedom, to fit into any work structure. One might have expected conflicts, clashes, all-out battles to be waging constantly in her mind and heart. But it was not so. Miraculously she juggled and jigsawed, and all the diversities formed an admirable unity. Perhaps in her reconciliation of opposite forces she was not all that unique among women. Nonetheless there was an intensity about everything she did that certainly rendered her somewhat special.

My proffered information about the project was so much verbiage. At the time in question, Karen, and indeed most people in Uppsala and probably all over Sweden had heard about my plans for a trip to Ireland. I had allowed the word to spread in the form of a rumour, hoping thus to arouse the desire of the ambitious and curious to find out more about the project and even to participate in it. I had succeeded in instigating plenty of gossip but not much else. The idea of sailing across the North Sea to Ireland in order to excavate sites buried under mountains of nuclear ash had provoked professional envy and spite, but so far nobody in the Swedish archaeological world had been sufficiently embittered to offer to steal some of the glory and limelight from me.

"There'll be two or three others, at least," I continued. "To staff the boat, you know."

"Who are they?" she demanded, in an unnecessarily abrupt tone. Among her many other strident characteristics, Karen possesses a deliberate, downright, and rather affected forthrightness, which frequently amounts to little more than bad manners.

"I can't tell you at the moment," I said truthfully. "I'm still in the process of interviewing candidates. Lots of people are interested in taking part in such an important dig, you know. It's going to be important, Karen. It's going to be of real historical importance. I don't know how important, yet. But even the attempt - the attempt is significant in itself. Even if we find nothing, it's crucially significant." I paused, exhausted by my own meaningless rhetoric. "It'll take time to narrow down the applicants and pick out the right ones."

The latter sentence was entirely false: sometimes it is necessary to tell a white lie or two in the interests of a greater scientific truth.

"Hm!" she said, crossing her legs, which were encased in shocking pink tights. "I bet it will."

She drained her cup and handed it to me for a refill, which I willingly donated in the cause of science, although real coffee was a commodity rarer and more valuable now than gold.

"I don't know," Karen drawled, to emphasise her doubt, presumably. "I have a funny feeling about this whole idea. It's too bloody dangerous, isn't it? I mean to say - Ireland! We probably wouldn't survive there for a day!"

"It is a risky project," I agreed. "And I do think you should take plenty of time to think it over. But of course I feel you'd be an invaluable asset to the team because you are, quite simply, the best field archaeologist in Sweden. That's not all, though. More than professional skills will be required on this trip. The people involved will need to have all kinds of other qualities in order to survive the rigours of it. Life skills, as it were. And I really believe you have the right qualities, Karen. I believe that, and that is why I am approaching you rather than anyone else. But you have to make the decision. You have to think it over and finally decide for yourself whether my assessment of you is correct, after all. Whether you are actually ready for a trip of this - well, for want of a better word - magnitude? You must be very very sure that this is for you, before you make the decision to go ahead."

"Yes," she said thoughtfully. The second mug of coffee had already vanished, and I sincerely hoped I would not be obliged to make more. Deep inroads had been made into the golden bag, with its picture of a fat Dutch maiden presiding over a fat china pot, its promise of fecundity and relaxation. I did not want to sacrifice my precious memento of a more caffeine-rich past too quickly. So I did not break the silence which followed Karen's monosyllable, but sipped most delicately from my cup, and waited for her to speak again. Which she did, eventually.

"I'm confused. I'm really awfully confused. I want to go. And I don't want to go. Do you know what I mean? I know there are all sorts of pros and cons that I should be able to sort out myself. But I haven't been able to do it, not so far anyway. And then there's Thomas to think of ..."

"You're worried about Thomas?"

Thomas was Karen's seven-year old son. She had had this boy at the relatively late age of thirty-five, and soon after his birth became divorced. As often happens in such cases, he became the be-all and the end-all of her existence. She was obsessed with him and his needs, so that he both justified and ruined her own life. Not surprisingly, under such circumstances, he was an obnoxious brat.

"Oh yes! How can I leave him, for such an indefinite period?"

I felt that any sane human being would welcome the opportunity to be parted from him for any period, the more indefinite the better. And if he didn't like it, well, serve him right. I could think of few things which would be better for him than a prolonged stretch of misery, preferably in solitary confinement in the kind of prison which has not existed in Sweden for almost a century. I doubted, however, if being parted from Karen would upset him all that much. My experience of him was that his only ambition in life was to stuff himself with as many bars of chocolate as his quite big stomach could hold, and he was not particular as to the identity of the donor of the goodies.

I was not, of course, foolish enough to be frank with Karen on the subject of Thomas. But no coward soul is mine, and I took the not inconsiderable risk of offering her some advice.

"Look, frankly, I think he will get on very well with his childminder. And," I added as an afterthought, "his granny." (I make a point of familiarising myself with the minutest details of my staffs' domestic routines. It is astonishing how frequently scraps of such apparently trivial information can be put to good use).

I continued: "It'll do him no end of good. And it'll do you good, too, to be away from him for a while. The relationship will improve enormously."

"Do you really think so?"

"Yes, oh yes, I really think so. I was practically brought up by a childminder myself, and it did me nothing but good. So do not worry one little bit about Thomas. You'll miss him a bit at first, but it'll all work out for the best, you'll see. However," I paused again, "I would like to qualify that by saying one more thing, and that is the following: I think the most important lesson we've learned from the disaster is that human feeling is extremely significant. More significant than scientific truth, for instance. So, once again - and I do want to stress this - please consider the whole matter very very carefully, before making a final decision. Consult your feelings. Allow them to instruct you."

I stared at Karen, straight in the eye, and allowed this gem to sink in. She was by now considerably more confused than she had been to start with. In short, my strategy had worked.

I picked up the urn and poured the final drop of coffee into her mug.

"I will interview my final selection of other candidates for the project this evening, and tomorrow I will complete my list of personnel and set to work. Maybe you could drop in to see me at some stage?"

"What time?" asked Karen, in a steady but thin voice. She picked at her tights with one long red nail.

"Oh, the same time as today. I'll be free then."

"All right," she said, getting up and walking lugubriously towards the door. "Thanks for the coffee."

She left my room.

It lost colour immediately, I observed. It was a grey room, with black furniture and some plants on the window sill. But these did not add much life to it. Karen, in her bright pink tights and pink and black and yellow jumper, had glowed like a lantern in the sombre surroundings. The glow emanated, not just from her clothes, but from her inner self. Although she was sloppy, confused and indecisive, she had

11

a certain strength, certain warmth, a certain motherliness, which were very appealing. The project needed her, for more than one reason.

Or so it had seemed, at that point. Now I was not so sure. What good were a warm heart and bright clothes in the middle of a poison ocean, where the essential characteristic for survival was simple stoicism? Karen's grumbling was natural and human, but that did not render it any more appropriate to the situation.

"Who knows what we'll find, further on?" Karl asked, with a chuckle. He had a tendency to chuckle, even when making the most banal remarks. He seemed to feel it incumbent upon himself to extract from life the maximum quantity of humour, and, even when this was beyond him, he liked to pretend that even the most banal or uncomfortable situations were comical. The effect of this habit could be disconcerting. But he was very funny as often as not, and was on the whole an engaging creature. So I had considered, at least, in the early days of the voyage, and I congratulated myself on having had the perspicacity to select him, too.

Not, indeed, that I'd had any choice. As I have previously pointed out, my comment to Karen during our fateful interview had fallen short of the truth, which was, to put it bluntly, that not a single person had applied for a place on the project at that stage, although I had been advertising furiously for well over a month. But fortune smiled on me, as is its habit, in the nick of time. Karen had not left my office for more than five minutes when the telephone rang, and a male voice made an enquiry about the Ireland Excavations. That was Karl's voice: deep and masculine, which I always like, and tinged with an American twang, which I am also rather fond of. He came to my flat on the very same evening, along with his friend, Jenny. They were both extremely presentable: he robust, with substantial quantities of curly brown hair on his head and face, she tall, slender, beautiful, and perfectly silent. He looked like a friendly bear, and she like a medieval madonna, wooden and serene. Karl gave me their credentials, which were more than adequate, under the circumstances. Before the short visit was over, I had offered them the job, and they had accepted. Jenny I was not sure of, but she came with Karl, so to speak, and, since he seemed to have her under his thumb, I did not feel there was any cause for concern.

So far she had given none, although her persistent taciturnity - I could not go so far as to call it sulkiness, although that is perhaps what it was - was disconcerting. It was, however, preferable to consistent complaining, and I was willing to put up with it, for the time being anyway. I knew that the time would come when she would become more vocal, and looked forward to it with curiosity, as one waits for a child to say its first words. With Jenny, as with a child, it was a matter of maturing. She was still the quintessential maiden: as long as she had Karl there as her spokesman, taking responsibility for her, she was too lazy to bother asserting herself. Laziness, that was what she suffered from, I decided after a few days' acquaintanceship with her. And this discovery somehow made it easier to live with her.

Chapter Two

Since my crew was, of necessity, so limited in number, I was forced to require of it the operation of a rigid and demanding rota: twelve hours on, twelve hours off, two people always navigating in tandem. Some of my personnel, notably Karen, objected to this on the grounds that it imposed excessive strain: "That's the sort of bloody routine that drives people round the bend!" she muttered petulantly, glowering at me from behind her frizzy blond fringe. Jenny blinked her saucer-shaped eyes, possibly in agreement, but she did not say anything, being as yet, I think, too unsure of her position, naturally too timid and anxious to please, to give voice to any opinion whatsoever. Karl, fortunately, felt that I was right, and did not see any problem.

"We'll be exhausted, that's the problem, isn't it? We'll be knackered after four days, just you wait and see! Don't you believe me? Can't you see it coming?"

Karen had the habit, an endearing or an irritating one, depending on how you looked at it, of almost always finishing any statement with a question. She tried to force a response from everyone, to force acquiescence from them, by the use of this device. And the unfortunate thing about it, the most irritating thing, was that it worked as often as not. But not inevitably:

"Hell, we can sleep for twelve hours out of every twenty-four, that should be enough for anyone. It's not as if there's a whole lot else to be done around here," suddenly Karl lost his temper and spoke gruffly and angrily. He was, I was gradually discovering, given to abrupt mood swings, very shocking in effect. Luckily he did not display his uglier side very often, so it had not caused me undue concern, and at this precise moment I was grateful enough for it. Any show of solidarity with me was as nectar to a parched throat, because, already in the period of preparation, I had realised that I was in a boss versus staff situation. Karl, Karen and Jenny saw me as an enemy, from the word go. Really I do not know why. Perhaps every captain, every leader, feels that the underlings are always in league against her, or him. But I hadn't felt it before, not to the extent I did on this expedition, and therefore I was overly thankful for any support that might fortuitously come my way.

"You don't understand" Karen tossed her head and pouted. Then she pursed up her lips and refused to discuss the matter further, a technique often employed by women defeated by perfectly logical arguments, I have noted, and not one calculated to get them very far. But it does have the merit, if such it is, of ending the conversation. And so my original arrangement prevailed, willy nilly, and Karen was, after all, too experienced and conditioned an employee, too much the efficient worker bee, not to stick to it. In any case she must have realised that it was essential, especially in the early stages of the voyage, that both she and I, who were not experienced sailors, should learn as much as possible from Karl and Jenny, who were.

The arrangement was, then, that Jenny and Karen should always work together, and that Karl and I would share the alternative stint. And this order would have continued for the duration of the voyage, had not Jenny, who occasionally gave proof of being less innocent than was customarily apparent, manipulated a change at a certain stage in the journey, and rescued Karl from my dangerous clutches (as she no doubt would have put it herself).

On our very first night at sea, however, Karl and I were on duty together. I had looked forward to the opportunity of having a *tête à tête* with him, and of getting to know him better, but, alas, perhaps there was something in Karen's criticism of my roster because, when the time came, I was too tired to feel much interest in anyone. All I could do was sit in the control room in the most comfortable seat available, and concentrate on keeping awake. Karl was exhausted too: after all, we had had a very early start after what had been for me and probably for everyone a sleepless night, and our curiosity had not permitted us to take the naps we needed during the day. He did not sit, however, but stood at the control panel, examining various buttons, fiddling with the compass, and eating a packet of potato crisps, his favourite food. I decided to postpone my first lesson in driving the *Saint Patrick* until I would be feeling more receptive to information, and thought that I would be better employed for the present in amusing myself. I had not had an opportunity to do so in many weeks. So I opened a novel, in German, that I had brought with me for this purpose. I do not, I must admit, like novels, or any kind of literature: my favourite reading material has always been that which is relevant to my profession. Nor do I like foreign languages much: actually I hate them. Swedish is so flexible, so malleable, so sonorous! And so easy. But whenever I go on a dig or any trip abroad, I take only foreign books, usually literary classics which I feel all cultured individuals are expected to be familiar with. I know that if absolutely nothing else is available I will be forced to make the necessary effort, and peruse the stuff, no matter how unsavoury. I think I can safely say that I have a working knowledge of several tongues on account of this habit, which I can highly recommend to anyone interested in improving their linguistic range. Besides, I have managed to assimilate, if not enjoy, the most important literary works of most writers of the past three centuries, although I have not yet attacked Chaucer, Boccaccio, or - somewhat to my shame - the Icelandic sagas. Time is on my side, however, and I have included them in a long-term plan which will cover every work in the literary canons of Europe and America. When I have worked through my programme, I will certainly be the best-read book-hater in Sweden, if not in the world.

What I opened now was a long and heavy account of the adventures - though that is hardly the *mot propre* - of a diseased man, which was supposed to be an allegory for a diseased, twentieth century society. I found the German hard and the pace slow, and besides, I was feeling itchy in my protective suit, which, although designed for comfort as well as safety, inevitably became irksome when one was at a low ebb. The odour of Karl's crisps, that pungent mixture of grease and onion, was an additional irritant, as was the sound of his noisy mastication. All in all, conditions conspired to make concentration on German literature difficult.

After a couple of hours, long long hours, when night had closed in on us and the hero of my novel was still, incredibly, introducing himself, I found myself slipping into that state of half-sleep which is always so intoxicatingly pleasant and almost impossible to arouse oneself from. It is a kind of drug, that delicious languor, and like a drug, it is the state which usually inspires the most vivid and delightful dreams.

Now, although I willed myself to get up, to snap out of it, I could not, I was paralysed. And before my half-opened eyes the knobs and buttons and levers and lamps of the control room dissolved, and transformed slowly and inexorably into quite other objects of the most brilliant colours: purple, yellow, pink, blue, every hue the very essence of itself. At first these things were nebulous, they had substance but no form, but gradually their shapes became defined. They were flowers on a green field, the greenest field I had ever seen, and the vision was so perfectly beautiful that I felt myself bathed in happiness.

This warm sensation gave way as the image took on a more distinct form, and as my mind began to question it: a field, sloping down to the sea, and in the sea three islands, two long and low, and one having the shape of a hump-backed whale. My languor went and was replaced by a fierce curiosity, a powerful desire to know exactly what that field was, where it was, what the names of the flowers were. I knew that I possessed this information, but it was for the moment buried somewhere in my subconscious and although I strained after it I could not retrieve it. I could see names and titles printed on labels but I was illiterate in the language they used, I could not understand them.

Suddenly, my striving switched abruptly, and instead of looking for information I was being pursued by a person: a woman, black-haired, white-faced, something like Elizabeth Taylor or Scarlett O'Hara in that film: she had those histrionic brunette good looks, a kind I have never encountered in reality. I ran from this woman, through what kind of landscape I am not sure, the scenery was not specified at this point. Of course, she followed me, no matter where I ran. I ran, I ran, and voices spoke to me, but I couldn't hear what they were saying.

From a dark brown shrub, at the side of the field - which returned to the dream - a creature emerged. A small brown animal, with eyes that were not round and timid, as the eyes of arboreal animals are, but elongated, piercing, vindictive. The animal would attack, I knew, and I ran away from it now, I ran wildly, chased like a hare by both the woman - I knew, although I didn't see her, she was no longer in the dream, that she was after me - and the horrible unspeakable animal.

"Robin!"

Karl was shaking me, none too gently.

I was frightened. And yet, surprisingly reluctant to let go of my dream by waking up.

"Robin! You nodded off."

I opened my eyes. He was standing over me, looking mildly amused.

"You know, I thought you'd want me to wake you up."

He shrugged, and walked away, leaving it to me.

"Yes, of course."

I shook myself and stood up, feeling cold and miserable.

" Thank you, I don't know what came over me there."

He looked at me quizzically.

"You were shouting in your sleep, that's what alerted me."

"Hm," I said, "How interesting." Which it was, I thought.

"You seemed to be calling out some name. I couldn't catch it though, I couldn't hear what it was."

"What a pity!" I felt relieved, although I wished I knew the name myself. It would have given me some connection to the dream, which would soon slip from me, vanish. I often feel lost, bereaved almost, after dreams, no matter how horrifying they are - and many of my dreams are, for some reason, of the nightmare variety.

"Like a cup of coffee? Might wake you up!" Karl spoke quite kindly, but casually: he did not like to make any kind remark, offer help, without being off-handed about it. It was as if he was afraid to be too much the decent chap, as if he thought there was some danger to his dignity in that.

"Good idea," I said, also off-handedly, since this was the best way to deal with him. "Please do."

He poured boiling water onto instant ersatz coffee, and we sat and drank the steaming, tasteless liquid from melamine cups. I do hate melamine cups, they remind me of picnics with my mother in my youth! And I hate ersatz coffee, too. Its horrible powdery taste always reminds me that I shall never drink real coffee again, that no one in the world will, not in the foreseeable future. I find this thought somewhat depressing. But the drink, containing stimulating chemical additives, revived me, just as real caffeine would have done.

"Feeling yourself again?" He really was in an exceptionally humane mood tonight. And he had stopped eating crisps.

"Yes thanks," I smiled at him and looked him in the eye. How ruddy he looked, how healthy, with his thick brown hair, the rough, pleasant features, his eyes which were sometimes brown and sometimes blue, and always flecked with yellow. His characteristic aroma of garlic, tobacco, and sweat. Sometimes men of Karl's age - he was twenty-four - seem to epitomise what is strongest and best in humanity. They are the very emblems of brute force, fertility - all that is powerful and virile in the world.

"Hasn't been a picnic, these last few weeks, has it?"

Picnic. The word caused me discomfiture, but I could not at that moment understand why. So I dismissed it.

"Not exactly," I said. "We are all very tired, as is only natural."

"You've been at it longer than the rest of us, though. And it must be a real big deal for you, getting started and all?"

"It is, of course," I nodded, "a very big deal." Then I added, conversationally, although it was not particularly true: "I never thought I'd see the day, as a matter of fact."

"Yeah," Karl sighed, and looked off into the night sky, which was visible through the large window of the room. "Yeah, it's good that it's all happening."

He paused for a minute, and I drank my coffee in silence.

"Yeah," he sighed again, and scratched his mop of hair. "It's a sort of vindication for what's happened, this trip. That's how I look at it anyway. Know what I mean? It kind of helps to get rid of some of the guilt you feel."

"I know exactly what you mean," I nodded solemnly. "I couldn't agree with you more."

It was true. I had not, indeed, personally experienced any guilt at all as a result of the Ballylumford affair, and so did not require purging. But I'd heard so much about the "Guilt", I heard my colleagues and friends talking about it at such length, I'd read so many features on it in the newspapers and seen so many discussions of it on television, that I did know precisely what Karl was talking about, all too well, since it all seemed a bit childish, nauseatingly so, to me.

It was normal enough, I suppose, in no way novel or unique. I have read that survivors of the Nazi concentration camps, of the Second World War, felt this same strange sense of responsibility for those who had failed to survive, and a disgust with the ingenuity or adaptability or, as it more often was, the sheer good fortune which had delivered them from conditions in which the majority of their peers perished. The survival instinct, for which I have boundless admiration, is not an especially pretty quality, and my theory is that most people, even those who possess it in no small degree, cannot come to terms with it easily. They are not essentially nice people, they are not selfless, but they wish they were. Like most people, apart from the very very strong, such as me.

This was, I think, Karl's position, and that of most Swedes at this time. They survived because the Swedes are survivors. Sweden tends to have foresight and to plan for the future, unlike many countries who, traditionally or owing to unpropitious circumstances, govern by crisis. Sweden was prepared for nuclear disaster when many countries, such as Ireland and England, were not. Due to our farsightedness, our long years of preparation, we had a large efficient network of shelters, enough for the entire population, by the time disaster struck. Moreover, we had been pursuing a policy of de-nuclearisation since the 1980s, and simultaneously ensuring that our environment became both clean and safe, insofar as that was possible in a world where many countries continued to ignore the danger signs, where every year brought some fresh environmental or nuclear disaster. We had abandoned fossil fuels, nuclear fuels, oil, and harnessed natural resources for our energy supplies. As in the pre-industrial Scandinavia, most of our power came from water: the rushing streams of spring and autumn, to which we now added the power of the sea and the wind, gave us electricity, light, heat, everything we needed to maintain our position as the world's healthiest, although no longer richest country. But of course, we had noted in time that the definition of wealth was changing.

Trend-setters, rather than sheepish followers of fashion, we realised in time that iron and coal, oil and gold, would no longer count as riches in a world which was being eroded by ozone depletion, where the only aid to survival would be clean forests, clean waters, plenty of old-fashioned flora and fauna: the traditional property of the poor and under-developed. And lucky old us, we've always had plenty of trees anyway, as well as iron and coal and oil and all the latter day demons!

When other European countries, panic-stricken in the face of the Greenhouse threat, had adopted policies of rapid nuclear expansion, as the lazy easy alternative to environmental destruction, we had had the courage and the strength to abandon them, and take the difficult step of befriending nature instead. Our seas, a few decades ago the worst in the world, were almost unpolluted; our animals, far from becoming extinct, were multiplying at an almost too rapid pace: in what other European country do wolves howl in suburban backyards on winter evenings! Where else is the wildcat as common as the kitchen puss! But so wise had we been, we accepted the fact, we realised the truth, that only de-nuclearisation and a policy of environmental protection could save us in the long run. Most other countries either opted for nuclearisation, to stave off environmental disaster, or opted for environmental suicide, in attempts to avoid nuclear accidents. Hobson's Choice, they said. And now? South America is flooded, Africa is prey to drought, flood, famine, plagues of every kind. Half of western Europe has vanished.

But not us. We did not think, Hobson's Choice, and throw our hands out in despair. We planned and worked, and restored our country to what it had been two hundred years earlier. And it seemed that, in return, nature had rewarded us. In the wake of the Ballylumford Incident, we had not only been safe, thanks to practical foresight, we had been lucky. Not only did we survive, we survived unscathed. The winds were on our side: only a tiny amount of radioactive material was blown towards us, and we were able to deal with it immediately. On the other hand, the heavy black clouds which gathered in our skies soon after the bases in Ireland and Great Britain exploded were rapidly dispersed by strong gales, which sprang up at just the appropriate time, although it was already summer. We escaped, through good management and good fortune, scot free.

And that was unbearable, for most Swedes.

No doubt, it is horrible to die from radioactive burns, but, apparently, many felt that such a fate would be preferable to the psychic pain they, the saved, were obliged to endure. Swedes are, perhaps, even more than other peoples, ridden with guilt, and the constant, half-repressed suspicion that they really deserve to suffer. They could not, on this occasion, face the fact of their innocence, the very reason why they had not perished. And in what did this innocence consist? Friendship with nature, from where it counts, the seat of power, parliament. For many years, government of Sweden has been the joint responsibility of the Social Democrats and the Greens, both parties equally strong. So we had been, in our legislation, rather than in our opposition groups, on the side of the good and the natural, as well as the good and the technological (for only fools believe that the latter is wholly malign, and we learned how to harness nature to machines, as our ancestors have always done). Virtue was rewarded, it seemed to me, and nature and technology, which we had allowed to coexist in a reasonably peaceful union for at least a decade or two, repaid us. But Karl, and most Swedes, would have preferred hellfire to the heaven we had made for ourselves.

This awful, silly, vain guilt was something that seemed to increase with the passage of time, rather than the reverse. Initially, in the immediate wake of the Incident, people had been simply stunned and in fact afraid. Although all the official news indicated that the danger was past, they continued to fear that something else was bound to go wrong, and that doom awaited them. And I must admit that I shared these fears.

We emerged from our underground shelters - I had felt quite at home in mine, and I suspect that this was a common sensation - blinking uncomfortably at the sun. It was spring. The birches were veiled in the tenderest green, the grass was encrusted with the deep blue scylla, the yellow crocus. The rivers roared into the millstreams, the moose bellowed, the waves in the archipelagos danced.

It was, simply, too much.

The silly frippery of it, the vulgar carnival of rejuvenation. False, we thought, because nothing was to come of it, there would be no summer, no harvest. It was a travesty. We faced nuclear winter, and the grave. It was after all what we had heard so much about, and desired.

But the mints deepened to emeralds and then to bottle, and our brittle numbness had to relax, we had to accept our fate. Survival. And then we had to ask "why?"

Wasn't there something uncanny about it all, people asked, at their coffee mornings, their cocktail parties - the old rituals were quickly restored, although the provisions were often not up to pre-Ballylumford standards. They began to view the Swedish friendship with nature as some sort of diabolic pact, such as medieval witches enjoyed - and had suffered for. They began to suspect that such leagues are less natural than the other, spontaneous kind of behaviour, which ends, inevitably, in destruction. The natural thing to do, after all, looking at humans as the embodiment of nature, is to flog nature and all natural things, including humanity, to death. That is what the great powers had done from the beginning of history. And what is history, after all, what is official textbook history but the story of humanity's intolerance of earth and all that is on it: the Romans had their circuses and galleys, the Spaniards their Inquisitions, the British their factories and coal-mines and institutionalised brutality, the Americans their Indians and slaves, Hitler his concentration camps, Pol Pot his, the Chinese their special oriental tortures, their three million strong army mowing down every individual dissident voice ... and now all contemporary powers their Bombs, the ultimate in universal psychological and potentially physical torture. So most peoples had continued until now to behave in the authentic human mode, and so had reached the goal they naturally desired: annihilation. Small boys fight, big boys fight, the world explodes in a mushroom of smoke. That is what is truly fitting for humanity.

But we Swedes? Effeminate, false, witches, hags. We should have been burned at the stake.

And we were, or most of us were, but it was in a bonfire of the mind, and psychiatrists were kept busy helping people to endure the pain of those flames. Because of course no Swede, however crazy, was actually suggesting that we should do away with ourselves, that we should shoot every man woman and child, or systematically blow ourselves to bits. Oh no. All they were saying was, we should carry on, but not on any account enjoy it.

But, eventually, inevitably, the guilt became less, because nobody can continue to harp on an old sorrow forever. By autumn, as the bounty of berries and nuts and mushrooms, the flash of the capercaillie's feathers in the undergrowth, the hint of frost in the air, let people know that all was not doomed, there was less worry about what had happened and what might yet happen. And by the time the winter wolves were howling outside the suburbs of Stockholm, people had begun to concern themselves with their usual affairs: the argument for and against wolves raged in the house of parliament, as it did every winter; two children were eaten, everything was back to normal.

Not Karl, apparently: he needed more than time to absolve him.

"Well," I played with my empty cup, "it's good that your feelings about the expedition are so positive. You will get a lot out of it, I know you will, but it's going to be tough."

"I guess!" he laughed and reached for my cup. "here, let me take that!"

His hand brushed mine as he took it, and I felt a tingling, a faint tingling, and I laughed too.

Chapter Three

Our cabin arrangements were the following: Jenny and Karl shared quarters in the stern of the launch. Karen had an extremely small cabin next to theirs, amidships, and just opposite hers, mine, the main cabin, lay. To the fore were the galley, the control room, and the deck, upon which Karen hoped, vociferously and often, to sunbathe. This meant that the couple who were on duty in the controlroom or on deck - as happened during the day - were separated from the sleeping compartments by the galley. The latter was quite a spacious room, serving not only as a kitchen but also as a space for relaxation: it was furnished with some soft seats, a television, compact disc player, an exercise bicycle, as well as other aids to leisure and there, as a rule, people who were not on duty were to be found cycling, eating or watching TV. Otherwise they would be asleep, in their respective cabins.

On the day following my conversation with Karl I slept heavily until about one o'clock. Then I went to the galley and cooked a meal of spaghetti bolognese for myself and Karen and Jenny. She wanted to call Karl, who had not yet emerged from his cabin, but I forbade it, on the grounds that he probably needed as much sleep as he could get. We ate the meal in silence. Karen was sulking, because I had reprimanded her for not keeping her part of the vessel shipshape, and Jenny was supporting her, even though she stood to suffer if Karen failed to maintain regulation standards: Karen had shouted at me that such demands were relics of ancient naval customs, that free people required no such rigid standards of cleanliness, and that she was already so overworked that she would probably drop dead if she had to spend her spare time tidying and cleaning and doing the sort of chores she had come on this trip to avoid. I asked her to lower her voice. From then on she had said nothing to me, and a great deal to Jenny, in a very low voice indeed. As soon as the meal was consumed, they both left the galley and took up their posts on deck, whereupon I, secure in the knowledge that they would not return for some time, put a video on the recorder, turned up the volume, and went aft, to Karl's cabin. The room was dark: the blind was pulled down over the porthole. He lay on his berth, breathing lightly.

"Karl!" I said, softly. "Can I get you some lunch?"

There was no response.

"Karl," I decided, since I'd trespassed anyway, to try once again, "are you hungry?"

"No," his answer was lethargic. "Come here, come on over."

I took the invitation for what it was worth, and climbed into his berth. His breath was soft and sweet, his eyes still closed. For a few moments I stroked their lids: there is something so appealingly vulnerable about closed eyelids, they have always aroused my tenderest emotions. He responded by grunting, a very negligible grunt, such as a very young piglet might make. Then he buried his head in my hair, and caressed my legs, which were, unfortunately, completely covered in thick cloth.

"Jenny, Jenny!" he murmured softly, nuzzling the nape of my neck. I smiled silently and did not enlighten him. I felt his lips on my skin and the sensation, although I presumed it must give away the secret of my identity, if it were, in fact, a secret, as too enjoyable to permit me to speak. I felt certain that the immediate consequences of my visit, whatever about the ultimate ones, would be quite rewarding.

Unfortunately, I was doomed to disappointment on this occasion.

"Robin, Robin!" Karen screamed in a very loud and hysterical voice, from the stern.

"Jenny Jenny!" whispered Karl, with a hint of desperation.

I slid away quickly, turning my face away from him as I moved towards the door. (Although in retrospect I realised that he must have recognised my body. It is true that I share certain characteristics, such as height, and slimness, with Jenny. But anyone, even in the dark, even half asleep, would know the difference between us.)

I went up to the control room. Karen was standing at the panel, staring out the window.

"Oh, Robin, look!"

Jenny lay, crumpled up in a little heap, on the boards of the deck.

"What's the matter with her?" I asked.

"I don't know. She just suddenly sort of dropped, or collapsed or something.. She won't say anything."

"Does she ever?" I asked. "Well, let's get her in."

We half-carried, half-dragged her into the galley, and then, on a spurt of inspiration, down to her cabin, where we laid her on her berth. Karl woke up immediately and came over to inspect the damage, in a state of some shock. She was quiet and pale, but not, I thought, looking very different from her normal self.

"What happened?" asked Karl, in a tone which sounded genuine. We told him.

"She'd better rest for the remainder of the afternoon," I said. "I'll take over for her now, and we can arrange a new roster when she's feeling better."

"Sure," said Karl, kneeling at the bedside, all concern. What an accomplished liar! I thought, admiringly. I was about to vacate the room once again, when he exclaimed:

"Hey! Wait a minute! "

"Yes?" I paused, politely, in the doorway.

"You and Karen can't be on together: that's one of our rules, remember."

I was about to object that the rule could be waived in an emergency like this, but thought better of it.

"You're right," I said. "Well, what should we do?"

It was obvious, of course. He went on with Karen. I would have the pleasure of Jenny's company later that night, if she were well enough. As it happened, I had it for the rest of the voyage.

It did not take long for me to realise that there was very little the matter with Jenny: she had probably staged the fainting fit, suspecting, how I do not know, that something was afoot in Karl's cabin. I remained at her side, keeping very quiet, until she opened her eyes. I stared into them: big brown cow's eyes, full of guile, and, I had to admit after this close examination, outstandingly lovely. She did not speak and neither did I, but we understood one another perfectly: I knew, when I looked into her eyes, that she knew, and that she had played a trick. Silently I congratulated her for her efficiency, and immediately left the cabin.

I amused myself in the galley by cooking the evening meal. I am an excellent cook and very fond of the art, which I learned as a child at my mother's knee, more or less. The ingredients available were limited, but I had enough to make a dish of which I am fond: Chicken Provencale. I love olives, and as a result favour Mediterranean cookery, which could be a problem since there is no longer a Mediterranean, or, rather, there is too much Mediterranean and not enough *terre* down there. But luckily olives and most other sun-loving vegetables and fruits can be grown in Sweden now, thanks to the escalating temperature. We had a generous supply of oil as well as tubes of garlic paste, dried onions, frozen chickens, and red wine. I tossed all these things together in a big casserole, prepared some garlic bread and left a pot of rice ready to boil, and spent the short period before dinner listening to Sibelius and drinking a glass of wine: it was the least I could allow myself, in the way of a treat, under the rather terrible circumstances: I was still physically smarting from the sudden rupture of my liaison with Karl, and psychologically shaken as well, as was only natural.

At a quarter past five I invited the entire crew into the galley, for dinner. They were surprised and clearly delighted at the little treat I had prepared.

"Isn't that just wonderful! We're having a party!" Karen exclaimed. She is the type of woman who loves to state the obvious, and gushes in a most insincere manner as a matter of course whenever any social event occurs.

"Let's hope it doesn't poison us!" Karl muttered, with a grin, as he sat down and tucked his napkin under his chin. I considered the remark to be in bad taste. Or perhaps it was the grin that seemed ominous.

Jenny picked up a fork, turned it over, as if to check its cleanliness, and put it back on the cloth. Satisfied with the inspection, she smiled smugly at me.

"Cheers!" I raised my glass.

We all began to eat.

"This isn't too bad!" Karl said. "Did you open the cans yourself?"

"Thank you," I murmured. "Are you interested in cooking?"

"Cooking and cleaning are for servants. Or women," he chuckled, but not with much confidence. "Hence I do it all the time. Jenny won't besmirch her lily white hands with such trivia, will you, dearest?"

It did not seem to bother him that she made no reply whatsoever, but sat, like a mute, stuffing her wide pink mouth with chicken and rice.

"You live in Gothenburg, don't you, usually? Do you have an apartment there?"

There was plenty I did not know about Karl and Jenny, and it seemed opportune to pry at this juncture.

"No, we have a so-called house. Just outside the city, place called Molle, do you know it?"

"No, not really."

"Well, why should you? It's not Sunset Boulevard or 5th Avenue. Though it's not bad and we've got an OK house. Jenny's mother gave it to us, as a kind of wedding present, I guess."

"Are you actually married?"

"Aw, no. But she wishes we were. Giving us the house was a bribe, which I knew very well. We just took it and ran. We've been together for years, who wants to get married?"

"I do," piped up Jenny. We all ignored her.

"I understand. You were highschool sweethearts?"

He looked mildly taken aback, but replied anyway.

"No, we met in college. In Gothenburg."

Karl bent to sustain himself with a few mouthfuls of food and draughts of wine, which he consumed, I noticed, three times faster than anyone else. Then he continued to talk.

And now he stared at and addressed his remarks exclusively to me: Karen and Jenny became an anonymous audience, in the gods, as it were, while I was a guest of honour. For his own part, Karl dropped his curiously unsatisfactory bantering style, and became serious.

"I'm not from there, you know, originally. I was brought up in Copenhagen. I thought I'd mentioned that at the interview, or on my CV or something?"

"Oh yes, yes of course you did, silly of me to forget."

I hadn't read his CV carefully and did not have a copy with me on board: there is a limit to the amount of rubbish you can take on a long sea voyage, in a small craft.

"You see, my father was American, as you know, and my mother was actually Danish. They met when he was over on a business trip: she worked in a sister company to the one he was with in the States. A computer firm. She was keyboarding, he was an MD. True romance!"

"Keyboarders always marry MDs. Or if they're lucky they don't marry at all!"

"This one did. Then they went and lived in NY for a few years. That's where I was born."

"How long after the marriage?"

"Three months. They stayed for a few years anyway, so I learned to walk and talk in New York."

"When I see you walking, I invariably recall a song my mother used to sing:

Yankee Doodle came to Town
Riding on a pony
Stuck a feather in his cap
And called it macaroni.

You know that song?"

"Yes. Everyone does. Anyway, after a while most of her next door neighbours had either been murdered or had flitted off to Vermont, so she decided she wanted to move back home."

"Wives frequently do."

"He didn't want to."

"Husbands never. Too lazy."

"Well, he'd been born and reared in the Bronx. He really believed the world ended at the Washington Gate Bridge. But anyway he gave in and managed to get a transfer in the end, and back they came. He was on the go a lot, I recall. Hardly ever at home. But she didn't seem to mind. She was crazy about Copenhagen, thought it was just about the centre of the earth."

"It is."

"You don't say? Spent much time there?"

"Oh yes. I've often attended conferences in Copenhagen, and I've spent periods doing research at the Institute of Archaeology from time to time. Kirsten Bramsby is a close friend of mine, actually."

Copenhagen. Wonderful wonderful. It is true that I am fond of it. Indeed it is probably true that it is my favourite city. And not just because it has - had - all sorts of truly delicious characteristics: beauty and bustle and a cosmopolitan air. A tremendous casual self-confidence. I mentioned these qualities to Karl, and he agreed with me that Copenhagen possessed them in no small degree. What I did not bother to mention, considering it indelicate, under the circumstances (I've noticed people wince when I talk about my past, and especially about my husband) was that I'd met Michael there, at a conference at the Open Air Museum in Lyngby. He was giving a paper on the cruck truss in Atlantic fringe areas, and I was delivering one of my old and tested standbys, on cinema sites in mid-twentieth century Norway. We gave our papers on the first day of the congress and after that abandoned it entirely: I recognised it as an event of no cultural or political importance, in fact it was the sort of conference it would have been better not to be seen at, if such a thing truly exists. Anyway, since Michael and I had fallen in love more or less at first sight, we had more important things to do than listen to dull lectures on ploughshares and oatmeal bread. Instead we had a ball, visiting all the most wonderful places and restaurants and theatres, staying at the Hotel Angleterre in Kongens Nytorv, which had always been both my favourite hotel and favourite square in the city. Michael had never been to Denmark or anywhere in Scandinavia before, and it compounded my delight to show him this particularly brilliant jewel of the North. And the novelty of the situation - of being in this place, of his being a complete stranger to it and to me - enhanced our physical and psychological relationship. Tivoli! Ferris wheels in fairy-lit trees. Lobster Thermidor. A huge bed covered in white linen. The smell of roses and of Poison, the perfume I was wearing that week. Michael's crinkly, reddish Irish skin. His smoked tweed jacket. His meerschaum pipe. Copenhagen evoked all that. The very name meant that much, to me. I could not mention Michael to Karl. It would be, simply, a turn-off.

"Well, I'll bet my bottom dollar you've never been in the part of Copenhagen I come from."

"No? Where is that?" I was not at all interested. Suddenly, I had caught sight of the other faces at the table: Jenny was simply staring at the sky, as if hypnotised by what she saw there. Karen was removing scraps of leftover food from the serving dishes and eating them, with a furtive air: she was heavier than she liked to be, I knew, and considered herself a glutton. The boredom I saw painted on her and Jenny's faces infected me. But Karl was immune to it. He was becoming progressively drunker: talking did not stop him swigging from anything in sight that contained a drop of alcohol. He seemed to prefer it even to crisps.

"Place called Albertslund. Know it?"

"Well ... no."

"I knew it, I knew it. Nobody, but nobody, has heard of Albertslund. It's a ..."

"Could you pass the bread please," Karen said, pointedly. Karl did not take the hint, but continued to regale us with a description of his childhood home, his parents' characters, his life at school, his deeply influential relationship with a teacher when he was eight, and so on. The wine had clearly gone to his head. So much so that, after his fit of garrulousness, he suddenly became truculent, and argued very trenchantly with me about the route I had selected for the voyage to Ireland.

"It'sh dumb, going this round the world way," he said. His voice was slurred at this stage. "It'sh the dumbest thing I ever heard of. And it'sh bloody dangerous too."

"Oh nonsense!"

I can't bear inebriation. It bores me to distraction.

"Only a real idiot would chart that course. Only somebody who knows absolutely zilch about sailing ... it'sh a laugh, but less hope the laugh'sh not on us."

Karen was looking cross and Jenny worried.

"You're drunk, Karl," I said firmly. "I never take advice from people who are drunk. Why don't you go to bed now, and we can discuss this again when you're feeling better."

"Discush it now, discush it now, you dumb twit!" he yelled. "You bitch! You stupid wildcat! Discush it now!"

He drained a whole glass at one gulp, and slumped across the table.

Later that night, I tried to open up some line of communication with Jenny, who was still an enigma to me. Indeed, although we had now been working together for almost a month, I knew as little about her as I had known on that first night, when she and Karl visited my flat, to be interviewed. In all that time, she had not addressed more than one or two words to me, and I had rarely heard her speak to anyone. And naturally, the more silent and obdurate she was, the more urgent grew my wish to break down the barriers which separated us. I did not, at first, know how I could even begin to draw her out of herself. I sat, ostensibly reading my difficult novel, thinking how dull sanatoria were and how, in some ways, they resembled ships, occasionally looking at Jenny, who stood at the controls, slender and almost luminous in her green suit. "What a delightful night!" I ventured, not, it is true, very brilliantly, round about midnight. It was certainly a lovely evening: the moon was full and making delicious silver tracks in the black water.

But she did not reply, or deign to look at me.

I resumed my reading, half-heartedly, since after midnight I simply cannot stomach German, or death. Ten minutes passed. I tried again.

" The night shift is difficult!"

This time she turned, and looked at me, somewhat contemptuously.

"You can sleep if you like," she said.

"Are you mad?"

I was annoyed, not only at her dismissal of me, but at her flagrant and brash disregard for what she knew I considered an important rule. What *was* an important rule!

"There's no real need to have two on, when one can do the work just as easily," she remarked, dispassionately. "Anyway, twelve hours are too long, for a shift. "

This was undoubtedly correct. I had realised it after my first stint on duty, and if I'd had any experience of sailing I wouldn't have organised matters in that way. But I'd made the regulations and it is an iron policy with me never to change anything.

"It's essential to have two people on simultaneously. What if something goes wrong? Like this afternoon?"

She made no reply, or gesture. The path to a revealing conversation, the way to a meaningful relationship, had been snarled up. We did not speak to one another again that night.

At dawn, the coast came into view. The English coast. (Karl had been a day too late with his objections to my plans. Anyway I knew he would never have the guts to question them when in full possession of his faculties. He was, and I acquired further proof of this as our relationship progressed, a coward. A sheep in wolf's clothing.)

Now here we were. East Anglia, where, I recalled, my ancestors had landed and battled with the Anglo-Saxons more than a millenium earlier. It looked, probably, much as it had always looked from a distance: even, dull, devoid of any scenic interest. Nevertheless, something about that landscape had always attracted me. It seems so quiet and calm, so modest and yet so self-assured, like a certain stereotype of an English lady - like Jane Bennett, or Dorothea's boring sensible sister, in *Middlemarch*, was her name, Grace or Mary - some nonentity, whose face and name are soon forgotten, but who has what the heroines lack. Consistency. That was what the eastern shore of England appeared to have, it looked, in spite of its open aspect, quietly invulnerable. Who would want to attack such a boring landscape? But of course it was not, and people did, and all you had to do, as far as I could remember, was sail up to within a few yards of the coast and wade ashore, or gallop out of your ship on horseback, and there you were. How easy it had been for them all, the Saxons and the Romans and the Vikings! As easy as breathing, to land and colonise. So why was there all that bother at Maldon? Some nonsense about tides and rivers, I can't remember, it must have been an exceptional case.

The light on that coastline is unusual too, interesting, and I seem to remember that it had been a haunt of water colorists. It is a watery sort of light. It has, still, some of the aqueous luminosity of the air over the open sea, but mixed with deeper tones, from the sands and grasses. Although the land is hardly higher than the water, and seems to be not much different in texture and tone from it, it exerts its own influence. Almost hypnotic.

I had arrived in England this way before, quite often. The last time, with Michael, just five years before. We were on our way to Yorkshire, where I was to deliver a lecture, and afterwards we went to see Michael's mother, in Ireland. We'd sailed on the ferry from Gothenburg, taking much the same route that I had selected for my present journey. Only of course it had been much quicker, thirty six hours as opposed to five days, on account of the greater size and speed of the ferry ship. And it had been more fun, naturally, for all kinds of reasons which are no doubt obvious enough, and also because voyages on that particular line were always enjoyable: the ship was luxuriously appointed, there were a number of comfortable bars, a disco, a cinema, a swimming pool, excellent restaurants, and so on. The highlight of the trip for most people was a huge "Traditional Scandinavian" breakfast in the deck-top restaurant. Michael and I, who normally skipped this meal, gorged ourselves on cheese, salami, French bread, Danish butter, coffee, Viennese breads, yoghurts, and many foodstuffs which I remembered with a pang since they were no longer readily available. After this gargantuan repast, we walked on deck, and participated in a little ceremony which even at the time had moved me. As the low coast of England came into view, all the passengers on the ship gradually moved towards the prow, where they congregated in a special glass walled room, designed for viewing. There were plenty of seats in this chamber, but hardly anyone sat down. Instead they stood silently, to attention, as it were, and watched with some sort of reverential awe, until we were actually in harbour and ready to disembark.

"How lovely! How patriotic!" I had thought, joining in. In fact, the majority of the passengers were probably Scandinavian, so it was not, strictly speaking, a patriotic gesture. Nevertheless it was touching. Sea voyages bring out what is best and most traditional in people, above all, the love of land.

Chapter Four

Sailing around England was a painful and disturbing experience for me, for more than the most obvious reason. True enough, simply observing the scene of general devastation which met our eyes was would have distressed anyone, and it was clear that all of us suffered abundantly at the sight of so much waste and ruin. Even Karl, who liked to hide his feelings behind a cheerfully stoical persona, looked unhappy. Jenny was in a slightly bluer study than usual - seemed, in fact, to be communing with some distant and less than congenial spirit, and Karen complained shrilly at frequent intervals: "Jesus, what a bloody shame!", or "God, wouldn't it make you sick!" I had never noticed that she professed any religious belief whatsoever, if the adoration of her son, Thomas, were not some sort of private faith, but she had always been very adept at blaspheming. This did not worry me in the least, but Karl sometimes looked uncomfortable, almost shocked, when Karen went on to an excessive extent, and Jenny, I thought, also occasionally underwent a subtle, barely discernible change of expression when hearing her more outrageous obscenities.

In the event, what we were witnessing justified them. Because England had vanished, it simply no longer existed. For any Swede, or for any European, I imagine, it is more or less impossible not to have some sort of strong feeling about Great Britain. The nature of the sensation no doubt varies from nation to nation, but for Scandinavians it is almost always positive. England, after all, saved most of our grandparents from Hitler. We were brought up feeling a strong debt of gratitude to its citizens, for that reason, and of course we are also all brought up learning the English language, and becoming familiar from an early age with many aspects of British culture, through the pervasive influence of the media in all its varieties and through the even more powerful effect of daily exposure to school-books relating to England and English.

The rule of the road is a paradox quite
In driving your vehicle along
If you go to the left, you're sure to go right
If you go to the right, you go wrong

This was what my mother had learnt at her first English lesson, when she was already sixteen, and old enough to understand words like "paradox". But before I even understood the rules of the road I was perfectly at home with Caroline and Bobby, their corn flake breakfasts and their fish and chip suppers, and the fascination of their father with football matches and of their mother with cups of tea and the hairdresser's. Before I was ten Noddy and Big Ears, Paddington Bear and Eastenders, Alice in Wonderland and the Queen Mother, were household characters for me, as familiar as Pippi Longstocking or my own mother, as well-known to me as the vagaries of English and the simplicity of Swedish orthography. And in this I was in the same position as every Swede of my age.

It was not only because of that sense of familiarity and of national affection that I had a soft spot for England, however, and it was not because of that that I felt deeply depressed when witnessing its decay, for it was now a corpse, rotting, with no grave, even, to cover it.

England reminded me of my mother.

I could not banish her from my thoughts, as we passed those bleak shores. Asleep or awake, she was in my mind, plaguing me.

She'd died of cancer, my mother, three years earlier. I hadn't seen her for many years before that, not since I was about nineteen. Not since the day of my nineteenth birthday, to be exact, the day I left my home town, Lulea, to go to Uppsala, as a student.

I'd lost contact with her. For the simple reason that I didn't like her. And the feeling was mutual.

My mother. Emily Lagerlof.

Her real name had been Inga Olsson, but she had it changed to Lagerlof, because Olsson was so common, at a time when people were being persuaded to adopt unusual names in order to discourage bureaucratic confusion. And she simply changed the Inga to Emily, because she was an Anglophile. A totally incurable, chronic Anglophile.(Inga was common, too, of course, but so in fact was Emily. That didn't matter: it was as English as you could get, in Lulea).

Emily Lagerlof ... the surname had literary associations, and she liked them, because she was snobbish: I doubt if she'd ever read a book in her life, apart from some linked to her profession, of public relations, and they were few enough. But she was very familiar with the contents of the works of such standard English novelists as Jane Austen and Charles Dickens, and she professed to adore Evelyn Waugh, whom she regarded as being, somehow, more quintessentially English than honest Protestant authors: she assumed that in England, as in Sweden, Catholics were rather unusual and exotic, which of course was partly true, as long as they were rich as well. My mother's acquaintance with the works of these great figures had been acquired in an unusual manner: in brief, she knew them through the medium of film, and that exclusively: she was forever borrowing videos of *Little Dorrit*, *Pride and Prejudice* and *Brideshead Revisited*, and possessed a fairly vast video library of films based on literary works of one kind and another. I enjoyed many of them myself, I must admit, and actually to this day would rather watch a film than read a book. I have inherited my mother's impatience with literature. The books always seem so stodgy and dull, I really don't know why people bother to do them any more, unless they are, like me, scholars: scholarship has remained rather conservative, which is, it seems to me, a pity. But it is true that we do not know what the life of a film really is, whereas we are sure about the expected duration of a book's existence (not long, for most. But mine are always printed on special long-life acid-free paper, as is only proper, and will be almost immortal, if it is not, of course, destroyed by some environmental disaster before their own span has been exhausted, which may well happen).

Emily Lagerlof worked in a match factory, in Lulea: that was the most significant fact about her, the one of which I was most conscious, even when I was a tiny girl of two or three, toddling along through the winter snow to the crèche where I passed my entire childhood. Mother, efficient, clever, dedicated - and ruthlessly ambitious - talked about this match factory, Olsens, as if it were the world's only source of fire. Apart from England, it was her favourite topic of conversation and one of the few which she broached with any enthusiasm. Indeed, she was not a very talkative woman: when she was at home, she tended to clean the house, briskly and so effectively that our home, which had the potential to be beautiful, was always clinical in atmosphere. It was never a comfortable place to be in: on the outside, it was ordinary enough: a two-storey wooden edifice, painted copper red, to emulate the traditional style of the early Lulea settlements, and with a very busy, very delicious garden. But inside, the house was not traditional Nordic, or Swedish, or even English - somewhat surprisingly. Inside, it was all empty spaces, palest grey floors, snow white walls. There was little or no furniture, and what of it there was was designed to strike the eye rather than comfort the body. The chairs were pieces of avante-garde sculpture, bony structures of black leather and glittering steel. The dining-room table, which sat, perfectly isolated, in the centre of the room, was a triangle of white plastic supported by three fine gilt rods which had been implanted in the floor. The dining-room chairs consisted of six black stools, arranged neatly by one wall. Apart from these, there was no other furniture. Of course, some clutter necessarily invaded the bedrooms and kitchen but as little of it as possible, and in general the house was bare. What filled it, was the cold light of the north, in which the strange shaped of the furniture protruded dramatically, even startlingly, like black trees in snow. It had its beauty, certainly, but it was a beauty of a cold, merciless kind, of pure light and form. No comfort, no mess, no fuss. It was this which appealed to Mother, no doubt. She had some bleak aesthetic ideal which she tried to express through one of the few art forms available to her: interior decorating. She loved the house as much as Papa and I hated it.

So when she was in it, she cleaned it, and watched videos, and most of the time she wasn't in it anyway. She was at work, or she was at a conference or a meeting, or abroad somewhere. Probably it was mainly owing to her constant absence that I never got to know or like Mother. Possibly I resented her apparent lack of interest in me, and certainly I consciously resented her blatant boredom with Father, of whom I was extremely fond, as a child. Because in retrospect I understand that there was much to admire in Mother. Everything, much much more than in Father, whom I did love, at the time. She was attractive, for instance. Well, to be fair, I gave her credit for that, and on the odd occasions when she showed up at the crèche or at a school event I felt hugely proud of her: she was six feet tall, Mother, and always kept her figure, even though it was fashionable at that particular period not to bother too much about that (a reaction to the obsessive slimming rages of the seventies. Something to do with feminism, too). Her hair was white-blond, and she wore it long and wrapped in plaits around her head, and her clothes were always understated and lovely: plain grey or white suits for work, white or pink shirts, sludgy velvet leisure suits for around the house. It is in retrospect again that I appreciate her good taste: at the time, while I could recognise, and envy, her beauty, I thought the clothes dull. They were, indeed, one of the aspects of Mother of which I most disapproved: I saw them as an expression of her cold insipid personality, of her unwillingness to commit herself to any human being. She was, it seemed to me, interested only in Olsens, or rather in some image of herself as a superwoman, selling more matches than anyone else in the world (she succeeded there, I think, or came close). And then the English thing, which she used to provide herself with a contrast to the factory and her life there, to provide herself with an alternative image. Emily the Little Match Girl. What could be less industrial, less feminist, less inflammable, than Evelyn Waugh or the stage image of the Englishwoman? Cool and *sportif* and county, at weekends, busy and smart and vulgar during work, that was how Mother saw herself.

Well, I should have been grateful. She gave me riches: and she wrote me, once, in a letter that I read a few times but did not answer, that she had worked hard for my sake, because she wanted me to have everything that she had not had during her childhood, and Father, she pointed out in the letter, had not been successful professionally. This was true, and it is true that thanks to Mother's success in her field we had a somewhat more luxurious lifestyle than we would have had had she been less ambitious. But in reality the difference could not have been all that great. Nobody in Sweden has been poor, not since after the Second World War. Even if neither of my parents had ever worked - I had class mates who belonged to unemployed families, whom Mother derided and Father I suspected even then and know now, deeply envied - I would have had more or less the same kind of upbringing that I had anyway. Was it all that important, to have the most expensive clothes Lulea could offer, when they looked exactly the same as the department store's cheapest anyway? Did we need to eat all that many real Swedish crayfish, when the imported Turkish kind tasted just as good? Was it essential to have the very latest Volvo all the time, and renew it once a year, when all Volvos, treated with normal care, will last half a lifetime? Yes it was, according to Mother. The best and nothing but the best. And one benefit of the extra cash was that we did have many holidays abroad, not one package trip annually to Majorca or Rhodes, which was what the very poorest child in Lulea enjoyed. No, thanks to Mother's money and also to her keen interest in holidays, we visited all kinds of places, from the time I was able to take the faintest interest in anything besides food and Mother. Before that, in my earliest years, she was not adventurous, and satisfied herself with trips to Grand Canaria and the Costa del Sol: anything more enterprising would have been next to impossible for parents burdened with a child such as I was: never sleeping for more than an hour at a time, having an appetite which required assuagement every twenty minutes, and notoriously lively, energetic and precocious in every imaginable manner - as is the way with exceptionally gifted infants, I have since learned. But from the time I was three we began to visit real places, which the Lulea milkman was unlikely to penetrate. By the time I was fourteen, and no longer willing to take vacations with my family, I had been in at least as many countries: practically everywhere in Europe, including Russia; I'd been to China, to several places in Africa, to Malaya, to Argentina, and outer space, admittedly, in the case of the latter, on a short and very overcrowded package trip, which I have no desire ever to repeat.

I'd been to London seven times with Mother, mostly for weekends, which we spent in a big modern hotel called the Tara, and during which we shopped on Oxford Street and in Harrods, drank tea at Fortnum and Masons, saw shows at Covent Garden, and did as many things that Mother considered to be properly English as was humanly possible, including riding in St James's Park on a Sunday morning, an activity which must have cost almost as much as the trip to space, but was certainly a lot more fun.

So I had much to thank Mother for. The seeds of my anthropological zeal were undoubtedly sown by her, during those many trips to so many different and fascinating lands: indeed, even to be with her on the trips was enjoyable in itself: abroad, she came into her own, in some strange way, and was very interested in what she saw and experienced, and eager to discuss all aspects of wherever we happened to be with me. Father, on the other hand, whom I adored and with whom I spent almost all my free time at home, was totally boring when abroad. He always made it plain that he thought the whole thing was a drag and a waste of time, and longed all the time to be back in Lulea, pottering around in his garden: his favourite activity. But I was not grateful to Mother, I was not, and even though it was not she who betrayed me in the end, I have always blamed her for that. She drove Father to it, away from me. She was too perfect, too driven, too cold. No child could have responded to her. And no man, least of all such a soft and gentle man as my father, could have stood it for ever. A woman who never said "I love you", never in my hearing, in nineteen years. A woman who never kissed him, not in my presence, never never never. No man would have stood for it. Not if he'd had a choice.

And what a choice.

I do not like to remember it. The bleak shoreline I witnessed recalled all these events to me, but I tried to suppress their memory. It was simply too irksome to have to ponder experiences which belonged to the distant past and were unbearably unpleasant. Besides, I realised that we were entering onto the third and busiest stage of our trip: soon we would be in Ireland, and about to embark upon the excavation which was our goal.

"How long do you think it'll be, now?" Karl asked, at supper.

"I'm not quite sure. About a day, I suppose."

"Gee, that's just great! I can't wait to get there."

"I, for one, am not looking forward to it," said Karen, with her most pained expression.

46

Jenny smiled. Karl and I exchanged a look, of exasperation on my part, at least. Really, what was the point in being so negative and so infantile about the whole thing at this point? It was not as if there was any going back.

I wished most sincerely that I'd left Karen at home. Hateful woman! Everything about her annoyed me. Her whining voice, her strawlike hair, her garish pink lipstick. The large brown freckles, or age marks, which speckled all her visible skin. Oh, how I hate and distrust that dry transparent spoiled skin! How I suspect women with fat behinds and thin birdlike legs! And what is it I suspect? Their unconquerable feminine power, the strength of their wombs, wobbling in their big capacious bodies, feeding their characters with irrationality.

"Would you like to go home, Karen?" I could not resist it. Anger was surging up in me, I had in ten seconds gone beyond the turning point myself.

"Yes," she said, with an insolent grin. "This is a bore, and it's dangerous, too. I'd really like to go home."

"You're probably just premenstrual!" I said lightly, and, leaving the table, went directly to my cabin and slept.

Karen and my mother were in the flower garden, sitting on the grass, talking. Karen was knitting something. I was in the picture, at the edges, hiding in a bright hedge, trying to hear what they were saying. "Leonore," Karen said to my mother. "A girl called Leonore is Thomas's best friend now. He met her at the swimming pool."

Oh I hate swimming, I thought, I hate swimming. And I could feel the water, cold, cloudy, stinking of chlorine, clogging up my nose. I screamed. Mother, mother. I'm drowning. Mother, tell me something ... say it! Mother looked up in surprise, but continued to sit, and Karen did not look up, but knitted on.

Lena was in my mind when I woke up, after many hours: she was such a pleasant thought that I lay and tried to hold on to her. I was with her in the kitchen of the crèche, Lena's crèche, which she ran and where I had been minded for twelve years ... from the time I was six months old until I was almost thirteen, much older than most children are when they stop having a minder. This kitchen was my favourite room throughout my entire childhood: it was furnished with golden pine cupboards, and had orange tiles on the wall and rich brown tiles on the floor. It faced south, and the sun poured into it in the afternoons. *The sun poured in like butterscotch and stuck to all my senses!* was a line from a song Lena liked to sing. As I sat there, on one of the kitchen stools, having a cup of tea, and relating to Lena the events of my day at school, she would listen, comment, work at whatever she happened to be doing: mixing flour and eggs for the evening's pancakes, making drinks of orange for the small children, heating bottles. And she would hum snatches of this and of other songs, old pop songs, from her own childhood. I was able to tell her anything. She always responded in the absolutely correct way: interested, low-key, understanding, warm but not too involved for comfort. She was everything my mother was not, Lena, my childminder. No wonder I loved her! I had her, now, for some moments, in my mind: she was small, fair-haired, sallow-complexioned. Her face was impish and attractive, though far from beautiful. Ugly-attractive, *joli-laid*. And the clothes were always such as appeal to children: casual, funny, bright. Yellow and red, green and pink, these were common combinations with her. I pictured her now in red jeans with a yellow and blue sweatshirt, upon which a big daisy was picked out in silk thread. Her hair was tied up in a yellow spotted scarf, on her feet were red canvas lace-ups. Eminently unsophisticated, she looked like an aged toddler. Smiling cheerily, like a happy toddler. But unlike any toddler, even those in her crèche, which was so well-run, so excellent an environment for the young, she never cried.

Why did she do it?

She slipped from me, as pleasant thoughts do, and I could not get her back. I awoke with a sour taste in my mouth, a lump in my belly. If I'd been able to, I would have gone for a good long run, to tire myself out and put the depression at bay: my doctor has often recommended this method to me, and I found, during my deep depression after the bomb and Michael's death, that it worked.

But there was nowhere to run, on board the *Saint Patrick*. I stood on deck, with Karl, who was smoking and eating crisps again and Karen, who was drying her nail-varnish, as we sailed across the Irish Sea.

Chapter Five

Already we could see the Wicklow Hills in the distance, blue elevations traced on a papery sky. The knowledge that the end of the journey was imminent effected a change of mood on board the *Saint Patrick*, as the prospect of change always does: the present becomes more endurable, it becomes positively pleasurable, simply because its end is in sight. The long hours in the control room no longer seemed so interminable, the atmosphere at meals in the galley lightened. Karen laughed and chattered gaily to everyone, even to me, anticipating events in Ireland, giving us all sorts of detailed and unnecessary information about her life at home, about Thomas and her ex-husband, her problems with his access times, about her mother, who owned a cake shop in Stockholm and was, apparently, stunningly attractive, and the object of many rich businessmen's desire. The elusive, unattainable object, it seemed, from Karen's gleeful descriptions of her diva-ish ways. I guessed that most of this stuff about her mother was custom-designed for Karl's benefit, and was interested to deduce that Karen was attracted to him. What went on during their periods of shared duty, I wondered? I'd met Karen's mother, a dumpy little woman, dressed eternally in a blue gingham overall, with, it is a fact, frills on the cuffs and collar, giving off an aroma of sugar and cream which could, no doubt, be attractive to men with sweet teeth. She had not struck me as being particularly devastating, however, and I found Karen's depiction of her as some kind of geriatric *femme fatale* unlikely to say the least. She presumably hoped to impress upon Karl that she had exciting genes. He lapped it all up, eagerly, too. Indeed everyone did, because when Karen got going in this fashion she was immensely entertaining: her prattle was full of colourful idiomatic expressions, jokes, and puns. What Michael would have termed "Great crack", a term I instinctively hated.

"What a woman!" Karl exclaimed admiringly or perhaps sarcastically and Jenny nodded, smiling an uncertain little smile. She liked Karen, but she must have understood what the latter was up to, and, as I had good reason to know, she was not interested in Karl-sharing with anyone. A more democratic attitude on her part would have saved us all a lot of trouble, but Jenny was sexually young and green, and it was too much to expect her to be as wise in the ways of the world as I, for instance, with so much more experience, was.

Jenny herself, although not going as far as to volunteer any detailed information on her personal sensations, was obviously very relieved that the first leg of our project was nearing its end. Her facial expressions, her gestures, and even the way she moved about the boat lost a certain stiffness which they had had. Her body seemed to be at peace, for the time being, and one could only assume that her mind was in the same condition. In confirmation of this, perhaps, she was even heard to speak on a few occasions. At a long chat we all had one day on deck, as we sat in a gentle and pleasant sunlight and observed the coast of Ireland drawing ever nearer, she uttered two complete sentences. The first was

"You were a good medical student" and the second:

"I don't like Gothenburg very much."

This was in the course of a long discourse by Karl on his academic life. Like many graduate students, or recent graduates, he dwelt a great deal on various courses of study pursued by him in the past, wondered about choices he had made, thought of the other roads which he might have travelled, if he had chosen differently. He was young enough to care, and to believe that it mattered, not only to the world, but to his own state of well-being, what he did. To imagine that he could design his own life. At twenty five, neither he nor Jenny knew what Karen and I simply accepted as a fact: that our lives are governed, not by our own will, but by contingency. Accident, or at best, a confusing admixture of accident and heredity, plots the path of the individual life. My own experience, for instance, has been that my eventual "choice" of occupation was almost entirely arbitrary. I could have been a doctor, or a lawyer, or a civil servant, as comfortably as an archaeo-anthropologist. All that was ordained was that I was likely to be very successful, no matter what career I followed, thanks to the sense of perfectionism which I have inherited from my mother. (What have I inherited from my father? I do not know).

"Why did you choose archaeology, Karl?" I enquired, not from honest motives of curiosity, since I must admit I have little or no interest in other people's motivations, however odd. And actually it had struck me that archaeology was an odd choice for Karl: it is not, of course, that lively handsome men are never attracted to it as a career. They are, more so than to other academic disciplines, even. But they are as a rule also rather brilliant men, which Karl was definitely not. His marks, I could remember, from my cursory reading of his CV, were in no way impressive. He would certainly have had much greater chances of career success in some non-academic field, such as television, or sales, or politics. But the young are often stupid when it comes to selecting careers. Youth is wasted on them: by the time people learn how to make realistic choices, they are usually too old to have them.

He scratched his head, looked into my eyes with a serious hard gaze, and said slowly:

"Do you really want to know?"

"Why yes!" I exclaimed, politely and untruthfully.

"Well..." he sighed, and looked at Jenny sadly, "It was sort of accidental, believe it or not. I started off doing medicine. I really had a big thing about being a doctor. But I found out during the pre-med year at Gothenburg that I just hated the course."

"Why?"

"It was so bloody boring. Nothing but lists of facts, fact after bloody fact, if you'll excuse the pun. I couldn't take it. I really can't stand being bored."

"I see."

"That was when I met Jenny - she was majoring in archaeology, and sort of persuaded me to change over. I sure am glad I took her advice."

He gave her a look full of gratitude. She smiled shyly and turned her eyes to the floor. The attitude, which I normally find despicable, suited her very well.

"That's interesting," I could hardly bring myself to say it and was unable to suppress a yawn. I kept myself awake by observing Jenny, who seemed to be becoming more vibrant, in an internal, subtle way, as the days progressed. Beautiful she had always most blatantly been. But now her beauty began to acquire depth and tone.

"I think people who follow their dreams are marvellous!" Karen's tone suggested that this was probably not an opinion which I was likely to share.

"Oh, yes, " I said, "as long as they know what their dreams are."

There was an uncomfortable silence, and a damper descended on the conversation momentarily. Karen, however, her high spirits irrepressible, revived it, and soon was in full spate once more, telling stories of the great adventures of Thomas. In a way, these tales were more entertaining and less embarrassing than people's memories of their own pasts, which often seemed to me too private for general consumption. Thomas, however self-centred and obnoxious, could also be funny, and rather clever: good conversation material. He asked nice questions, such as: "How do babies get into the mother's bum?" and "Why are chickens called chickens even when you're eating them?" He was also quite an expert on theological matters. "God's a spirit, " he would say. "That means he can't sit down. If he sits down, he disappears into the ground." "When you die you don't turn into somebody else. You stay the same, only you can fly." I knew Thomas, of course, all too well, and had never felt the slightest fondness for him as an individual. Still, as a type, as a representative of childhood, he had traits which were attractive in spite of himself. It is, I suppose, impossible for any child to be consistently unattractive, physically or intellectually, so staunch, so universal, is the appeal of the fresh! And so powerful that I had occasionally, when in his company, against all my better judgment, wished that I'd had a child of my own. The desire, fortunately, was invariably short-lived, and tended to vanish as soon as he reverted to being an individual rather than a prototype of youthful humankind. Then I would thank my lucky stars that there was no longer any chance that I would reproduce.

Bray Head, the Little Sugar Loaf, the Big Sugar Loaf, Lugnaquilla, Three Rock Mountain ... I picked them out, darker now, more solid, rising from a milky sea, the rounded haunches, the pointed breasts. The humps. Lumps. Tumours.

Hills had not been levelled by the blast. Should I have known it would be so? I think not, I am sure that they could have been flattened. After all, they were thrown up there by a blast to begin with, they are no more permanent or durable than houses, forests - in theory. But they have something going for them, and they were there, enabling me to recognise our locations without recourse to laser or compass.

And, although I had not finalised my decision as to the precise location of my dig previously, I knew, as soon as I saw that landscape, the humps of Bray riding like camels across a desert, that that was it. Bray. It seemed perfect, inevitable, and fated.

I had been there before. Not with my parents, who, whenever they visited Ireland, vacated Dublin and the east coast almost as soon as they landed. "Dublin is not Ireland!" my mother would shrug, disdainfully, as she headed westwards at high speed She was wrong, of course. As I'd realised as soon as I visited the place for a reasonable length of time, with Michael. Michael was not himself a Dubliner: he had been born and brought up in Portadown, in where both his parents had been primary schoolteachers. Catholic and of the strong old-fashioned nationalist streak endemic to their class in that place, at that time, they had never felt truly at home in Portadown, although their ancestors had lived in its vicinity for several hundred years. Not enough, it seemed, to get used to their Presbyterian neighbours. Anyway, it was desirable to avoid the Troubles, so they went on early retirement when Michael was still at grammar school, and moved to the south. As far south as they could go, in fact: they bought a small house in Dunquin, a national park on the Dingle Peninsula in Kerry. Their constant view was the Blasket Islands, and they were also as far west as they could be, which seemed to satisfy some deep-seated occidental aspiration shared by both of them. From the age of fourteen, then, Michael had spent his summers wandering around the picturesque, tourist-packed environs of this idyllic spot, and his winters riding on the school bus to and from Dingle, where he was a pupil at the Christian Brothers school. It had all been quite good fun, in its way, once he'd got over the culture shock: life in Kerry was surprisingly different from life in the North, and not only because of the absence of the Troubles and the disconcerting experience of living in a Park and feeling like an exhibit in a folk museum for most of the year. Tourists, Irish, drinking, talking, not working, were all so much the way of life, in Dunquin, that it had seemed like a foreign country to him, in spite of his parents' protestations to the contrary. For their own part, they, the initiators of the move, never actually got used to their new lifestyle. They liked the look of the place, all right, but they did not learn to be at ease with its inhabitants, and spent the remainder of their quite long lives frantically growing vegetables organically, milking prize goats, freezing yoghurt. Mrs Madden had even taken up weaving, and bought a loom, upon which she made lengths of crunchy porridge tweed, which a dressmaker in Dingle sewed into baggy skirts and punitive dresses. This enterprise became successful, surprisingly, considering the cut and scratchiness of the garments involved, but in another sense comprehensible: success was inevitable for anyone who worked as diligently and carefully as Mrs Madden did. She couldn't avoid it, and found herself making money which she neither needed nor particularly wanted. Cursed with the golden touch.

Michael did not inherit it. The children of the diligent rarely do. On the contrary, he had the opposite characteristic. He was spendthrift, lacking in basic prudence, almost lazy. When he left the Christian Brothers, after two goes at the Leaving, he went to Dublin, to take an Arts course, Irish and Folklore. Both were second nature to him, on account of his Dunquin background: he had learned next-to-perfect Irish from his neighbours, and the whole place was most self-consciously steeped in folklore. He'd been attending summer schools, autumn *éigses*, winter lecture series, scholarly weekends, heritage courses, and other similar events, throughout his childhood, because holidays had been spent in the place, even before his parents retired there. There really wasn't much he didn't know about his two subjects before he set foot in college, and he did remarkably well on, by his own account, remarkably little work. Luck was with him, too, in that he happened to graduate during a good economic year in Ireland, when instead of freezing posts, as it had been doing for the past twenty years or more, the university was filling a few, one of which he got. Assistant lecturer in folklore: the only one to be taken on in a thirty year period at University College Dublin. Lucky Michael!

Which explains his presence at the Copenhagen Folklife Conference, where I first bumped into him. Soon after that, six months later to be exact, we had married during the long summer holidays, and he had brought me to Ireland, to meet his family. Most of the time we'd been in Dunquin, in their house, which was really quite perfect, the only truly charming house I'd ever been in, in Ireland. I got on more or less well with his parents, although his mother, naturally, in accordance with the universal law, hated me. She was, however, sophisticated enough to try hard to hide her dislike and to treat me politely if distantly. His father was most congenial: we fished together from rocks at the end of his road, from a particular rock, actually, called Thomas's Slab. Fat pollock, not too badly deformed, but a fish which is not very tasty, was all one could catch there, but of course it was something: and Michael's father - his name was John, John Madden - insisted that it was a very unique treat, because it was much freer from contamination than any fish one could obtain in the Irish Sea - if one were lucky to find a fish there at all.

Once when I was with him he caught a baby seal, a small fat black creature with wide childish eyes, frightened out of its wits. I had been astonished, first of all at sighting a seal at all, since they were very rare at that point anywhere in Europe, and were all but extinct in the Baltic, and secondly at the horrific circumstances: few animals look comfortable hooked to a fishing line.

"He'd nearly talk to you!" Michael's father said, gently removing his hook from the animal's fin. The seal was in fact crying, quietly and persistently, like a truly miserable child. "There!" said he, throwing him back into the churning black water, none too gently. "He'll recover before he's twice married, and no harm done!"

I remember being surprised that such a kind and gentle man could be so callous. I had not yet learned that almost every man is callous. That is partly what maleness is all about. Not its only or most significant trait, of course, but a vital one nevertheless, and one which I came to envy.

Michael was not callous, not very. Neither was he very male. I do not wish to discredit the dead, especially not the dead who have been related to me, but I have to admit - to myself - that Michael lacked something which I felt a man needed to have. It was not that he was in any sense impotent or sexually incompetent. On the contrary, he was an excellent lover in every technical sense. Physically, he was curiously attractive: his features were fine and small. He had black eyes, surrounded by black-rimmed spectacles and placed rather far apart on either side of a rounded, beaky nose His hair was black, curling neatly over his forehead. He reminded me strongly of a puffin, an effect which was exacerbated by his deferential gestures: due to his short-sightedness, he was always peering from side to side, shyly and distractedly, as I imagine a puffin does. And, since I have always loved those birds, and since Michael was kindness itself, I am not to blame for having fancied myself in love with him, in the exotic setting of Copenhagen. By comparison with the middle-aged, bespectacled crowd attending the Folklife Conference, he was a true Apollo. But he lacked something, and I think my later decisions with regard to my own life, my own ambitions, were born partly of my acute sense of frustration at Michael: I knew I could live his life so much better than he was doing it himself. Given his advantages, almost anyone, I sometimes felt, would have achieved more than he.

Such an inveterate weakling!

"Michael, " I would say, sitting at the breakfast table in the Dunquin house, munching toast and butter, gazing at the turquoise ocean, the Great Blasket basking in it like some fat lazy whale. "What shall we do today?"

"Oh!" his voice was thin, it was too small for his body, which was six feet tall. "Whatever you like."

"Mm." I would observe the field outside the window, that well-tended acre, with a vegetable garden at one side, three goats at the other. The back part, however, the bit farthest from the house, had been allowed, mercifully, to remain in its natural wild state. It was a sanctuary for thistles, ragweed, millefeuille, foxglove, which rose above the many varieties of grass like airy pennants fluttering on a blue-green sea - from the house, one saw them, swaying in the wind, feathery light, softly coloured, delicate symbols of all that is fresh and free.

"Mm. Well, perhaps we'll go to Dingle today?"

"Sure, that's a good idea." Michael would smile at me, a child looking for approval. Currying favour by being acquiescent. He hated Dingle. He'd never told me as much, but I knew, from the way he looked whenever we even passed through it, that he loathed its narrow traffic-jammed streets as much as he was likely to loathe anything.

"No, no!" It irritated me so much, that he always gave in, that he was so afraid of me. And not only of me. "Let's not go. It's much too nice a day for that. Let's go to the island instead."

"OK" he would shrug, with a smile. "OK" was an expression he used often, with me and everyone. Michael was an OK man.

"OK," I'd say, feeling deeply disgusted. "OK, let's get ready then, let's go."

And we'd get ready. And we'd go.

And, if it was a day on the island, we'd have a heavenly time, because the island was heavenly, in spite of being the most intensively marketed part of the National Park. And in my pleasure at the clean silver strand, the moss green hills pocked with rabbit warrens, the rabbits themselves, bobbing about all over the place, like frisky stuffed toys, I'd be happy with Michael, and my minor irritations would be forgotten. Temporarily. It would seem not to matter, that he had no mind of his own, that he was a chameleon, borrowing his colours from the surroundings, always ready to accommodate other points of view, to compromise, to back off, always ready to say "yes", unless he suspected that the correct answer was "no". And he was very clever, very sensitive, he invariably judged correctly what was expected of him, he was an expert reader of mood. So that now, when our marriage was four or five weeks old, he already knew what I had tried to keep a secret. He knew I despised his weakness. And that made it harder for him, it made him more afraid. He did not know how to be other than what he was, a brilliant, spineless creature. Doomed. No matter what, doomed.

A chameleon, with me, and trying to be me, trying before my eyes to be what I was. It was too much to suffer, the indignity was too great, I found it unbearable and knew, even in those early, early days, that I would have to avenge this sin, the sin he committed in being me.

I don't know what caused him to be such a non entity. His father and mother were strong personalities, as is often the case with primary school teachers: asserting their wishes had been their job for forty years, they were adept at asserting them at home as well as at school. Although Mrs Madden grated on me, mainly, I think, because she spoke very loudly, shouted, all the time, I found myself getting more and more fond of John Madden. He was strong without being rowdy, sensitive without being vulnerable. His interest in archaeology was nil, and he made no effort to pretend any, as Michael did, most irritatingly, it seemed to me. What Mr Madden was interested in was fishing, observing flora and fauna, and drinking pints of Guinness in the local pub three nights a week. I found it very enjoyable to participate in all of these activities, and did so. Michael, of course, usually joined in, too, but after about a week he was taking the role of gooseberry. It was not that I felt any sexual attraction towards his father: although I was beginning to realise that I was probably a woman who preferred either older men or younger men, but not contemporary ones, Mr Madden was old enough to be my father, and I did not find him especially attractive. His skin, as a matter of fact, was too mottled and weather-beaten from constant exposure: it put me off. When I imagined brushing my face against his, and I wonder about this in connection with almost every person I know, it is an acid test, I found a slight repulsion surging through my body. No. I did not wish I'd married the father instead of the son. But I certainly found the father a more congenial companion, and I did begin to regret having married at all. A marriage between a woman such as I and a man such as Michael could not last for long, I thought.

But I was, for once, wrong.

Chapter Six

What had happened to Ireland? Simply this: a nuclear power station, one of a number built during the 1990s in an effort to control the energy crisis and to deflect the Greenhouse Effect, as well as solve some of Ireland's economic problems, suffered an accident, later termed the "Incident". The station involved was situated at Ballylumford, on Islandmagee in County Antrim, and had earlier been an electricity generation plant. The cause of the "Incident", as is ever the case with these matters, was unknown. Media reports initially took great care not to rule out sabotage, and indeed it was clear that the British Government, insofar as it commented on the event at all, wished to stress that the IRA was behind it, as it might have been, although as a scapegoat that organisation seemed to me to be too obvious a choice. Still, it was, by now, both sophisticated, disgruntled, and callous enough to perpetrate such an act, which had consequences nobody could have anticipated: to be aware of the possibility of chain reaction is not the same thing as understanding the exact position of all the links in the chain, or their extent. That is something which the human brain, even in a cool and calm state, finds next to impossible to gauge. Heated the brain is incapable of calculated judgement. Even if the IRA were the culprits, the ultimate cause of the incident was human error, since security should have protected the nuclear base from any assault, internal or external. As far as I could deduce from the Swedish reports, which were no doubt among the most accurate and objective, a series of minor accidents at the plant culminated, on 22 April, 20--, in a massive overheating of core material in one of the Ballylumford reactors.

The first I heard of this was on 23 April, when I noticed a small column in the foreign affairs section of *Svenska Dagbladet* indicating that a minor fault at Ballylumford was now under control, but that people living within a twenty-mile radius of the plant had been put on alert: an evacuation might be necessary, simply as a safety precaution, over the next day or two.

What actually seemed to have happened was that as soon as the overheating began to occur, technicians in the control room received inaccurate or at least confusing messages about the exact temperature of the reactor, and as time passed the confusion deepened: in short, the emergency system did not work at all, and when experts were called in, it emerged that there were no experts any more: just an assortment of human beings, unable to cope with a technology which was rapidly becoming almighty. Things in the saddle, as they say, rode mankind. On 24 April, three thousand people were evacuated from the Islandmagee area to Derry, some sixty miles away. This was described as a temporary measure, a precaution, to protect the public from any incident which might occur while the Incident was being dealt with by the experts.

It was on this day that the British Prime Minister, Ms Bennett, made a public announcement; she reassured the British people on both islands that the problem at Ballylumford was very insignificant, but that every effort was being made to ensure that the most skilled and gifted scientists in the United Kingdom would deal with it in the speediest and most efficient possible way, and that in a matter of hours it would be under control. The important thing now, she said, was for the people of Great Britain and Northern Ireland to keep cool and not to lose their heads, to stand together and keep their spirits up and the flag flying.

She spoke from California, where she was at a meeting with the President of the United States and the Irish premier, to discuss, ironically enough, the question of a new Anglo-Irish-American agreement.

By coincidence, the King, Queen and most members of the Royal family were also abroad, in various far-flung parts of the commonwealth. The only representative of that large body left in England was the Prince of Wales, who spoke for a moment on television and announced his intention of visiting the evacuees in Londonderry in a few days time, if they were still there. In the meantime, he was flying to Turkey to confer with his father.

On the night of the 24 April, when, fortunately for him, the Prince of Wales had reached Ankara and was having dinner with his parents, the main reactor at Ballylumford reached meltdown stage. Within hours, core material had reached temperatures hot enough to burn through the base of the reactor, through the earth beneath, down to the watertable. As soon as it came into contact with water, the first massive explosion occurred. This had the effect of devastating everything within a hundred and fifty mile radius. Since this area contained several other nuclear bases, for instance, Windscale, Calder Hall and so on, the chain reaction was quick and inevitable: these stations blew up, destroying vast areas surrounding them, until within a short space of time most of Britain and all of Ireland had been wiped out.

Ms Elizabeth Bennett, speaking from a mansion in Beverly Hills, commented:

"To err is human, to forgive divine." Then, with tears in her brilliant eyes, she said: "We must now try to build on what we have left to us. We must not give in or despair, but remember that Great Britain has always been the leader among all nations. There will always be an England."

She did not mention Ireland.

Chapter Seven

Bray had been, when I'd last visited it, a strange combination of common garden suburb and splendid Victorian bathing resort: in it the doggedly modest and the magnificently pretentious met, on the shores of a broad shallow bay twelve miles from Dublin. They met and did battle, and in my opinion the older and more worthy part of Bray had been losing ground fast to the banal and the modern. The esplanade had been a festive mile: on the coastal side, a sward of lawn stretched, its patched and well-worn surface broken by bandstands, rain shelters and gaily-striped kiosks, the latter dangling bunches of beachballs, buckets and spades, inflatable dolphins, and all the heartlifting paraphernalia of old-fashioned holidays at the shore. On the other side of the road was a long parade of great Victorian hotels, their windows mullionned, their gables Gothic, their piazzas Romanesque: the Shangri La, the Beach House, the Grand, were marshalled up side by side, a phalanx of vulgar comfort warding off the ozone and the east wind. But the hotels were down at heel: there were numerous old folks' homes, which lent to the resort their own sad morbidity, and the snooker centres and gaming halls were more in evidence than the genteel family guest house. The railings along the seafront, which seemed to cordon off the sea and make of it a public park, were rusty, badly in need of a lick of paint. The beach itself was nothing but a heap of stones: the breakwaters which had in the heyday of the bathing place kept them at bay and ensured that Bray had possessed its golden mile of sand had broken and never been replaced. So there was no beach, worthy of the name. Brave souls picked their way painfully over the round grey pebbles and had their icy swims, and at one end of the bay paddle boats, red and pink and yellow, were punted about by delighted children. But there was no serious bathing or sunbathing or sandcastle-building to be done at Bray, as there had been in the 1890s, or whenever it had been truly fashionable. By the time I first visited it, it was, at best, a place where people from south Dublin went for a stroll on Sunday afternoons, at its worst, a terminus for those whose poverty would allow them no better destination for a day trip from a city centre flat.

What lay behind the seafront then was a country market town and a huge suburban sprawl of housing estates, and the real centre of activity in Bray was in this area, not in the part of it which was most picturesque and unique. The mean Main Street was thronged with shoppers and traffic, while the noble esplanade was often abandoned. It had often seemed unfortunate to me that the two parts of the town had failed to marry successfully. In Sweden, they might have done, I could not help thinking: the old resort would have become a favoured amenity for the new suburb. But in Bray, that had not seemed to happen. Certainly not in a very graceful way.

Still, the town had appealed to me, when I had been there before. It had been lovely still, not least because of its setting, the type of magnificent romantic scenery the Victorians revelled in: savage rocks, majestic peaks, roaring rivers, as a mount for the prettiest craftwork: the lawns, the tearooms, the slapstick "amusements". Even latterly, when I had been last there - here - one had had a clear impression of what had been, and that lent the beauty of the place a nostalgia which of course made it almost overpoweringly poignant: Bray had been then a foxed mezzotint, blurred and weary but not without romance.

It touched me deeply, to see what had become of it all.

"Ah! Just in time for my constitutional!" Karl said, grinning, and adopting his idea of a posh accent, which he had a habit of doing when in very good humour. We were all standing together, close together, clinging together, almost, gazing at the new scene : it was one of the rare occasions when we had a sense of intimacy as a group. Few experiences could have the energy to unite us now, but this first sense of pain and fright did.

We had already anchored in a sheltered rocky cove, close to the foot of Bray Head, a little to the south of the town, or of the site of what had been the town. Had the railway snaked its way around that mountain, its tracks neatly embedded in a narrow shelf on the cliff? Or was I thinking of something else, perhaps? Just a path, maybe ... my memory of the place was not as precise as I would have wished - I had after all only spent a short time in it.

Now, we lowered ourselves into our dinghy and rowed towards the tiny shingled beach which cushioned this enclave from the hostile-looking landscape behind it. Trying to avoid all contact with the water, we rowed right up onto the beach before disembarking. Then we pulled the dinghy into a narrow cave and left it there, out of reach of the tide, before setting off on our first exploratory walk. We climbed up from the beach to the side of the hill, and then walked around it until we had a full view of the flat land which stretched from the Head to Killiney, and back towards the Sugar Loaf and the Wicklow Hills.

Although, as I have already indicated, the basic contours of the landscape were just as I remembered them, there was no other resemblance between what had been and what now existed. Our first impression was quite simply that we had landed in a desert, of a particularly featureless and gloomy aspect. As we walked, we heard beneath our thick boots a hard crunchy sound: this sand had the texture of cinders, as well as their very dismal colour.

Gradually, however, as is often the case, our perception became more discriminating: it was as if we had been looking initially at a black negative, and were slowly moving it against a light, so that its intricacies became revealed. The analogy is inexact, of course, since there simply was not all that much detail to take note of here. But we soon began to notice that the land, which had at first seemed perfectly flat, was not so at all. On the contrary, it undulated gently all around us. And besides these soft wavy slopes, a number of hillocks, in size and shape somewhat like medieval mottes, dotted the surface. These were by no means as regular as the waves, nor were they distributed with any regularity, but they cropped up at random intervals here and there through what I recalled to have once been the town. Behind this urban area, the steep hills still rose to the sky, and it was clear even from a distance that parts of them consisted of bare granite, which had escaped being drenched in the filthy ash which was everywhere else evident. One of the higher peaks was snow-capped: the temperature was quite low for the time of year, but it often is, in Ireland.

"What can have caused them?" I mused aloud.

"What?" Even Karl seemed shocked, and spoke as if he had just been awakened from a sound sleep. We had been walking in total silence for almost an hour, and a sort of sleepy solemnity had descended upon us. It was as if we were in church.

"Those mounds in the landscape"

"Oh!"

"I hadn't even noticed them, I must say," Karen said impatiently, annoyed, it seemed, that I had broken the silence and spoiled the pleasantly miserable atmosphere. "What do you think they are?"

"I think they must be houses," I stated flatly.

"Oh, do you think so? Is that really what you think? " Karen's cold disagreement was as automatic as it was covertly expressed. Why she had never learned the simple art of being honest I do not know. But she hadn't: she was mistress of the innuendo, the knife in the back. "Could any house have survived the blast - why would some of them have remained standing, and others not? I think, now it's just my personal opinion, you might have another idea, but I think they could be just heaps of rubble - houses, all right, but not houses, if you see what I mean. Do you see what I mean?"

Karl laughed.

"Look!" he whispered loudly, "footprints!"

Jenny and Karen jumped out of their skins.

"Where?"

"There, over there! In the sand!"

We all stared.

There was no footprint. But the prank had upset us, and we took it as a signal to return to the boat, which suddenly seemed like a safe haven. The only home we'd got.

As we trudged back to the beach, I realised I was happy.

My discovery of the houses struck me as immensely exciting and significant, and I was filled with a sense of joyful anticipation. I had come to Ireland to conduct a survey, primarily, and had planned no more than a fairly rough excavation. What I had expected to find under the ash or rubble was the debris of the Irish way of life ... this was what Karen, and I suppose the other pair, still expected. But it had naturally never occurred to me that it might be possible to uncover an intact house. I don't know why the possibility hadn't struck me, certainly excavations of complete buildings had taken place often enough before, and usually in circumstances as like this modern one as nature had allowed in the pre-nuclear world. Volcanic ash, nuclear ash, what is the difference? Presumably it was simply owing to the fact that I'd never taken part in a Pompeian type of dig that I'd forgotten such things existed. Any excavation I'd personally participated in had been on a much less grandiose scale. The closest I'd come to finding a house was unearthing the foundation of a bothy in Shetland.

I'd reconstructed the whole thing, of course, using bits and pieces of material I'd found in the process. It had looked quite impressive, in the end. But I'd never actually found an intact building, or anything that wasn't broken. Indeed, it is true to say that prior to this I'd dealt exclusively in smithereens.

And now?

Supper that evening was a gay affair: in spite of the bleakness of our surroundings, we were triumphant and relieved to have arrived, cast anchor, and made an initial survey of the field.

"It's like being on the moon," Karen opined. "Isn't it? It's just like being on the moon! This is what I think the moon must be like. Probably I'm all wrong but that's how I feel! It's weird. Isn't it really weird?"

"Weird is what it is," Karl countered. "And of course it's all bloody tragic and so on, but it's more or less what we expected to find, let's face it. I mean, that there was an Ireland, with real live people walking around, going to work and having kids and all that shit is something I can't really come to terms with, here. It's as if that Ireland never was, never had anything to do with this place. Yeah, I guess it is like the moon, as far as I'm concerned, it is the moon. But more fun. I've seen the moon, and it looks pretty boring. I mean, there's no mystery to the moon. But who knows what we'll find under those mounds?"

He ripped open a packet of potato crisps and handed me one.

"Houses," I said. "No thanks. You should know by now that I hate crisps."

But of course men like Karl never pay any attention to other people's likes and dislikes.

"Sure, houses. But what houses?" He paid no attention now either. "Whose houses? It's a mystery. That's the great thing about archaeology, you never know what you're going to find once you get in there and start digging."

"Robin has been here before. You've been to this town, haven't you, Robin?"

"Well, yes. "

Jenny had addressed me by name. An exceptional, an unprecedented event. Curiously enough, nobody else seemed to notice it. I wondered if she had been chatting in a normal fashion to everyone except me all along. In spite of myself, the sound of her voice, addressing me directly and without apparent hostility, appealed to me. I knew why: simply by being sulky and withdrawn, Jenny had earned respect. The cheapest, the easiest form of power, but, as many a cunning schoolgirl knows, power nevertheless, in all its purity and attractiveness. I knew this, always, and now, about Jenny, but I could feel myself warming to her involuntarily: she had not spoken my name before, in that slow silvery voice of hers, and I was grateful, overwhelmingly relieved, to hear it uttered.

"So, you know what the houses are like. You know what we're going to find."

"Well. I've never actually been in any of these houses, you know. I visited this particular place for a day, that's all. Michael and I drove out from Dublin once - he wanted to see it, for some reason."

The reason was that he'd been to Bray as a child, and had loved it, because of the bumpers, the chairoplanes and especially the ghost train, which he'd actually tried to persuade me to try with him. But I didn't. If there's one thing I've always hated, it's ghost trains.

"Michael?"

"My husband. You know."

They knew. Karl and Karen looked acutely embarrassed. They did not want to hear any reference to Michael, because of the change in me since his death, and perhaps also because of his death. Even in this ghost country, where everyone was dead, the idea of a particular dead individual frightened or disgusted them. Or was it the idea of the bereaved one, the one left behind, with the stigma of death clinging, that put them off?

Jenny did not recognise the taboo, or if she did she ignored it.

"Where is he now?"

She knew, I was certain.

"Here."

"Robin!" Karen's bony hand flew towards me, as it always did when she was agitated with someone. She thought her touch had some healing power in it, and of course she was right, up to a point, although for me it did not function very effectively.

"I see," said Jenny. "That is very sad. It's very sad about all of this. It's horrible. But most of all about Michael. Your husband."

"Yes. Well, yes. It is, really."

And it was true. I felt sad, deeply, inconsolably, for Michael, and Michael's parents, and everyone I had ever seen in Ireland, who were no longer there.

Because of me.

Although our marriage was not a roaring success initially, Michael and I had stayed together. I was not passionately in love with him, after the first couple of weeks, indeed, by the time we married, my love for him had already disappeared. But, I asked myself, can any love, no matter how intense, last for very long anyway? Love thrives on the novel, the glamorous, and marriage is never either of these things. Ours most certainly wasn't. On the other hand, Michael appeared to continue to be very dependent on me, and this dependence he called, with a good deal of accuracy, "love". He was eminently co-operative, giving in to me on everything. As I have pointed out, this was a trait which did not arouse my admiration, but it certainly made him easy to live with. I never understood what his real feelings were, about me or anything else, and I doubt if he understood them himself. But he behaved, mainly, as if he adored me. And this was an experience which I felt to be too much to my advantage to give up.

Soon after our marriage and our wedding trip to Ireland, Michael resigned from his position in UCD, with some slight reluctance, because he realised he would never get such a job again. But he said he would prefer to live in Scandinavia, he'd had enough of Ireland for a while, and so he came to live with me in Sweden. We got a flat in an old apartment block on Glunten's Grand, which was very convenient to my place of work at the university, and very good value as well. It was not a luxurious flat, but it was spacious and more than adequate for our needs. Michael thought so, too, at least initially.

For our first few months at Glunten's Grand, Michael merely pottered around Uppsala, getting to know the town, and thinking about what he would do. He thought about opening a shop for Irish goods, and approached the Industrial Development Authority in Ireland, who were enthusiastic. But he decided that he would not like to spend his days behind a counter, packing tweed ties and woollen hats. Then he thought about getting a job teaching English, but there were not so many of those available just then, so he gave up that idea too. Finally, on my recommendation, he enrolled at the university as a PhD student in anthropology. It seemed that this was exactly what he'd wished for all along, but had been afraid to suggest, because he disliked the idea of depending on me financially. He could not get it into his head that in Sweden no one depended on another individual for basic needs. The state guaranteed all citizens, even foreign ones like Michael, a decent lifestyle. For an Irishman, this was incredible, and I don't think he ever realised what it meant (that Swedes were free, as most people of other nations were not, to choose their way of life).

Nevertheless, he was happy as a student. It gave him a sense of purpose in life, and a sense of importance. He was the sort of person who needs some sort of prestigious position to bolster up his confidence in himself: he valued himself according to the importance with which he imagined others accredited him. Of course, this was in reality very little. People, on the whole, care very little about how important or unimportant anyone else is, being much too concerned with their own place in the universal pecking order. But Michael admired PhD students, he admired academics, he believed they were more glamorous and intelligent and imaginative than other human beings, and therefore it suited him to be one of them, on any conditions.

For the first year after his enrollment, our life progressed uneventfully but contentedly: I was totally absorbed in a book on an excavation of a bombed cinema site in Norway which I had been working on just prior to my marriage, and Michael was having fun finding his way around the department of ethnology and making the first baby steps in research on his chosen topic, which was the custom of whale slaughter in the Faroe Islands. He enjoyed taking Swedish lessons at a downtown language school, becoming friendly in the process with various Poles, Turks, Italians and other aliens, from whom he picked up terrible grammatical errors and various prejudices against the native population, as well as some excellent recipes for ethnic food, which he often used at weekends: he was a good cook and a good housekeeper on the whole, traits which also served to enhance his usefulness as a husband. He also liked meeting students at college, drinking coffee and eating marzipan cakes at Ofvendahl's, conferring with his supervisor once a week, and sitting in at undergraduate lectures, just to get the hang of things.

A whole year passed before I realised that he wasn't really doing any work.

At that point, he went on his first field trip, to the Faroe Islands. He was to spend three weeks there, participating in the *Grindadrab*, as the custom was called, and then conducting interviews and observations in order to learn about people's attitudes to it. I was very interested in this custom myself, and, having never witnessed it, although I had been to the Faroes with my parents, I was tempted to accompany Michael. He had no objection to this plan, but finally I decided not to go through with it, since frankly the prospect of three weeks in Uppsala without Michael attracted me even more than that of butchering whales. Besides which, I knew it would do him good both to be without me and to be forced to do some hard-core research on his own two feet, or sea-legs, since the whale slaughter was conducted from small fishing craft.

One morning in April, he set off, flying to Copenhagen, where he would catch a plane to Thorshavn. I settled in the flat, savouring that wonderful feeling of peace and space which descends upon a home when at last, after many months of sharing, you have it all to yourself. My plan was to spend as much of the three weeks as possible at home, winding up my book and simply enjoying myself.

But my holiday was shortlived. Within a week, Michael was home.

"It was too ghastly," he shuddered. "I just couldn't face it."

"Hm" I nodded thoughtfully, not knowing whether he was referring to the whale business or to the islands themselves.

He passed a hand across his brow: he was slumped into a sofa, his parka coat and waterproof trousers still on. The pale green stuff of which they were made were spattered with brownish spots. Blood?

"I disgraced myself in Thorshavn, I really made a right eejit of myself. So I just had to turn on my heel and go. "

"What did you do?" I was just faintly alarmed. Michael's behaviour could affect my reputation, for better or worse. So far, he had done nothing which had had a positively negative effect. But ...

"I fainted."

He blurted this out, as if it were a confession of murder, and hid his face in his freckled hands.

"Oh!" I was relieved. And revolted. "That's not so terrible, is it? I'm sure it's happened before."

The custom of *grindadrab*, for those who are unacquainted with it, is this: once or twice a year, when the grind, or pilot whale, are at their most populous, the people of the Faroes gather at the harbour, arm themselves with harpoons and spears, and sail out to just beyond the mouth of the harbour, where shoals of the smallish whales are swimming. Taking up position behind the animals, they chase them into the harbour and up onto the beach, beating them on with their weapons, screaming, shouting, and killing as many as they can. As the whales are beaten and speared to death and the whole air is filled with fairly horrific sounds. The water turns burgundy, the beach soon becomes covered with carcasses, which those who are not in the boats carve up, in preparation for the real butchering, which is carried out by skilled craftsmen.

The slaughter is followed by ring dancing and carolling around the town, and all sorts of festivities.

"Apparently it's never happened before," Michael ceased to be distraught and spoke with great seriousness. "Lots of other people like me have taken part in it, blokes doing thesises and articles and so on, journalists ... but they've always loved it. At least, that's what they told me."

"You can never believe people about things like that. "

"No." He looked surprised, as if he'd never thought of doubting them. "I suppose not. But, still - they say its all so exhilarating, and thrilling - which it obviously is, its clear that for them it's all absolutely the most deadly fun. Men, women and children, they're having a ball, they go berserk. I can't understand it."

"I can."

It struck me as being perfectly natural, to enjoy a whale slaughter. It's the sort of thing all peoples have always enjoyed.

"Well, I can't. And as a matter of fact, I don't think I even want to write about it anymore. I can't imagine why I chose it as a subject in the first place."

His supervisor had suggested it. I'd been surprised myself, and wondered if it were quite the best thing for Michael. But, comforting myself with the theory that it doesn't after all matter what anyone's thesis topic is, that what counts is how they treat it, I'd let it go.

"Change, then," I advised, sensibly. "It's not important."

Michael, however, did not change. He could not bring himself to tell Fanny, his supervisor, that he was rejecting her suggestion. He struggled on, or pretended to struggle on, and in the end, after another year, more or less dropped out and ceased to work on the thesis at all. The work he had done lay in a filing cabinet in our bedroom, neatly stored in pink and yellow cardboard envelopes - he was quite tidy, Michael. He began to stay in the flat more and more, indeed, he became a housewife.

This suited me admirably, although it was disconcerting to have a companion who was so clearly discontented with life. This, however, seemed a small price to pay for having a full-time unpaid servant, who took all domestic responsibility in return for some food and a roof over his head. And pocket-money. But Michael's pocket-money requirements were small: he had no real interests once he'd stopped being a student, that was his main problem. Indeed, if he'd had some passion, however, expensive, our life together would probably have been more successful. It must be said, however, that in Uppsala it is not easy to have any sort of life outside the home, if one is not attached to the university in some capacity or other, or if one is not an old age pensioner. Michael, I knew, although he never admitted it, was now embarrassed to visit Ofvendahl's or any of his old haunts. He became paranoid, and imagined that people everywhere were laughing and mocking: "See, the fellow who fainted at the whale slaughter!" "Look, the failed academic!"

Uppsala was largely populated by failed academics, but how was he to know that? They mostly didn't know it themselves.

So, he stayed at home, and made the bed and cooked Greek and Turkish dishes, and cleaned and shopped, and went for walks, and was, unaccountably or not surprisingly, depending on how you look at it, miserable.

And I, for obvious reasons, was not.

My career thrived at this period, partly due to normal development - I was in my early thirties, building on the solid foundations I had been laying since my childhood, consolidating what had been then begun - I was, I felt, at an intellectual peak, I felt I could tackle and complete anything. But my success had something to do with Michael, too. He was in the background, doing my ordinary living for me. Unlike most other Swedes, male or female, I had no domestic duties or responsibilities at all. Michael was astonishing: if he noticed that my suit needed cleaning, he brought it to the dry cleaners. He washed my blouses every day, so I always had clean clothes. He made appointments for me at the hairdressers. He paid all bills, dealt with the bank manager, wrote Christmas cards to relations, kept in touch with friends of mine who needed to be kept in touch with, remembered to have the car serviced twice a year - in short, played the role of the sort of wife which ceased to exist in Sweden, or anywhere, for all I know, forty years ago. With such a back-up service, anyone would have been successful, even if they hadn't had my formidable ability. As it was, I soared.

But I made a mistake, I went too far. That is why I feel guilty now, that is why I blame myself for Michael's death.

About a year after he had dropped his thesis, I opened his filing cabinet and began to browse through his notes, from motives of idle curiosity, merely. He was out of the house at the time, I can't even remember what it was he was doing, although it was a rare event to have him absent. Probably at a Swedish lesson - his Swedish continued poor. I tended to speak English to him, since it was useful for me to keep that language in good working order and easier to communicate with him in it anyway. Anyway, as I thumbed through the pages, I realised that the subject was quite interesting and worthwhile, and that I would like to take it on myself. I had had no training in anthropology, ethnology or folklore - but what the hell? Those are the sort of pseudo-sciences that any intelligent person can learn in a week, if they read a few seminal articles and a simple introduction for first year students, preferably published in Totnes, New Jersey, or by the University of California. The more I thought about taking on the book, and what it would mean to me in terms of intellectual development, broadening of skills, the more attractive the challenge seemed.

So I threw in the glove.

Of course, I did not tell Michael about this, I wanted to protect him, I knew it would hurt him too much. But I felt I owed it to science to undertake this work, which I could do so very well - I postponed thinking about what would happen when the time to publish the book arrived. A pseudonym, perhaps? Perhaps.

Eventually, when publication date was imminent, I did not have the courage to go through with it, while Michael was around. So I encouraged him to take a well-earned holiday with his mother - his father was dead by then - in Ireland.

And that, of course, was that.

"Did you love him very much?" Jenny asked. Karen and Karl had ceased to look embarrassed. Now they seemed amused.

"Well," I shrugged, hardly knowing how best to answer this, hardly knowing whether I should simply snub Jenny roundly for asking such a ridiculous question. Really, what an idiot. But I suspected that if I gave the sort of answer the question deserved that she'd escape into silence again, and I was too curious about her to allow that to happen.

"Well, yes, I did, I suppose I did," I said.

"That's the important thing!" she gave me a bright encouraging smile, like a well-wishing schoolteacher prompting an awkward pupil.

"Sure is," said Karl, taking Jenny's hand and giving it a kiss (he'd had a bottle of Beaujolais at this point). Over her narrow shoulder, he winked at me and grinned. But I was not sure what that grin meant.

Chapter Eight

We were rocking gently, back and forth, back and forth, in a wooden chair.

Sleep my baby, don't you cry,
I will sing you a lullaby,
Sometimes low and sometimes high.
Sleep little baby, don't you cry.
Sleep my little baby!
Sleep my little baby!

Sun shone through a window, the room was filled with golden light. On a wooden cupboard door, the shadows of leaves danced, in a dappling, winking pattern. Water gurgled somewhere in the background.

"We'll go walkies now, baba come walkies with Papa!"

We get out of the rocking chair and I am put into the buggy. My sun-hat flaps over my forehead.

"There's a lovely girl! Oh what a beautiful little girl!"

We open the door and walk down the path onto the roadside. There are trees overhead, leaves bow, bend, swoop, I hear them swishing in the breeze. The sun is hot on my nose, my white hat does not protect that, I can feel my skin burning, pleasantly, reddening, browning. The road is quiet, few people are about, a car passing is an event.

"See the motie car!"

"See the motor car, Thomas, see the Volvo!"

"Yes, Papa, I can see it. Its lights are off. Why are the lights off, Papa?"

Thomas was running through the woods, my father in hot pursuit. A fowl squealed and flew up from the undergrowth with a great flapping of wings. The leaves were russet, brown, gold. As the bird scattered them they coughed dryly.

"The Volvo is sick, Papa."

"Yes."

"It has asthma."

The brakes screech,, the brake fluid has dried up, there's a desert there in those brakes, they cough like a child with pneumonia.

"Say it, Mama, say it, say it!"

The record on the stereo player plays Haydn. With words:
Sleep little baby, don't you cry,
I will sing you a lullaby...

The needle swerves, ploughs across the disk, my ears shiver.

"Say it!"

The boat rocked, barely rocked, in the soft black bay.

I got out of bed and walked out to the galley, thinking that perhaps I would make myself a cup of tea. When I got there, I switched on the boiler, and, while I waited for it to heat up, I went out on deck.

It was the first time during our trip that this experience, of being alone on deck was possible.

The water was black, the sky was black.

There were no stars. Our lights cast lambent patterns, like sheerest chiffon, gold and silver, draped over the corrugated water.

There were no sounds, apart from the plashing of water against the side of the boat, and the purr of the other water, boiling.

I walked from one side of the deck to the other, gazing into the sea.

When thoughts concerning the expedition - what I should find tomorrow, how significant or insignificant such finds would prove to be, the new dangers ahead - came to my mind, as they inevitably did, I quite deliberately pushed them away.

"Do not think of work," I said, more than once. I was practised at this exercise, I had developed a power over my night mind, my mind full of useless anxieties. I could by sheer effort of will get rid of all that garbage, use the night for what it was intended.

What was I doing, out here on deck, in my pyjamas? Unprotected.

I was waiting for Karl.

Perhaps he would come out, perhaps he would wake up, just like me, and take a stroll. Perhaps he would be curious, perhaps ... he would walk out, onto this dark cool lovely place, and the rest would continue to its logical, natural conclusion.

I sat down, hugging my knees, savouring the night. And my longing. I could have purged that, I could have said, "Do not think about him," and it would have stopped. "It's a waste of time," I could have said, and of course it was a waste of time. He might not come, the chance of one thing happening were as strong as the other. There would be chance where Karl was concerned. He did not care enough, I was not nothing to him, but I was not a lot, and I was dangerous. Karl would not court danger. Few men do.

I knew all this, but I sat, and hugged my knees, and half-hoped.

When dawn was beginning to creep over the horizon, in a faint rose flush, I took my cup of tea and went back to bed.

I was not in despair. My disappointment was slight, Karl was not truly important to me. If he were, I would not continue to play with my lust, I would have had to put it aside, suppress it as a danger. But now it seemed to me that what I felt for him was harmless: a mild amusement, a sideshow at a carnival. Bumpers. Merry go rounds. An Aunt Sally, to be knocked down if the whim took me, to be ignored otherwise.

After all, I, and not Karl, was in control of this and every aspect of the situation.

When I awoke I heard his footsteps, heavier, of course, than either of the others', in the galley, and although I had slept only for three hours I sprang out of bed and went out.

"Good morning!" Jenny's soft voice, sweet and girlish, crooned.

"Good morning," I replied, carefully editing the faint disappointment I felt from my tone.

"We're just making breakfast. What would you like?"

"Coffee please."

Jenny poured me a cup of coffee, and placed a plate of freshly defrosted bread and butter in front of me. Her hair was not tied in its usual plait, but instead looped into a pony-tail: it flowed down her back, rich and shining: how did she keep it so clean, since washing facilities were limited? She seemed to have that hair which remains thick and clean for weeks. Her face had the relaxed gentle expression often seen on the faces of those who have had a holiday after a period of intense activity and stress. She was in every way a different person from the Jenny I had got to know.

For that moment I hated her, as I must always hate the rival. I could feel my animosity in my stomach, a lugubrious bomb. But at the same time, I knew that my interest in her was growing. Why? Because she had been stupid, and now seemed less so? Because something in her demeanour hinted at a depth of understanding, which, even if not intellectually based, might have its own instinctive brilliance, a reason to match my own?

Merest hypothesis.

And not a good enough reason to allow her to complicate my emotions . I turned away from her and concentrated hard on my breakfast.

Karl sat down facing me, and began to eat. When he had had a roll and a cup of coffee, he looked me straight in the eye.

His eyes seemed to hold promises and I became aware of positive vibrations between us. But was my sensation false? Was all the aspiration on my side only? I had believed myself expert at gauging such feelings, understanding these messages. In the past, I had never failed to interpret the silent signals correctly. I had been able to judge with precision the time required to bring a relationship to crisis point, and the skill to use the critical moment to my best advantage. But in this situation I found myself losing confidence in my critical abilities. Karl was a slippery fish, I simply did not know where I was with him, I was, really, at sea.

"Nice day," I said, pointedly pointless.

"Could be worse, I guess. What's the great plan?"

Jenny came and took his head in her hands. He allowed it to loll back, and he closed his eyes as she rubbed his hair. It was very difficult for me to remain seated and calm.

"Well..." She began to caress his cheeks, and to press his eyelids with her long fingers. I got up and walked over to the porthole, through which I surveyed the landscape. Since the angle limited my perspective, I went out on deck and gazed at the shore through my binoculars. What I saw was what we had seen yesterday: a desolate desert, greyish sand, mounds of various sizes dotting it.

I returned to the galley, and was gratified to note that in my absence Jenny seemed to have abandoned Karl and was now at the dishwasher, stacking plates and cups, while he sat, still breakfasting, and talking to Karen.

"What we will do is this: first of all, we'll photograph the whole area, using the stills and the video cameras. Since we haven't got the equipment we need for a proper aerial survey, the ground photography will have to be carried out very carefully."

I sighed. The reason we did not have equipment for an aerial survey was that the Swedish Commercial Bank, which was funding my enterprise, had been rather mean, and refused to supply enough money to hire a specially equipped plane for the excavation. In any case, it is likely that I would have been unable to find a crew for such a plane.

"We can also take soil samples, depth measurements, and so on. And we can think about selecting a suitably limited site for excavation." I paused. They were all staring at me, nodding silently, like zombies. Although I have been managing personnel for years, I am nevertheless always taken aback when it is brought home to me how very manageable people are, in professional situations. Karen, Karl, Jenny: three human beings of strong and stubborn character, thorough individuals, contrary , unpredictable in every personal contingency, when dealt with like schoolchildren in a classroom responded as schoolchildren. Was this a reflection of their professional incompetence? Or merely of their need for an infallible omniscient guide? A god?

"I suggest that we begin by taking out the cameras and the other equipment, allocating the various tasks to various individuals, and then simply setting to work. What we must bear in mind is that our work must be meticulous, and done to the highest possible standards, since this is a once-off project, and the very first of its kind. There is no point in doing anything in a slipshod manner. I know, of course, that you are skilled professionals, and that there is no real likelihood that you will make any mistakes. But we are working in stressful conditions, in a situation which is completely alien to us and which we naturally mistrust. We are also in a hurry: we have a month in which to carry out our excavation, another three weeks in which to conclude the work and return to Sweden. When we consider that many traditional excavations are carried out over periods of years, even decades, we see what a difficult, even impossible, task is ahead of us. So we must tread carefully, do as much as we can as well as we can, and keep our heads."

I mopped mine, with the back of my hand, and hoped I had sounded convincing. The look of scepticism on Karen's visage, coupled with Karl's expression of mild surprise and Jenny's plain admiration, indicated to me that I had, as usual, done quite well. I have a gift for rhetoric and human relations, which often surprises even me, since with some exceptions I am not so fond of the human race.

"Does that sound OK to you?"

"Sure," said Karl, and Jenny smiled sweetly and nodded her head vigorously. Karen did not respond, but from her that could be taken as acquiescence.

"All right, then," I said. "Let's go."

We collected our equipment and went ashore. So the Ireland excavation began.

Chapter Nine

We spent the entire day surveying an area covering a few square kilometres and situated close to the part of the shore where we had docked. We did not discover anything which we had not noted during our walk on the previous day, but took satisfaction from our realisation that we were at last embarked upon the task which was the goal of our mission: we were beginning to make a permanent record of the physical state of this section of Ireland. Posterity would thank us for it.

The work was arduous, and we did not stop to eat until it was evening: as yet, we were wary of the crisp, cindery substance which crunched under our feet everywhere we went, and the idea of sitting down on it, even with a protective sheet, was repugnant to us. And certainly we were in danger: it was obvious that the whole superstructure was heavily contaminated by radioactive particles, and as a matter of fact we knew we were exposing ourselves to some of them even by walking around. That, however, was a risk we had prepared for. But we were not - not yet - willing to expose ourselves to any unnecessary danger. So we worked on, until we were too exhausted to do any more.

As a result of our tired state, some us were in the doldrums at dinner, which we ate on deck, as the sun, fiercely crimson, descended behind the distant mountains.

"I feel so depressed," Jenny said, uncharacteristically.

"Why?" I asked.

"It's all so horrible here. Isn't it? Don't you all feel like me?"

"Oh, yes, I think it's ghastly, I really do, I know it's not very sensible to say it, but that's how I feel, I can't help it." Karen jumped in to agree. Possibly she did share Jenny's attitude to some extent, but it was clear to me that she was not excessively anxious about her situation. On the contrary she seemed to be taking it all in her stride, confirming one of my suspicions about her character: that she was basically too egotistical to be moved deeply by any external circumstance which did not bear directly on her own emotional experience. The expedition *per se* did precisely that, of course, and it was to the latter that Karen's "ghastly" was applied. She did not, however, suffer as Jenny did for the sake of Bray, or of Ireland, or of any place or people or ideal external to herself. She was the sort of person - I have known several, I am one myself - who would commit suicide from despair over a lost lover or a failed examination, but would observe the massacre of a million human beings with a calm and scarcely moved eye.

Karl did not speak but gazed, admiringly, I noticed with some anguish, at Jenny. Who was, after all, the other kind of person. The philanthropist. Rare and eminently admirable.

"I've known it was all horrible all along, right from the time it happened. Before that. But it hadn't really hit me before. Before today. And now I just feel physically repulsed, I feel sick, actually."

"I hope you're not coming down with some bug!" I laughed, perhaps a little hastily. But I found Jenny's lamentations disconcerting and even embarrassing. "No!" Jenny was too sad to be irritated, but Karl and Karen gave me filthy looks. "It's nothing like that. It's just that I suddenly feel bleak. And hopeless. I mean, look." She waved her long arm towards the shore. "We did that!"

"We?"

"Yes. We let it happen."

"It had nothing to do with us," I said. "It came about as a result of British carelessness, we all know that."

"Everyone's carelessness," Jenny said, in a more belligerent tone. "We've been allowing an armaments industry, nuclear power industries, to develop in Scandinavia for years - we let it all happen. It had to come to this."

"It hasn't come to this in Scandinavia, has it? And anyway there aren't any nuclear stations there, as you know."

"That's what's so doubly disgusting about it. We protect ourselves, but not those who are less developed - like the poor Irish. They didn't even have any arms, or nuclear stations, or anything until a couple of years ago."

"But that was their problem, and their fault. If they'd been productive, like us, you can be sure they would have had just as much as we had, before we started to get rid of them. More. As a matter of fact, the Irish were doing their level best to destroy themselves anyway, long before this happened."

"You mean, the North and all that shit?"

"No, I mean pollution and all that shit. They had wrecked their rivers, ripped up priceless valleys looking for gold - can you imagine, gold? Who wanted gold, in the 1980s? The Irish, that's who - they couldn't understand that what they had, then, was worth much more than gold, even in purely financial terms. And people ... they put such a tiny price on people, they allowed a kind of erosion of humanity to take place right up to a couple of years ago. They were positively pushing people out, you know, to America, Germany, Japan, any country that could be prevailed upon to take them. Exactly as they did in the middle of the nineteenth century, when they managed to halve their population."

"They weren't to blame for that, were they? And they weren't to blame for this either. It happened simply because they were poor and vulnerable, for no other reason. And we were saved for the opposite reason."

"So what's new?" asked Karl, rather sensibly if insensitively.

"It's true. There's nothing new about it. But it's wrong anyway. And I can't bear to be part of this mess. I'd rather be dead too, really, I'd much rather be dead than have to look at this."

The sun was just about to vanish, and the sky had the appearance of a very creamy peach melba .

"See!" I pointed at it. "The sun still shines here. That means there's hope, you know. It means there's life."

"I'm afraid I don't believe that," Jenny pursed her lips. "I'd need more evidence than the fact that the sun actually shines. That means nothing. The sun will go on shining when the whole earth is as empty as this place. And as far as I can see, it's only a matter of time until it is."

"Hey, I thought you were an optimist!" Karl put his arm around Jenny's waist, and pulled her to him.

"I thought so too. But no realistic person could be optimistic here."

She looked back at the skeletal landscape. Then she addressed Karl directly, as if Karen and I were not present.

"It's as if I've been running away from this all my life, being optimistic was just a way of pretending that this was impossible. But now, when I'm face to face with it, it seems like this is the only real thing - the truth."

"Not likely, really," Karl said in a rather off-hand manner, scratching the tip of his nose with his thumb. "It's just that this is so lousy that nothing could be worse. It's the bottom of the pit, you see, and there's always a sense of recognition when you get to the bottom of the pit, like you've been there before. And like you're safe, too, at last."

"I don't think I've been here before," Jenny said slowly. "I really don't think so."

"Lucky you," Karl did not smile. "I guess most of us have, you know."

"But how?"

"Oh, childhood, I guess. Being born is like this, I'd say - and then there are all the desolate events you know, of childhood."

Karen got up and left the deck. Jenny looked at her retreating back in some surprise, and asked:

"Why did she go?"

"Oh, well one must never mention childhood or children in Karen's company. I thought you'd have noticed that by now. It always reminds her of Thomas."

"Oh yeah," Karl shook his head impatiently. "She goes on too much about him, it's sickening, the way she has to martyr herself all the time, when obviously there's no problem. If there was she wouldn't be here."

Jenny, who had been twisting a strand of her long brown hair around her finger, suddenly pushed all of it behind her ears and, raising her voice an octave or two, most unusually, exclaimed:

"That's so unfair!"

"What's that?"

"It's so unfair, the way you refer to Karen's problem about Thomas as if it were simply a figment of her imagination. I hate the way you try to euphemise the whole situation out of existence, by using these words, words like "martyr" and "guilt" and so on. The way you try to pretend Thomas doesn't exist, except as a figment of Karen's imagination."

"Hey, wait a minute, I never said ..."

"I don't mean just you personally, I mean everyone, Robin, everyone in Sweden, even Karen herself, most of the time. Everyone pretends that children have no feelings, and that it doesn't affect them at all to be separated from their parents and homes for most of their childhood. Even though it's perfectly obvious that it must. And then, of course, you're the ones who talk about the pits of childhood despair, or whatever. It's so ... stupid. It's so much doublethink. Ugh!" She tossed her head so that her ponytail bounced up and down against her chest, over which it hung, gracefully, like Rapunzel's plait.

"Really!" I smiled, but was beginning to feel that terrible sense of boredom which overwhelms me when someone expresses a stupid and reactionary argument.

"Are you trying to tell us that Karen should have stayed at home with Thomas?"

Jenny looked cross.

"Yes, yes I think I am. I think that would be the best thing, for Karen and for Thomas."

I prepared to leave.

"OK, Robin, I know you're supercilious. But was your childhood happy? Was Karl's? Was mine? Yes, mine was, because I lived on a farm and everyone was around all the time - Mother, Father, both working, but both there, available, most of the time, and work was around, there was no alienation."

"How idyllic!" I said. "Unfortunately we can't all live on farms, and people who don't have the good fortune to be country bumpkins have to be alienated some of the time, if they're to get anything done. Personally I don't agree that Karen, or any woman, should have to be the loser, as soon as the family moves from the ancestral acre to the bright lights."

"Neither do I. But I don't see why Thomas or any child should be the loser, either. Karl was unhappy as a kid, weren't you, and mainly because of that?"

"Well ..." Karl was scratching his nose again, hoping to find inspiration in its bony contours. "I was probably just a gloomy kid!"

"You're not a gloomy adult, why should you have been a gloomy kid?"

"Well, anyway, as you know, there were lots of complicating factors. It wasn't just that my mother went out to work, it was other things too."

"Like what?" I risked, suddenly curious, and tempted to change the subject. Had I had a happy childhood? No, I had not, and I'd never imagined that I'd had.

"Oh, like Mother being such a gadabout, being unfaithful to Papa, that sort of thing."

How delightfully frank he was about his mother's private life! I thanked my lucky stars for my childless state, listening to him, but my curiosity prompted further investigations, for the sheer hell of it.

"And you were aware of all that?"

Jenny gave him a warning glance. But he answered.

He seemed to wish to spill the beans.

"Yeah, of course I was. I was Mum's friend. I was her accomplice in it all, she pulled me into it with her. We were really very close, Mother and I ... I was the only child, of course, and since she didn't get on all that well with Papa, after the beginning of the thing, I was her friend in the family. Her only friend. She used me, not exactly as a confidante, but almost. She talked about a lot of things with me, I knew more than I wanted to about the grown-up world when I was still a little kid."

"Who looked after you, mostly, then?" I asked.

"Oh, you know, a succession of women - a kindergarten, at first, in Albertslund, run by a woman called Kirsten and dozens of other staff, forever changing. Students, people down on their luck, as well as the so-called trained staff, who did usually stay a bit longer. Kirsten was real bossy, and ugly. You know, a big cigar-smoking Danish woman? The kind who owns one pair of grey cord pants and one Icelandic sweater?"

"Did she smoke cigars in the nursery?"

"No, no - just a figure of speech. She was a tough one, Kirsten. I got on all right with her. I think I was there until I started school, and then the minders at home started. That was pretty awful, although I guess some of them were OK. There was one, I remember, a man, an oldish man with grey hair who used to come instead of his wife. She was the one who had been taken on, of course, but he used to come instead half the time, and then go home just before Mother came in. He bribed me to silence with chocolate. Thoms Gold Bars. He used to give me about three or four Gold Bars every afternoon, when we sat in the dark watching TV. That's what we did, all the time, winter or summer. Watched cartoons on TV. Mother found out in the end, he went then and someone else came along, I can't remember who."

"Sounds a bit traumatic, all that changing," I said. "Didn't you have anyone who stayed long enough to make an impression on you?"

"Naw. Can't say I did. I did have a schoolteacher who made an impression on me, as you say, all right. That was all."

We waited for an elaboration of this statement, but Karl was staring at the sky, boring its pearl depths with dreaming eyes, and he seemed to have forgotten us for a moment. Jenny shrugged.

"It's all alienation, that's all I mean. This splitting up of life that people have had to endure for the past fifty years."

"Some people have endured it for longer," I said pedantically. "It's only people like us who have been exposed to it lately, isn't that what you mean? It's people like us who really matter."

"Of course it's not what I mean! I'm well aware of the fact of the Industrial Revolution, and all that shit, don't think that I'm not. And people saw the danger then, and were labelled sloppy silly romantics, just like I'm labelled a silly unrealistic reactionary, a crazy Green. But I'm right, I know I'm right."

Jenny was shouting, quite unnecessarily.

"For Heavens' sake, I'm Green myself."

"Everyone's green now. Green is the in colour."

"I know what you mean," I said, attempting to close the discussion. Exhaustion was overcoming me. It had been a hard day, and I was suddenly finding it quite impossible to maintain interest in the conversation.

"I'm sure you do," she snapped, and strode off into the cabins.

I sat down and spent some time observing the sea and the sky. A breeze had suddenly sprung up and the water was rippling quite energetically. Its colour had changed from blue to grey and dark shadows raced across its surface. The land, too, was affected by this wind, and I could see dust rising in fine quick veils, being whipped along for a second and then falling back. At first I appreciated the new development as a welcome break in the monotony of the surroundings: even for me, schooled as I am in stoicism, the boredom of the colourless, featureless, lifeless environment was beginning to tell. Anything which would add the faintest soupcon of interest to land, sea or sky, was desirable as an alternative to their habitual sameness and emptiness.

But after a while, as the wind rose and the dust veils climbed higher and ran faster, I felt alarm. For one thing, I did not exactly relish the thought of a night or longer on a storm-tossed ocean - we had been lucky in that regard so far, and nobody had experienced any sickness. In the second place, I worried lest the dust should prove dangerous to us, and finally I could see the danger of it drifting. Indeed, it was perfectly obvious that it did drift, and it struck me that the mounds we had observed did not contain anything at all, but were simply dust dunes, created by the wind. In reality, it was this idea which disturbed me more than the other two.

"Why didn't I think of that before?" I said aloud, stamping my foot.

"What's that?" Karl had been in a kind of waking reverie, and now he jerked out of it and looked at me kindly.

"Oh, nothing. I'm worried about the wind, that's all."

"Hm" He looked around him, as if hoping to catch sight of the wind, walking by, clutching an umbrella, perhaps, or puffing out of fat fluffy cheeks, like an obese Edwardian gentleman, as in children's story books.

"Well," he said, his voice deep and soft with consideration. "I don't think there's anything to worry about. They don't get real storms here as a rule, do they?"

"No," I said, touched not so much by the "they" as by the expression on his face. "They don't."

"They don't get real weather, even, do they?" He crossed the deck and stood very close to me.

"A lot of rain," I said. My heart had begun to race, and I felt my blood run. I am hot blooded, I am hot blooded and natural. No matter what they say. "We've been lucky," I said, huskily (I think). "So far."

"Let's hope our luck holds." He placed his hand on my shoulder.

"And don't worry, the storm won't harm us," he said, his voice very low, "I know it won't."

Then he, too, walked away.

Chapter Ten

Contrary to Karl's reassuring expectations, a full scale storm developed overnight, and next morning the waves were rising as high as houses, while the boat was tossed from crest to hollow, from hollow to crest, the wind roared like an angry beast and the rain lashed down in frenetically writhing blasts and gushes. The vessel was sound and I had no reason to fear for it, but I am no sailor: I dislike the sea, and each time we lurched into a hollow and saw the next wave tower above us, waiting to crash down over us in all its frenzied power, I believed in my heart that our hour had come. In short, the storm terrified me.

It did not, however, make me sick. Both Karen and Jenny suffered agony; they took to their berths and lay there, covering their heads with pillows, devouring travel sickness pills and sipping water and honey. Karl and I played nurse to both of them, but there seemed to be very little we could do, except keep up the supplies of pills and drinks and mutter words of encouragement concerning the probable ending of the storm: it could not last more than a few hours, Karl said, it could not last more than a day. We were close to the shore, after all, we were in a sheltered area, it was just the beginning of May. There was no reason to be pessimistic.

The weather did not facilitate work. Going ashore was naturally out of the question, and, when I tried to write, I found my microcomputer slipping about the table - I felt it wise to take the precaution of placing it in a sealed cupboard for the duration of the storm, since I would need it urgently later in the expedition, and, while the sea continued rough, there was a danger that the boat would capsize. It was guaranteed not to, but any sailor I had ever spoken to was sceptical about assurances of any kind. "There is no guarantee against the sea. Look at the Titanic", my Mother, a keen sailor in the archipelago at Lulea, used to say, from time to time. And I could remember myself one appalling occasion when I, against my better judgment, was accompanying her on an afternoon voyage around some of the more adjacent islands in a twenty-one foot Firebird which was supposed to be self-righting, finding myself and her swimming in a suddenly angry sea beside a large upside down craft, which we had the greatest difficulty in setting upright again. I remember the event because it was horrifically traumatic for me, and also because it was one of the last times - although not the last - that I allowed myself to be dragged off by Mother into the archipelago: it had the virtue of providing me with a good excuse for not venturing to sea again, which Mother had to accept, although she never, being an avid sailor, understood my fear or reluctance fully. This was one of the many aspects of character in which Mother and I, alike perhaps in a few ways, were fundamentally different.

There was, then, little I could do, so I decided to employ the time in relaxation: we had already worked hard so it was opportune to rest, and possibly, given that our schedule would be knocked out of kilter slightly by the storm and its possible repercussions on personnel and equipment, not to mention Bray, it would be one of the last chances I would have to do so for some time. So I watched videos and read a novel in English, *Robinson Crusoe*, which I had not tried before and which seemed apt under the particular circumstances. Also I am much better at English than at German, and I was bored with Thomas Mann and could not bring myself to read any more of *The Magic Mountain*, which looked as if it would never never end, and moved its mountains of difficult language and interminable sentences at a snail's pace across the long packed pages. I found Defoe more to my taste, and his descriptions of storms extremely realistic. The first storm in the book, when he is not far from Hull, seemed exactly like ours, and it was gratifying to note that it abated after twenty-four hours or so - Hull was situated in a position similar to that of Bray, I guessed, and I hoped this coincidence might augur well for the duration of our storm. I recognised, of course, that Defoe was not the most realistic of writers ... so delightfully different from Mann in this! In his descriptions of storms verisimilitude cannot always have been a factor granted much significance. Certainly I found it difficult to credit that so many squalls, tornadoes, storms could occur as often as they do in *Robinson Crusoe*, where the rate is one every three pages, each more violent than the last, until finally Robinson is thrown up on his island and the sea is allowed a well-earned break from its relentless activity. I got the impression that Defoe liked storms better than calm weather ... but after all, he had a difficulty, because what happens at sea unless it is a storm? For a novelist, a voyage presents this major problem, that of lack of scenery, and lack of cast. One can go on only for so long about the silvery and the blue and the serene, which, like holidays at Majorca, are pleasant for those experiencing them at the time, at least, for the first seven days, but really lack the colour and grit which make traveller's or any kind of tales interesting. Cook up a storm, seemed to be Defoe's method, and it worked, because a storm means noise and danger and flashing lightning and suspense. But even that palls after a while, and presumably it is for that reason that he does not waste too much time in finding his island, full of fruit and fertility and mystery. Such a striking contrast to our own!

Karl spent much of this time with Jenny, comforting her and reading aloud to her from some Swedish novel which I did not know - it sounded old-fashioned and sentimental, like *Selma Lagerlof* - until she implored him to stop. Then he contented himself with bringing her glasses of water and pressing her to take a bite to eat, which last suggestion made her shout at him with a sudden burst of energy : "Are you out of your tiny mind?"

At that point, he came into the galley and from then on whiled away the time watching videos - using the earphones in the video nook, so that he did not disturb me, to my gratification, because my feelings about him had changed radically, and I did not want to have him bothering me: an indication that I had never had more than a passing fancy for him, I suppose. Which is, perhaps, and I think unfortunately, all I have ever had for anyone. With a single possible exception, and then sexuality was not a factor.

Towards mid-afternoon a slight change came in the weather: the wind continued to howl and the waves to shudder, but there was a gentle lemon light in the sky, and one sensed rather than perceived that the storm was abating and that quite soon a calmer state of affairs would prevail. It was a very comforting time, these moments when one became aware of the reversal. One of those border times, liminal, when one feels that one has let go, temporarily but completely, of day to day concerns, when one is etherised by one's powerlessness in the face of nature and consoled by one's new faith in its benignity.

Karl turned off the video, came into the galley, and asked "Like something to eat?"

I had not eaten anything much all day, thinking it wiser to abstain, so of course I said yes, as I would have even if I'd been stuffing myself since morning. He began to take things out of the fridge and to fry them, singing to himself as he worked. I turned off my disc and listened:

Hey Mr Tambourine Man, sing a song for me ... seemed to be the main line on his song. I'd never heard this and asked him what it was.

"Oh, just an old song ..."

"Your Mother used to sing," I finished for him.

He laughed.

"How did you know that?"

"I just guessed. It's something you say very often, actually, didn't you know? Your Mother did this, she did that. She must have meant a lot to you."

"Sure, she did, I make no secret of that."

"And now?"

"My Mother's dead."

"Oh well, I'm sorry."

"Yeah - it's too bad. She died a year ago. One of those things, I guess. Stroke."

"She must have been young."

"She was forty five."

This was close to my own age, and I expressed shock again.

"Yeah, it was a real shock for me, and for everyone. My Mother wasn't the sort of woman you'd expect to die. She was very lively, you know, and she was very pretty. Feminine. She was always gadding about, a butterfly, she had nothing in her head really, except clothes and make-up and having a good time. You don't think people like that will be the first to go - they're like children. They act like children, and that's why, maybe, you don't imagine they're mortal".

"I thought you said your mother had a career."

"Oh, sure, but it was a career as a receptionist, it wasn't such a big deal. She did it, went to work every day, all that. She was good, probably, at dealing with the public and she got on all right. But it wasn't the sort of job you take home with you, it was limited, it didn't take over her life the way your job, for instance, would. And as far as I could see that was the way she wanted it. She wanted her job, although Father didn't see the necessity for it, to have her independence to do her own thing."

"Which was?"

"Buying clothes and furniture, and having a good time, basically."

"Having a good time? I never know what that expression means, really."

"Yeah, I know what you mean, I guess. In her case what it meant was carrying on with men, not lots of men but more than one. She had to do it, though, if you knew her you knew that. She was so great, my mother, she really was. She was alive, and she was beautiful. Monogamy would have been idiotic, from her point of view. It just wouldn't have made any sense at all."

"It probably doesn't anyway," I ventured.

"Oh sure," he said. "Sure thing!"

Then he put food on two plates.

"Burgers," he said. "Rough and ready. Hope they're to your satisfaction, !"

"They look wonderful," I exclaimed gaily and quite untruthfully, because they were a mess: overcooked, rubbery, sticking out of untoasted buns whose dryness had not been relieved by the application of any sort of sauce. Karl, however, produced the ketchup bottle, and I helped myself generously, although normally I don't touch the stuff.

"Pity we've run out of crisps," he said, pouring about half the bottle of ketchup over his burger.

"Yes indeed," I said, biting mine. Then, not wanting to relinquish the thread of the previous conversation, I asked: "What was your mother's name?"

"Ingrid," he looked up between mouthfuls, and then looked down again.

"I'm sorry. Does it bother you to talk about her?"

He'd already spontaneously talked so much on the subject that this hardly seemed likely.

"Yeah, I guess it does, sometimes," he said. "Hell, nobody wants to talk about their mother all the time. Would you? I mean, do you ever talk about your mother? What's she called? Does she have a job?" He looked rather ferocious, moved by the unfairness of it all.

"She was called Emily and she's dead, too, just like yours, though not so tragically, I suppose, since she was older when it happened. And it does bother me to talk about her as a matter of fact. It bothers me and it bores me, she didn't mean much to me. For you it was all different."

"My Mother died under circumstances which were not one bit funny." He chewed ruminatively and stuck his fork into his meat. "The fact is, I believe my father killed her."

"Oh, my! I thought you said a stroke."

"Yes, but he brought it about, I know he did. You see, the way it happened was this: Dad, in the end, left Mother. She was the one who had been playing about, as far as I know, but she did it in a kind of casual way. A natural way - everything she did was just so natural, she was absolutely uncalculating, and she couldn't help behaving the way she did. Really Mother was basically faithful. After her fashion. She would never have left him, not if he needed her, no matter how many lovers she had. But he, the paragon of virtue, fell for one of his secretaries, just like he'd fallen for Mother years before. I mean, he did this when he was nearly fifty, it was one of those so-called mid-life crisis kind of things, know what I mean? The girl was more my age, if not younger. Nice, really, very nice. So anyway he went off to live with her in an apartment somewhere in town, in Norrebro, you probably know it?"

"Yes."

"Real bohemian stuff, you know: like his last chance to try the good life he'd never had when he was young. So anyway after a year or so of this, during which Mother and I were alone in the house in Albertslund, she got fed up of the whole thing and started divorce proceedings. But for some crazy reason, he wouldn't divorce - he insisted that he was living alone, and that they should try to get together again, and so on."

"Maybe that was what he wanted."

"No, no. He was with the other woman, less than half his age, she was pregnant, even. It was just that he had some old-fashioned thing against divorce. Just didn't want it at any price. So he started to threaten Mother, that she wouldn't get the house, that he wouldn't give any support, and worse."

"Worse?"

"You know, veiled suicide threats, that sort of shit. The more the thing when on, the more he got to hate the idea, he got totally neurotic about it all. So anyway she dug her heels in. I don' know, maybe the pregnancy did it, was the last straw for her. She just insisted on getting that divorce and got her lawyer working on it. It was a cut and dried case, he knew it too. Dad I mean. The closer the thing got to completion the more he stepped up his campaign against it. So in the end she went away, to Greece, while the divorce was going through the final stages. Just to escape, you know, just to make sure it all went without a hitch. But he found out somehow where she was, and he barraged her with telegrams and calls and everything. Jesus, he even took a plane and went down there, trying to get her. Such a loon! Luckily she got back to Copenhagen just in time."

"And ...?"

"She got her divorce. And the day after the divorce, she got her stroke, and dropped dead. The mistress - Karen, her name was, too - found her, actually, on the kitchen floor."

"How horrible!"

"You get used to a thing like that. It is horrible, but you just grow accustomed to it. Like you can live with it, after a while."

"You've no choice."

"That's it, I guess!"

He picked up his plate and took it over to the dishwasher.

"Coffee?" he asked.

"I'll make it," I said, trying to sound kind. I deposited my plate in the dishwasher and put on the kettle. He went over to the disc player, and put on some classical music which I did not recognise while I stood leaning against the little counter, waiting for the water to boil. Then he sat at the table again.

I brought over the cups of coffee, and placed them on the table. I was standing more or less behind Karl as I did this. What I could see was the back of his head, his abundant brown hair. Almost involuntarily, my hand touched this mop and rubbed it. Just once .

"It's all right," he said, in a very low voice. "Keep doing that."

But I remembered, just in time, that I no longer cared for Karl in that way. And I stopped.

Chapter Eleven

The storm died down gradually, and by the following morning the sea was as smooth as polythene and there was little or no wind. I gazed on the blue water with great delight, as if it were the most beautiful scene I had ever had the fortune to look at.

Karen was feeling well enough to get out of bed, and she, looking rather green, had breakfast with me on deck. Jenny was a bit better, but too weak, Karl reported, to think about work for at least another twenty-four hours. He stayed with her in their cabin, and insisted that he would have to remain with her all day. She could not be left alone on the boat in her condition, he said, not looking me in the eye.

"You're quite right," I said, "I couldn't agree with you more. I'll continue surveying today on my own - I don't think Karen is ready for work, either."

In the event, Karen - showing that true grit which I had often observed in her, once she was in the field - decided that she was, and we spent the day making observations, drawings, and taking photographs. The storm had wrought considerable changes in the Bray landscape, but, most fortunately, the large mound I had had my eye on from the beginning had not changed in size or appearance, and I took this as evidence of its general stability and solidity. Karen returned to the boat at mid-day, unable, in spite of her keen interest in the work, to go on for longer, but I, refreshed by the inactivity of the previous day and faintly reluctant to face Karl, who was behaving in characteristically contradictory fashion and from whom the most recent vibes had been anything but positive, stayed on shore until dinner time.

Karl, as I had expected, was making himself scarce. Karen and I dined alone, and I spent the rest of the evening working at my log and making notes for my report on the excavation. The material was mounting up rapidly, and I always think it vitally important to keep records as I work, otherwise important details are lost forever. I wrote in my cabin and at one point, rather late in the evening, heard Karl and Jenny leave the boat and go ashore. I was asleep by the time they returned.

The following day, we were all at work, and we managed to finish the preliminary survey.

Our excavation was of a kind relatively new to archaeology - indeed there are those who would deny that it was archaeological at all, since there was nothing archaic about it. My answer to that accusation is that the definition of what is archaic is entirely subjective, and that in any case with the disaster which brought about the conditions we were investigating the world had moved very abruptly into a new era, rendering the past, although in one sense it occurred only yesterday, a million years ago from another point of view. Time, it has often been pointed out, is relative, and it is obvious to me that the pre-Ballylumford world was more different from the world in which we now live than that itself was from, say , the Middle Ages. And yet archaeologists of the twentieth century had no reservations about excavating medieval sites and calling them archaic. Much more archaic than these were the Ireland excavations, in my opinion, and much more germane to the true aim of scholarship, which surely is to provide information which will elucidate the past as fully as possible and which will provide humanity with knowledge which is useful for its future development. Medieval archaeology, or most other archaeology, for that matter, served both these requirements very partially.

Since, however, the work was new, experimental and pioneering, the traditional methodology of archaeologists was not considered appropriate, and therefore I did not waste my time applying it. And indeed a significant by-product of my researches in Ireland is the new technique which was developed there, methods which can be applied from henceforth in excavations and surveys of this kind throughout the destroyed parts of the world.

Traditionally, archaeologists have conducted digging in a painstaking fashion, manually removing soil or rubble or dust one spadeful at a time, sifting practically all covering material, extracting every object for cataloguing and analysis. For us, this *modus operandi*, demanding a large workforce and an extended period of time, was impossible. In any case, I think it would have been undesirable. What I wanted to do was to ascertain whether a fairly intact structure could be found, and, if so, to dig it out as quickly as possible. If not, the more painstaking method could have been employed on a selected location, just to discover exactly what, if any, fragments had survived the disaster.

I had selected the site I wished to investigate on the second day of my survey. From the variety of mounds and dunes which confronted the eye all over Bray, I had noted one which seemed to me to be in an ideal position: it nestled at the foot of the Head, which gave it an alluring situation from an aesthetic point of view, and also, it seemed to me, it had protection from environmental conditions which more exposed locations would not enjoy. My observations on the day after the storm confirmed my suspicions as far as that was concerned. The mound also seemed just the right size, not too big to present a huge excavation problem, not too small to be downright uninteresting. Besides, I fancied I remembered what had stood in that place prior to the disaster: if my memory served me correctly, it had held a terrace of big Victorian houses, of the north-western Atlantic model, typical of Irish and British cities , and therefore practically non-extant in the world. If the mound contained one of those houses, or bits of it, or any relic of it, our excavation would be of even more historic moment than it was anyway, of its very nature.

Karen raised some objections to the choice of site, complaining that it was too far from the boat, and would cause us considerable inconvenience if we had to work at it every day for a period of weeks. She thought it would be more practical to choose a smaller mound, closer to base.

Recognising in her objection nothing but an expression of her habitual hostility towards me, I dealt with it in the fashion most useful for dealing with such behaviour. I humoured her.

"All right, Karen," I said, ostensibly full of the co-operative spirit. "I accept your objection. It is valid. Would you like to select a more suitable site yourself."

"Yes I would," she replied with emphasis. "Yes, I would."

"Then you can do so," I offered. "It doesn't really matter, it's a random choice, anyway. We have no idea what's in these mounds, so we are as well off investigating one as another."

She made no response to these remarks. I waited, smiling gently, for a minute, before encouraging her further:

"Well, do you have any suggestions?"

"Not right now," she spoke too quickly, obviously still taken aback at my tolerance, and never having given a moment's thought to the choice of site. "I'd like to think it over a bit, naturally. Don't you think I should get time to think it over? Isn't that the least I can expect?"

"Of course," I said. "Well, perhaps you could let me have your views on it tomorrow morning: it is important that we begin the dig as soon as we possibly can - we haven't got a whole summer, you know, like most excavations. And we haven't got next summer either, or the one after that, as far as I know."

"Yes, yes," said Karen impatiently.

Next morning, on board, she told me that she had made her decision, and, using the binoculars, pointed to a mound quite close to the one I had originally selected and more or less equal in size.

"That looks fine to me," I said. "Let's go then, and start, shall we."

We set out. When we, with our various pieces of equipment, arrived at the proposed area, I began to dig at the site I had selected . Karen made no protest: I doubt if she'd noticed the difference, which would have been apparent only to someone as skilled in making scientific observations as I myself was.

First of all, we probed the ground with electronic metal rods, which would react to any mineral or organic substance beneath, and measure its depth. An hour or two of probing in this way confirmed my suspicion, namely that a house lay beneath the mound, possibly fragmented, but, if so, in fairly sizeable segments. Having completed this initial investigation, we proceeded to dig. For the heaviest part of this work, we employed the Volvo 9512 electronic mini-bulldozer, which had been given us, not, surprisingly, by Volvo, but by Anderson's, the nuclear armament company in Varmland, as a token of their interest in our project: as a matter of fact, Andersons had hinted that they might consider sponsoring some other more major aspect of the project, such as a second trip to Ireland, or, more likely, an Ireland Exhibition, arising out of this expedition, in the future. As it was, the mini-bulldozer was an extremely intricate and sophisticated machine, costing almost as much as the boat on which we and it had sailed across the northern seas to Ireland, and I was deeply grateful to Andersons for their sponsorship (they had, it should be added, a certain understandable interest in the scheme, since they had been the main suppliers to Ballylumford Power Station, and had been accused by some Greens of being the destroyers of Ireland: a nonsensical theory, needless to remark).

Karl had been trained in the operation of this machine at the Volvo Plant in Gothenburg just before we'd left, and now he showed himself quite adept in its management. He dug away at a rapid pace, removing fork after forkload of the grey silvery material, and dumping it a few yards away from the site. In a couple of hours, we could see what was emerging from the dust: it was, to my intense gratification, what appeared to be a fully intact house, substantial, and apparently in good condition. By the end of that day's digging we could see that it was a two storey building, with a slated roof - I felt I recognised it, that it was a house I had actually seen , when last in Bray. But it was still coated in dust and clay, and we would have to complete the excavation using the traditional tools on the morrow, so I could not be sure that my final suspicion was correct. Nevertheless, I walked away from what I will henceforth refer to as the Bray House a happy woman. So far, I thought, so good.

My good humour did not, it could not, survive the freezing reception given me by Karl. Jenny was polite, if distant, Karen was vaguely crotchety, as always, but he was cold and rude. I found it hard to understand. And, in another way, easy to understand. But certainly he was behaving oddly, by most standards. How can you flirt, or, practically, go to bed, with someone one day, and seemingly despise them the next? It was not a type of behaviour I was familiar with, although from what I had come to know of Karl, it was typical of him. He seemed to perform some sort of paradoxical courtship dance, something like one of those Irish ceilí dances, *The Siege of Ennis* or *The Walls of Limerick*, which I had done with Michael at dances in the school in Dunquin. "How Irish," I had laughed, "to call dances after battles!" He hadn't liked that, and why should he? " Many dances are called after battles," he protested. "It's a common international convention." But the only example he could come up with was *The Lancers* which is, I think, a Scottish dance, and not so different from the Irish anyway. Probably he was right in his point, I've never been concerned enough to find out one way or the other. In any event, these dances, in and out, back and forth, advance and retreat, provided me with a close analogy to Karl's technique, if such it was. I felt like suggesting that we all get up and tread the boards, do a sailors' hornpipe just to celebrate the successful start of the dig, on deck, and wondered if he would take the hint. But in the end I didn't bother. We were all tired, and anyway I felt fairly sure that he wouldn't understand the message, which would have been too subtle for many more sophisticated people than Karl. Moreover, he wouldn't care if he did understand it. And I, for my own part, didn't care any more either. There are limits to the path of lust, luckily. Otherwise the world would be full of lovesick middle-aged men and women with the emotional structures of teenagers. Perhaps it is? But I am not one of them.

We were, apart from the day of the storm - Defoe's seasoned sailors would have called it "but a capful of wind" - very lucky with the weather, somewhat to my surprise, since I remembered my previous trips to Ireland as times of rain and general climactic misery. But now the sun shone almost every day, and even when it didn't a delicate greyness, dry and cool and ideal for working in, prevailed. The sea, always changing, was almost invariably calm, one day grey as lead , with little dark scribbles scrawled on its even surface at irregular intervals, one day - or one hour, because it changed several times a day as a rule - a vibrant blue flecked with racing frills of snow white foam, often a turquoise lake, rich and powerfully cheering. Since the landscape , devoid of all organic life, was a totally predictable constant, always dull and always depressing to observe, the sea became our friend, our entertainer, our reminder of what could be. And the sky, too, of course, was full of interest, although for some reason which I do not understand it did not mean as much to us as the water. Maybe it was simply too far away and too ethereal to matter in the same way. In the mornings and the evenings it was splendid, a spectacular display to delight our eyes. But in between we didn't think too much about it. We were always conscious of the sea, however, always having an eye on its doings, always, really, aware of our dependence on it to take us back to civilization.

Because of the excellent weather conditions, work progressed very rapidly, once we had got started. In no time at all, we had completely laid bare the Bray House. Luck was with us where that was concerned, too: by some small miracle, the interior of the building was almost free from dust and debris. The doors and windows had all been secured, against the blast, probably, and only insignificant amounts of extraneous matter had penetrated the house through the chimney and various cracks and crevices. As a result of this, we felt quite secure in entering the building and beginning our examination of it almost as soon as we had completed the first leg of the investigation. This was very satisfactory from everyone's point of view, particularly in view of the enormous interest of the house, from architectural, archaeological, ethnological, and sociological perspectives.

At this juncture, in my account of the Ireland Expedition, I feel it is opportune to present the reader with my full Report and Analysis of the Bray House, before proceeding with the narrative of my adventures.

Chapter Twelve

Report on the Bray House

1. Introduction

The excavation at "the Bray House" was initially planned by
the writer of this report, Dr Robin Lagerlof, docent at the
University of Uppsala, Sweden, as a direct response to the
nuclear accident at Ballylumford, County Antrim, Ireland,
which resulted in the total destruction of the latter named
country.

The excavation was made possible by the co-operation
and financial support of the Swedish Commercial Bank, who
provided the team with a forty foot motor boat, equipped for
a lengthy voyage and for an excavation of the innovatory
type carried out in Ireland. Andersons, Varmland Ltd
provided a Volvo Mini Bulldozer 9512, and the University of
Uppsala paid the salaries of the team leader, Dr Robin
Lagerlof, and her Principal Assistant, Dr Karin Lundquist. It

should be stressed that a large part of the work was carried out by volunteers, namely Karl Larsson and Jenny Lind. To all of these, and to the many others, too numerous to name, whose assistance and co-operation made the project more than an ivory-tower dream, I would like to express my deepest and most heart-felt gratitude.

Since the excavations undertaken were of a radically new kind, concentrating on the modern rather than on the historical periods traditionally considered the domain of the archaeologist, ie the Palaeolithic to the Medieval, an entirely novel archaeotechnological methodology had to be developed more or less on the spot to cope with the demands of the work. Constraints of time and of environment were also of pressing significance and placed serious limitations on the scope of the project: with only two months at our disposal, and a tiny team of four, we had to carry out one of the most important and demanding surveys ever undertaken in the history of archaeology. When it is considered that the average "dig" at, for instance, a megalithic site can last for several years, using workforces of up to thirty or forty people, some appreciation of the strictures applying to the Bray House project will be obtained. Moreover, it should be borne in mind that the Bray House team worked in conditions which were highly dangerous, surrounded by materials the extent of whose toxicity has hardly yet been understood by modern science, and which meant that we were forced to take unquantifiable risks at every stage of the operation.

In order to come to terms with these difficulties, and to maximise efficiency, certain stages in the traditional archaeological method had to be by-passed, and others emphasised. What these were will of course become clear in the course of this report, but, to give one sample, it was considered useless to apply the radio-carbon dating technique to any of the Bray finds, the dating of which could be carried out in simpler, faster and more accurate ways. Nor was it considered useful to spend time on osteological or macro-fossil analysis, on palaeobotanical studies, etc. On the other hand, a trace element analysis was undertaken, as was a ceramics examination. The main analyses, however, were archaeological and ethnographical.

This dual emphasis may surprise some conservative archaeologists, for indeed one of the most revolutionary aspects of our excavation and analyses was its totally interdisciplinary nature. The archaeological analysis has gone hand in hand with a thorough ethnological study, and it is not overstating the case to point out that this excavation provides scholarship with one of the few truly and seriously interdisciplinary investigations ever undertaken.

Research Objectives

The aim of the Ireland Expedition was to survey the Hibernian region in the wake of the Ballylumford disaster, to estimate the extent of the damage from an archaeo-ethnological point of view, and to assess the possibility of future archaeological excavations in the area.

It was not initially expected that any full-scale excavation would take place, and the team had not prepared fully for such an eventuality, which may explain certain of the shortcomings of the work. Upon reaching Ireland, however, I, as team leader, realised that the most pressing and indeed the most practical task awaiting attention on the eastern coast was just such an excavation. I felt it to be my duty as a scientist and scholar to carry out a survey of the Bray area, where we landed, and to investigate thoroughly one building in that area, utilising my resources to that rather than to the originally planned end. The reason for my decision was that

(a) I realised that intact structures such as the Bray House could have a short life span, given the environmental conditions affecting them, and that full excavation of at least one sample of an Irish dwelling house was therefore an urgent priority

(b) I hoped that, in the event that future archaeological work in the Irish area is possible, my study would serve as a blueprint for eventual scholars and investigators.

Survey

During the first four days of the team's sojourn in Ireland, a survey of the region in which the Bray House was located, ie Bray, was undertaken.

The survey was conducted by means of ground photography, using four different film types: infra red black and white and colour film and conventional black and white and colour film. Aerial photographs were not taken.

Soil samples were collected at this stage and, upon completion of the expedition, taken for analysis to Per Lund of the Archaeological Research Laboratory in Stockholm.

Line drawings were made by Karen Lundquist. These, unfortunately, have not been preserved.

Physical Environment

Bray is situated on the east coast of Ireland, lat. 53.4', long. 7.8'. It is twelve miles south of the centre of the former city of Dublin.

At the time of surveying, the town had been completely submerged in nuclear ash. It is probable that substantial portions of the structures had been reduced to rubble or dust, and buried in this ash, and it is also probable that due to some influence not as yet fully understood, certain structures were buried intact. Further surveying will be necessary before either the extent of the damage or the number of surviving buildings can be known.

There were no traces of organic life of any kind in Bray.

The levels of radioactivity were as follows: Underground levels ranged from 200 to 500 bequerels per square foot. Overground levels ranged from 1000 to 3000 bequerels per square foot.

Excavation

One major excavation was carried out, on the structure known as the Bray House.

2. The Bray House

Site of the Bray House

The Bray House is located in the townland of Raheennaclig (Ir Little Fort of the Stones), in the parish of Bray (Ir hill) in the barony of Rathmichael (Ir Michael's Fort), County Wicklow (N. Little bailiwick). It is situated at 56.7' lat, 7. 8' long. on the grid for Ireland. The townland lies just north of Bray Head, east of the Sugar Loaf, and faces Killiney and the Irish Sea.

The site was covered by a mound of dust and ash, forty feet in height and sixty in diameter.

The excavation of the house which this mound contained was carried out in the initial stages by means of an electronic bulldozer, the Volvo Mini-Bulldozer 9512, which was operated by volunteer Karl Larsson. Two day's digging with this machine were followed by two days manual excavating, brushing and scraping, at the end of which period the Bray House was completely uncovered.

The dust and ash covering was not sifted or checked for archaeological artefacts. It is possible that these exist in it and desirable that more detailed investigation should be undertaken at some later stage in order to discover exactly what the material contains. But, for reasons already outlined, it was considered unnecessary to devote time to a close examination of the Bray House covering on this occasion. The scholarly morality of the procedure adopted is, I know, one which is open to question and I hope that in the course of the discussion of this Report which will be held in Uppsala later this year, my colleagues will put forward their own views on what is a most important subject.

The Bray House

The structure know as the Bray House is a two-storey Victorian style dwelling-house, bearing the date "1887" on a quartz stone over the hall-door. (A check of Thom's Street Directory confirms that the house appeared in the area sometime after 1886: prior to that, the street in question is described as consisting of "vacant lots")

The house is built of yellow bricks, with granite corner stones, the granite probably coming from local Wicklow quarries and the brick an import from Wales. In the centre of the front wall is an oak door, flanked by large bay windows on either side. On the second storey, there are four sash windows.

There are no windows on the gables of the house, and no doors.

At the back, there is a wooden door and a French window, as well as two sash windows on the lower floor, and four sash windows on the second floor. All windows were locked and intact.

The interior of the house had suffered no damage as a result of the Ballylumford disaster, and was a repository of numerous fine artefacts and documents, the examination of which afforded an illuminating insight into the life of the former occupants of the house, and provided us with materials for an invaluable microstudy of the Irish way of life.

The house contains eight rooms: four on the ground floor and four on the upper. Besides, there are two bathrooms, a hall, a stairway a landing and an attic. Any external buildings originally attached to the main structure are no longer extant: eg there are no garden sheds, indeed no garden, and no garage.

Briefly, the house contents consist of furniture, ceramics, glassware, cutlery, clothing, electrical equipment, toys, tools, books, tapes, films, discs, and various documents and records, printed, manuscript, and audio-visual.

Rooms

Drawing-Room

The floor of the drawing-room, which is the main reception room in the house, is covered by a grey-pink wool carpet, stained slightly in the area in front of the fireplace: analysis has revealed that these stains were made by coal dust, from which we can deduce that the house was heated by means of a coal fire. Since coal has not been mined in Ireland for almost a century, it seems likely that this fuel was imported from abroad. Poland appears to have been the main Irish supplier.

The walls of the drawing-room are covered by paper, white with a pale green stripe, stuck on with paste. The paper is peeling off the wall in one corner, but this is thought to be due to damp which affected the house in the past rather than to the effect of the recent disaster or of recent climactic factors: the house, as has been pointed out before, seems to have been impervious to any influence from the late events in Ireland.

One of the lower floor bay windows forms a focal point for this room: it is hung with both white lace curtains, of the type manufactured in Nottingham (machine bobbin net) and drapes made of a mixture of cotton and viscose, having the broken weave characteristic of linen and a shiny surface. The latter curtains are cream and patterned with illustrations of birds and flowers, in green, blue and pink. The effect is gaudy but in keeping with the tone of the room, which is fussy and Victorian, probably deliberately so.

On the interior wall of the house opposite the bay window is a fireplace, already alluded to. It is large and rounded at the top, made of black painted iron, moulded decoratively, and set with tiles. The tiles are multicoloured, and depict various fantastical and mythological flora and fauna: unicorns, stags and seabirds of unidentifiable species are among the items represented. The predominant colours of this fireplace are brown, gold and dark blue, and the effect is extremely rich and attractive.

On the walls of the room a number of pictures are hung: three oils and two water-colours, and six engravings. The latter are arranged in a group, over the sofa which will be presently described, and form a unit, while the oils and water-colours are scattered more or less at random. That the position of some of these pictures has been altered from time to time is obvious from some light-coloured patches, rectangular and square in shape, which occur in four different places on the wallpaper.

The oil paintings are the following:

(a) *Listowel Races*, by Bob Cairns (a stylised, highly coloured representation of a crowd scene and some horses on race track);

(b) *Fisherman*, by Carol Murphy (a romantic scene depicting a woman standing on the edge of a river bank, staring at the water, done exclusively in brown, green and grey);

(c) an unnamed portrait of a woman, signed by Carol Murphy. The woman is conventional in appearance, has black hair, a long nose and a red dress or sweater.

The water-colours are unnamed, but all of them are signed. They are:

(a) a picture of a table-top mountain, black silhouetted against a sky of peach and blue, by E MacHugh;

(b) a still-life (apple, cheese, jug) by Carol Murphy;

(c) a bog, stylised, green and brown, by E MacHugh;

(d) sheep on a mountain side, by Maria MacSimmons;

(e) a stylised cliffscape, by Arthur Nicholls.

The etchings or engravings are six prints, by James Malton, a well-known Dublin engraver, of various Dublin scenes, to wit:

(a) Christchurch Cathedral

(b) St Patrick's Cathedral

(c) West Front, St Patrick's Cathedral

(d) The Parliament House

(e) The Royal Exchange

(f) The Tholsel

The furniture in this room consists of a sofa or couch, four armchairs, all of which are covered with the same material as that from which the decorated curtains are made and which has been described above. Besides, there are two coffee tables, a standard lamp, a piano, a stereo record player, discs of classical and Irish traditional music, and one small set of three bookshelves, containing a variety of popular novels. There are also a few sets of English classics: a Dickens, a Walter Scott (the only hardbacks) and a few Brontes.

Dining-Room

The dining-room is located across the hall from the drawing-room and has the same dimensions. It is also, like the drawing room, provided with a bay-window, curtained and draped in similar manner, and a fireplace. The latter is simpler than that in the more elaborately furnished apartment, however, and is constructed of yellow brick, the same brick as is found in the outer walls of the house.

The floor of this room is polished maple, on which one large rug lies. This rug seems to be handwoven, woollen, and has brown, red and white stripes. It is rather dirty.

The walls are painted turquoise, and hung with a set of six willow pattern plates and an embroidered sampler of the alphabet.

The furniture comprises a square table with draw leaves and heavy carved legs, made from oak and plywood, a pine dresser, filled with an assortment of china and delft-ware, and six chairs, oak with rattan seats.

In the drawers of the dresser are two linen table-cloths, one white and one yellow, ten silver knives, eight silver forks, two silver teaspoons and sixteen silver soup spoons. There are also some crumpled up paper napkins, red, illustrated with boughs of holly and pictures of Santa Claus, some string, a packet of coloured elastic bands, two crayons, a used blue ballpoint pen, a spool of black thread into which a darning needle is stuck, and a copy of a woman's magazine.

Kitchen

This room is located at the back of the house, opening onto what was probably the back garden, by means of a French window and a solid door. It is almost as large as the reception rooms at the front of the house, measuring 20' x 15'. It is divided into two parts: an alcove, screened by a rattan curtain, which appears to have been the working space, and a much larger area, which probably functioned as a living room.

The kitchen floor is tiled with red stone, and the walls are white. It has one window, hung with brown tweed curtains. The walls are hung with the following objects:

(a) a calendar, Premier Dairies, portraying flimsily dressed women of exceptional beauty drinking pints of milk in scenic surroundings. The calendar is for the year 20-- and the months up to September, when the disaster occurred, have been pulled off and presumably discarded;

(b) a notice-board, upon which are pinned postcards, of Rome by night and a beach in Portugal by day, a programme of lectures for "Bray Women's Group", a notice from a hospital detailing symptoms of danger to look out for after a fall, a notice from Wicklow County Council concerning motor taxation, a notice from Wicklow County Council concerning water rates, a bill from the Revenue Commissioners for property tax, two theatre tickets (Gate, 22 October 20--), a recipe for gingerbread men, a shopping-list (listing: Jif, toilet paper, cocoa, potatoes, margarine lemonade, Alka Seltzer), a list headed "menu" (Mon: bacon and cabbage; Tue:pizza, icecream; Wed: beans on toast; Thurs: potatoes, fried eggs, cake; Fri: fish fingers, chips; Sat: toasted cheese sandwiches, chocolate Swiss roll; Sun: roast chicken, turnips, potatoes, ice-cream), an invitation to the opening of an exhibition of paintings by Christy Maginn at the Taylor Gallery, to Mr and Mrs Murphy

MacHugh, a docket from Bray Cobblers, for soles and heels, £10, a programme from the Bray Yoga Club;

(c) a spice rack, holding twelve small jars , labelled marjoram, oregano, curry, paprika, chilli, nutmeg, thyme, ginger, cummin, coriander, whole black pepper, meat tenderiser. All the jars were empty;

(d) a linen tea-towel, depicting a trout swimming in a weed-filled turquoise river, stamped Kilkenny;

(e) a reproduction of Van Gogh's *Sunflowers*;

(f) a shelf containing ten recipe books;

(g) a shelf upon which lies a selection of wine-making or home-brewing equipment, including a hydrometer, a packet (empty) of campden tablets, a plastic tube, a demijohn, two air-filters;

(h) an electric clock (stopped at 11.20);

(i) a rack of hooks, from which depend several items of kitchen equipment, eg egg-beater, ladle, fish-slice, etc;

(j) a carved pine shelf containing two flower pots, plastic, and a selection of mugs, bowls and jugs, illustrated with flowers and woodland animals, and clearly part of a collection of decorative pieces;

(k) a large wooden shelf containing six plastic flower pots.

The kitchen is furnished with fitted pine presses which are built along the two interior walls and are filled with empty receptacles for various foodstuffs, as well as kitchen equipment (all these are itemised in Appendix F.) It is furnished also with a rectangular deal table, very worn, and with six chairs, some of deal and some of oak, none matching, as well as one rocking chair.

In the kitchen alcove are found an electric cooker (ESB) and refrigerator (Novum) a dish-washer (Bendix), a washing machine (Bendix), a microwave oven (Moulinex) a sandwich maker (Moulinex) a food processor (Hoover) and sundry other items (see Appendix D).

Conservatory

The conservatory, which extended from the kitchen door to the dining room, is completely wrecked. Its area, equal in size to the kitchen, was adjudged from some broken material marking the site of the original outer walls. Shattered glass littered the floor area, as well as a number of fragments of flower pots. These were not reassembled, due to pressure of time, but it was deduced, from their quantity, that the conservatory had been filled which a huge number of potted plants. Remnants of a sofa or armchair were also found.

Study

The fourth room, apart from the conservatory, on the lower floor of the Bray House is the study or library. It opens off the dining-room, and forms a long narrow apartment at the gable of the house: indeed, it is an oddly proportioned room, more like a passage than anything else, and it would seem that it was originally fashioned by building a partition wall between the gable wall and the dining room: in other words, the study was not part of the original house.

It is lined with shelves from floor to ceiling, and stocked with some three thousand volumes, the predominant subject of which is law: although it was beyond the limits of our resources to make an inventory of the material, and no catalogue was found, it appeared that more than half the books in the room concern Irish and international, mainly British, law. About another quarter consist of parliamentary papers, and the rest are works of a miscellaneous nature, many of which are literary books by Gaelic or Anglo-Irish authors: names like Mairtín O Cadhain, Mairtín O Direáin, Seán O Riordáin, Eoghan O Tuairisc, and others, occur.

Apart from books and shelves, the study is furnished with one capacious green baize-topped desk, a swivel chair, a personal computer (Amstrad PCW 9512), an armchair, a footrest, a radio, a VHS recorder and television set, and six videos, the contents of which will be described later.

Of the numerous items found in the desk, and in other parts of the study, the following are considered most worthy of note:

(a) a pocket diary for 20--, the contents of which will be described at the end of this report;

(b) personal letters from Fiona MacHugh, Angela MacHugh, and Brian O'Brien, which are reproduced at the end of this report;

(c) professional letters, of a legal nature, from Mr Malachy Smythe, Dr Bill Leonard, Padraig Montague, and Mrs Rosemary Montague, which are reproduced at the end of this report;

(d) one whiskey flask;

(e) one silver cigarette case;

(f) one silver cigarette lighter;

(g) an airline ticket, Aer Lingus, Dublin-London, 15 April 20-;

(h) a copy of *In Dublin* magazine (9 April 20--), and several copies of *The Irish Eagle*. Relevant or interesting extracts from these are reproduced at the end of this report;

(h) two silver Parker pens;

(i) four glasses;

(j) one pair of spectacles;

(k) one black and white photograph of a teenage girl.

Hall

The hall is painted deep, midnight blue and the floor is covered with a red Persian rug. The room contains a hallstand of Victorian design, hung with several dozen coats and other outer garments, some of which appear to be extremely antique, with one chair and a small table, on which a telephone stands. A notebook beside the telephone contains various names, numbers and messages, which will be outlined more fully at the end of this report. One piece of paper, torn out of another notebook, stuck on the wall above the phone and contained this message, "Ring Brian !!!"

Bathroom

A small bathroom or cloakroom, containing a lavatory and a handbasin, as well as one small table upon which a plastic flower pot stands, opens off the hall. It is painted pink and the floor, wooden, is also painted, navy blue, with a pattern of flowers at the edges. The latter seems to have been done by an amateur and is rather clumsily executed, but attractive.

Upper Floor

There are four rooms and a bathroom on the upper floor.

Main Bedroom

This room is situated immediately above the drawing-room. Its windows open onto a panoramic view of the sea.

It is distinctively decorated, predominantly in shades of green, yellow and brown: the carpet is brown, the walls are papered with a pattern of yellow and green leaves on a white background, the curtains are a deeper shade of yellow. The room, facing east, is filled with an aqueous light, as a result of the curtains and the colour scheme: otherwise the rooms on this side of the house are lit very coldly, from the north-east.

The furniture in the room is of old stripped pine, cottage or farmhouse pieces. The bed has a brass headrail, and, besides the wardrobe, dressing table and chest of drawers, the room contains an old-fashioned washing stand, complete with large pitcher and basin. Besides, there are two small pine tables, upon which empty flower vases stand. The vases are of handthrown pottery, and are brown and grey.

The wardrobe is crammed to capacity with clothes, mainly women's clothes. They are a mixture of size twelves and fourteens, and mixed in style also. Some are conventional fashionable clothes, mini-skirts, suits, etc. But others are outdated hippy type "gear": cheese-cloth blouses, Indian skirts and dresses, harem pants.

Jewellery on the dressing table also manifests this distinctive lack of consistency of style: there are some valuable conventional pieces, namely one diamond bracelet and one brooch containing a sapphire, but there are dozens of wooden necklaces and other cheap and ostentatious items.

In the bottom of the wardrobe is a heap of some forty pairs of shoes, sizes five to six, in assorted styles and conditions.

There are, besides, a number of books, mainly on a shelf in a bedside locker, some on the dressing table and three on the floor beneath the bed. The books are paperback novels by Irish, English and American authors, all of which are female, by contrast with the authors found in the study, all of which are male, with the exception of one book on *Family Law in Ireland* by Mary Browne. The bedroom books are pushed onto the shelves in no particular order, and many of them have been maltreated, and are dog-eared, stained, and even torn.

Bedroom 2

This room has walls painted light pink, a dark pink carpet, and furniture in white melamine with gold touches.

Prints of popular singers - The Cancerous Fish, Rotten Apple, John Smith Jr - are pinned on the wall, as well as one textile hanging, in "folk art" style, depicting a gorilla, and apparently originating in Kenya. Also on the wall are four water colours, all signed Fiona MacHugh, and having as subjects:

(a) a waterfall, probably Powerscourt Waterfall, a straight silver line like a glacier in a mass of red and brown leaves;
(b) one branch of fuchsia;
(c) a bunch of wild flowers, rather loosely represented celandines and harebells, in a jam jar;
(d) a squirrel in a tree.

The room contains a single bed, covered with a pink quilt, a wardrobe full of clothes suitable for a teenage girl, and a chest of drawers, also filled with clothes.

The floor was littered with books, shoes, papers, jewellery, and other miscellaneous items, which the excavators decided could be moved and sorted out into tidy categories without injury to scientific standards.

Among the documents found on the floor and in the item of furniture supposedly designed to serve as a desk, were school exercise books, containing mathematical problems, mainly correctly solved, essays in French, English and Irish on a variety of topics, some letters, from a girl called Francoise, whose execrable English leads to the conclusion that she was not a native speaker of that language, and from a person signing him or herself as Beano, whose sex will be discussed during the analysis which follows this part of the Report. Included among these documents was a scrap-book, not apparently connected with schoolwork, into which had been fixed a variety of dried wild flowers, with their names in Irish, English and Latin, in most cases, handwritten in beside them, together with a description of the location in which the flowers had been found. This item is most interesting and valuable, including, as it does, samples of flora which are now extinct.

Minor Bedroom 3

This sparsely furnished room appears to have been a guest room, and one which was occupied by a visitor at the time of the disaster, or of the abandonment of the house, whichever occurred first. The evidence for the occupancy is a brown suitcase, containing some clothing, on the floor. A few garments also hang in the wardrobe. All the clothing, which is suitable for a woman, is extremely old, worn and unfashionable by almost any standards. Indeed, the clothes found in this room are almost sufficient to call into question the whole concept of fashionable dress and what it means, because they seem to be of a type which can never, at any time, have been modish. The actual items noted were:

(a) shapeless print dresses, with thin belts in their own material; a grey, straight, knee length, skirt; two cardigans in grey and beige; nylon tights and shoes made by Chapelle for the wider foot. Karen suggested, probably correctly, that they represented the wardrobe of an elderly woman. According to certain theories of folk costume, this selection of garments could be also described as just that: folk dress. In that it expresses the desire of an individual not to conform to any of the prescriptions of haute couture or current trends, but adapts modern styles to old-fashioned habits, the clothing in Minor Bedroom 3 is certainly of this kind.

The furniture in the room consisted of one single divan bed, one chair and one fitted wardrobe.

Its walls are painted white and hung with two Impressionist prints, by Monet, and one calendar. Hanging from the calendar's nail is also a set of Rosary beads, in green marble, Connemara marble. On the bedside table was a Catholic Truth Society pamphlet and a bottom set of dentures, in a kitchen cup.

Minor Bedroom 4

This room is hardly furnished. Apart from a kitchen table and a chair, it contains nothing at all in the way of furnishings. There is a typewriter on the table, however, and a selection of typescripts, containing letters and poems, of varying quality, under the table. A selection of these is included in the Appendix.

Bathroom

The bathroom is decorated in bright green and yellow: the walls are papered in white paper upon which are huge sprays of forsythia in yellow and green; the bath, handbasin, and toilet are green, and the floor is painted deep ochre. Towels of green and white hang on the radiator, and there are three empty flower pots on the window sill. A medical chest contains various empty bottles and phials, which originally held vitamin pills, Evening Primrose Oil, Milk of Magnesia, a depilatory cream, TCP and iron tablets. A packet of Durex was also found in this cabinet, unopened and dated 19-- (ie more than ten years old).

Chapter Thirteen

Documents from the Bray House

In this section of my report, I present a selection of written documents found in the Bray House during excavation. It has been impossible, regrettably, to include every item of this nature found in the house here, due to constraints of space. I have tried to choose as objectively as possible those which I consider to be most representative and significant. All other documents are stored at the Ethnology Archive, Uppsala, where they may be examined by any member of the public (please telephone the secretary to make an appointment; afternoons only).

1. Documents relating to Murphy MacHugh

(a) Murphy MacHugh's diary

This item was found in a drawer in the green topped desk in the study. It is a small brown pocket diary, published by

Collins, for the year 20--. Marked the property of Murphy MacHugh, *Thalassa*, Sea Road, Bray, County Wicklow, the entries on the fly leaf indicate that Murphy MacHugh's blood group was A, Rh Neg, and that he was not a kidney donor.

The following entries are made:

10 Jan: Fiona. 7.30. Savoy.
12 Jan: BOB, 5.00. O'Dwyers.
13 Jan: 1.00 pm. Shel. MM.
20 Jan: BOB 5.00 Dwyers.
1 Feb: Fiona, Macbeth Gate 7.45 pm.
4 Feb: Municipal Gall. Opening Eileen 8.00
5 Feb: Dentist (11 Harcourt St. 675532) 11.15 am.
6 Feb: BOB, Dwyers 5.
14 Feb: Fiona, Abbey. 8.00
19 Feb: Elinor's birthday. BOB Dwyers 5.30.
23 Feb: Dentist 11.15 am.
28 Feb: Wexford
4 March: BOB, Fleet 5.00. Dentist 11.15 am.
6 March: Newman House 8.00 Antiquaries.
8 March: Fiona, Screen 8.45.
10 March: Dentist 11.15. BOB, Dwyers, 5.00.
11 March: Lunch Moloney, Kilkenny. 1.00.
16 March: Wexford
24 March: Dentist 11.15. BOB, Dwyers, 5.00.
etc, to 20 April.

(b) Letters to Murphy MacHugh

The desk drawer contained a number of letters to Murphy MacHugh. The following three were deemed to be the most relevant to this study. The unpublished letters are stored in the manuscripts department of the Carolina Library, where they may be consulted at the discretion of the director of the Library.

The only personal letters in the drawer were those printed below, which were written by Fiona MacHugh, Brian O'Brien and Annie MacHugh:

(i)

Portsalon

5 July 20--

Dearest Da,

Sorry for the delay in writing. The weather is brill, as always, and I've been having a really deadly time. Even right now, I'm on the beach, completely covered, of course, in my cotton all-in-one, and covered by Total Block, of course. Although it's so much cooler here than at home, with such heavenly little breezes, that I really wonder if the total protection routine is necessary? It feels so comfortable and natural here, I can't believe it's risky. Still, better be sure etc.

I mean, I can actually walk around, in comfort, in July! I've collected some harebells for drying - I haven't got any, they don't seem to grow anywhere else that I've seen. There are a few other interesting flowers: some thrift left, and yesterday I saw an ox-eye daisy. But no fuchsia at all any more. Even I remember when it was all over the place. Isn't it astonishing? And not a single dogrose, and they used to be growing like grass here. The grass is still OK, by the way!

The birds are quite interesting, but there's nothing special, just mallards on the pond and seagulls on the beach. The rabbits are a joy, to me, Grandma and actually all the locals can't stand them and make every effort to get rid of them. But they seem to be immune to absolutely everything except shot, and shooting is a slow way of exterminating a million rabbits. It's like living in rabbit warren, in fact, they keep popping up and bobbing around at all hours of the day and night. Quite brill, honestly. You'd love them too.

We've taken time off from the beach to climb Knockrea, just once. Hot climb, but worth it. The loughs on top cool you, just looking at them. I've never seen anything so black, and so cold. A swan was swimming on one of the loughs, really spectacular, the white on black. The goats, with which the hills used to be alive, as you know, are no longer there at all, as far as we could see. Odd. I'd have thought they'd survive anything.

Went to Letterkenny last Thursday to shop. No fun. They've a cinema but nothing on ever. Crocodile Dundee 7, did you ever? Bought a few paperbacks, that's all.

I visited Gran as soon as I got here. She thanks you for the present, she liked it, although, she said, she doesn't wear woolly scarves in July. She said she hopes to visit you soon! Mum will be thrilled, I know!

Hope you're enjoying the summer. Don't work too hard! See you in a few weeks.

Love,
Fiona.

(ii)

8 Vernon Lawn,
Clontarf,
Dublin 5.

10 January 20--

Dear Murph,

Just a note to say I won't be able to make it on Friday: a family celebration has cropped up: Maria's birthday. See you Friday week instead, usual time and place.

Why haven't you been at work?

Brian.

(iii)

Bunnington.

[no date]

Dearest Francis Xavier,

Thank you very much for the £100 you sent with Fiona. It came in handy. The pension does not go far these times, I need not tell you.

Fiona is a grand girl. The image of her mother, God bless her. We don't see a lot of her in Donegal these times. Sure I suppose she's run off her feet, with all her friends and art exhibitions and night classes. I don't know how she gets the time for all that at all. Tell her I was asking for her.

The heat has us all killed. The crops are burnt in the fields. The priest offered up a novena for rain after Mass last Sunday, but half of them left the chapel before he finished. So it hasn't worked and is it any wonder? With the crowd that's going nowadays? Fiona doesn't come to Glenvar chapel, I notice. I suppose she goes to Kerrykeel. It's later. I always feel if I don't get mass in Glenvar I haven't got it at all.

My arthritis is better than usual, though still painful. God is good and His Ways Strange.

Johnny The Island is dead. He used to be in the class behind you at school. Do you remember, a big clumpawn of a fellow with hair the colour of boiled carrots? You might as well be teaching the wall, he had my heart scalded. God rest his soul. He left a wife and two weans, God help them, and her unemployed. Cancer of the skin. The usual, God help us.

I'm looking forward to seeing you soon. I might take a run to Dublin. With the free travel it's a pity not to take advantage of it and go on a run somewhere. Tell Elinor I was asking for her and I'll give her a ring when I make up my mind when it suits me to come.

Your Affectionate Mammy.

(c) Barring Order

A xerox copy of the following legal document was found lying on Murphy MacHugh's desk:

Mr Francis Xavier Murphy MacHugh may not enter the house known as *Thalassa*, Florence Terrace, Bray, from this day, 1 April 20-- until 1 October 20--, by order of Bray District Court. Signed, Cahir O'Connor, District Justice.

2. Documents relating to Elinor MacHugh

In Bedroom One and in Bedroom Four a number of documents relating to Elinor MacHugh were discovered. These consisted of letters and a Filocomputer, containing miscellaneous information on the owner's lifestyle, work, relationships, ambitions, and habits: in all, a complete archive relating to Elinor MacHugh, and a most valuable find.

(a) Filocomputer

A personal computerised organiser containing files under the following headings: Calendar, Day Planner, Weekly Planner, Addresses, Shopping Lists, Recipes, Flower Collector's Checker, Medical Record, Education Record, Home Entertainment, Restaurant Entertainment, Private Appointments, Writer's Notebook, Clubs, Societies etc.

(i) *Day Planner*

The Day Planner, dating from 1 January to 30 April 20--, had been programmed to remind the owner of the organiser of certain regular appointments and events. Apart from these, the Planner had been filled in only sporadically during January and February, and after that not at all. The solution to this mystery is to be found in other files on the Filocomp however, and does not mean that the owner ceased to have any plans in February 20--. It simply indicates that the nature of those plans changed.

The regular entries in the planner were for Tuesdays, Fridays and Saturdays, and read as follows:

Tuesday. 6.00 pm. Women's Studies Group Seminar, Belfield.
Friday. 7.00 pm. Art Workshop, Women Artists' Union, Merrion Row.
Saturday. 3.00 pm. Meeting of Greenpeace branch, Maurice's house.

The irregular entries mainly concerned luncheon appointments, dates to go to the theatre, and occasional parties. It is interesting and not without significance that these all stop towards the end of February, suggesting, on the face of it, that Elinor MacHugh's social life ceased then, completely, which is surprising to say the least. The luncheon appointments were all with two people, Marian and Carol, and the venue was always the same: the Peppercannister, Dun Laoghaire. Once, Elinor had an appointment to meet her daughter Fiona at the said establishment (that was at the end of January). She went to the theatre once only during the period in question, to the Abbey to see a production of Frank McGuinness's *Carthaginians*. There were, however, five parties, three in January, including a New Year's party, and two in February.

All of the parties took place on Saturday nights, except for the New Year's one, which occurred on a Thursday. The venues were Marian's (New Year), Carol's, Women Artists' Union (Merrion Row), Monica's (Bray), and Women's Group (Bray). Either the party at Monica's or at Women's Group, both in Bray, seems to have had important consequences in Elinor's life, and it is significant that after these events entries in the day planner cease.

(ii)   Weekly Planner

The Weekly Planner has been filled in, partially, between weeks 1 and 11, that is, during January and February. After that, Elinor MacHugh seems to have ceased having weekly plans.

The most heavily marked week is the first of the year. The entry reads as follows:

> Finish *Sisters* and *Fiona*. Buy large tube of yellow ochre and Blanc de Blanc. Plan video with Carol, and make contact with script writer. Enrol at Unislim. Run every morning, seven to eight. Discuss matters with Murphy and investigate legal situation. Visit sales for clothes and new pots. Organise party for weekend.

Further entries of interest are the following:

Week Three
  See Bobby Proctor and discuss video. Arrange meeting with Bill Whelan at RTE.
Week Four
  Finish *Fiona* and decide contents of April Exhibition.
Week Five
  Shoot first half of video in Wicklow.
Week Seven
  Shoot second half of video. Finish *Fiona*. Buy new microwave.
Week Eight
  Organise editing with Bill Whelan.
Week Nine
  See Bill Whelan re editing
Week Twelve
  Arrange viewing of video at RTE.

(iii)   Addresses

Carol Hannon, 85 Sorrento Rd, Dalkey 854730
Paul Campbell, 21 Windmill Crescent, Foxrock 880030
Eileen Byrne, 10 Castlewood Ave 973244
Maria Byrne, 1 Tivoli Terrace 807542
Monica 825596
Yvonne Latour, 10 rue Hardy, 78000 Versailles.
Suzie, 16 1 212 1759935
B. 825536

(iv)   Shopping Lists

The shopping lists were numerous: one for every week from 1 January to 15 April. With a few exceptions, they were almost identical, nevertheless a new one had been written for each shopping. The typical list is as follows:

Fruit: apples, oranges, bananas (?)
Vegetables: potatoes, turnip, tinned beans
Meat: mince (2), sausages, spam
Fish: fingers
Dairy: marg
Grocery: sugar, tea, coffee, flour, spaghetti, biscuits, jam
Bakery: bread.

An exceptional list appears on 23 January, as follows:

Fruit: pineapple
Vegetable: cabbage, onions
Meat: one chicken
Fish: frozen prawns
Dairy: cream
Grocery: six pack Harp, rice
Bakery: rolls.

(v) Recipes

This section, quite large, consisted of blank pages. Only one recipe was included, for high fibre bread.

(vi) Flora Collector's Checker

This section contained two lists, dating from the summer of 199- and of 202--, of flowers sighted in Kerry. The first list is as follows:

Early purple orchid
Wild violet
cowslip
primrose
heartsease
Irish orchid
buttercup
kingcup
thrift
bird's foot trefoil
marsh pea
bugle
bloody cranesbill
charlock
sheep's bit scabious
London Pride
ox-eye daisy
Ragged Robin
pimpernel
sea campion
sea rocket
wall pepper
yellow flag

foxglove
self-heal
tormentil
Montbretia
fuschia.

The second list is the following:

thrift
birds foot
celandine
self-heal
sheeps bit scabious.

(vii) Medical Record

Clinical History:
Pleurisy (20--)
Hibernian Influenza (19--, 19--, 19--, 20--)
Pregnancy: 19--, 20--
Varicose veins treated 20--
Angina Pectoris (20--)
By-pass operation: 20--. Bray Clinic. Consultant: Mr Blennerhasset.
Examination due: 2 March 20--, Bray Clinic, 2.30 pm.

(viii) Education Record

Year: 20--
Teacher: Iníon Uí Bhaoill
Class: 5th year
Remarks: weak at maths, German, science. Good at Irish, English. Lazy and unmotivated (teacher's comment). Needs understanding and encouragement.

(ix) Home Entertainment

Time: 8.00 pm
Date: 25 January 20--
Occasion: blank

Guests	Firm	Position in Firm
Carol	Own home	Boss
Monica	Bray library	bottom rung
Paul	Bray library	second rung from bottom

Bob O'Brien	O'Brien and Sons	Son
Melissa	St Ruan's	Teacher
Billy B.	National	MD
	Computers	

Menu
   Starter: prawn cocktail
   Main course: roast chicken, potatoes, cabbage
   Dessert: Pineapple with cream Coffee

Restaurant Entertainment
   MacDonald's, Fiona, 1.00, 22 Feb

Private Information
   Billie: 825596
   4 March, 7.00, Dun Laoghaire.
   Birthday: 5 May.
   Would like copy of Victor Hugo's essays.

(xii)   Writer's Notebook

This section, filled with unlined pages in green, pink and yellow, includes some very third-rate poems.

(xiii)   Clubs, Societies etc.

Here are entered simply the names of clubs to which Elinor belonged:

   The Bray Women's Group
   The Women Artist's Union
   Unislim

(xiv)   Calorie Counter

Elinor kept a day-to-day check on her intake of calories. She allowed herself 1200 per day, but usually overstepped the limit by two to four hundred calories, if not more.

Study

The study, as has been mentioned previously, contained some letters from a lawyer to Murphy MacHugh, viz:

Mr Sean Callaghan
O'Brien and Co Solicitors Ltd
Hely Chambers
Clare Street
Dublin 2

10 August 20--

Dear Mr MacHugh,

Further to our meeting on 5 August 20-- I wish to request you to furnish us with a copy of the deeds of your house and of any other property you may possess, a statement of your salary from MacHugh Ltd, and a statement of your wife's income, plus details of any property, investments, etc owned by her.

As soon as we have received the above information, I will arrange a further meeting.

Yours sincerely,
Sean.

Mr Sean Callaghan
O'Brien and Co Solicitors Ltd
Hely Chambers
Clare Street
Dublin 2

4 September 20--

Dear Murphy,

I have been unable to contact you at your office. Following our discussion on Tuesday, I have had my secretary make contact with your wife, and have asked her to come to my rooms to talk with me on Monday next, 11 am. I do not wish to pry into your relationship with her, but Kelly, my secretary, has suggested to me that your wife is not at all cognisant with what is going on. I feel it will ease matters considerably for all of us if you could brief her in advance, if you have not already done so. I am not, I need hardly add, a marriage counsellor.

Best wishes,
Sean.

O'Brien and Co Solicitors
Hely Chambers
Clare Street
Dublin 2

15 September 20--

Dear Murphy,

I have had a meeting with Elinor on Monday. She had not been prepared for my communication and it came as a shock to her. I really do not feel I can continue to handle this case if you are uncooperative. In any event it is going to be extremely difficult, since Elinor does not feel cooperative herself, and will oppose most of the conditions suggested by you. I recommend you to hire one of the best legal representatives in town for what promises to be an interesting and arduous battle.

Personally I would prefer to withdraw my services at this point, as is quite natural, under the circumstances. As I pointed out before, I am not a counsellor and cannot act as such. Given our long acquaintance, I will not pursue this matter further, but I am disappointed in your attitude, to me and to Elinor, for whom I have the highest regard.

Sincerely,
Sean.

3. Letters to Fiona MacHugh

(a)

798 Earls Court Road
London SW 1

2 Jan. 20--

Dear Feebie,

He who is bored with London is bored with life, and I'm not, whatever that proves. Having a real old ball, is what it proves. Saw three old Ayckbourns so far, plus the very latest

Grimshaw at the National Theatre. Stuffy, stuffeeeee! You'd like it.

Picked up something for you yesterday at Harrods. You'll just love it, I'll give you a clue, it's made of real, but real, gold. What do I get for pulling it off? You know what security's like at Harrods?

Also collected some books, from the British Library among other places. A nice first ed. of Jane Eyre which is, I gather, rare. A rare Eyre for me, dearie, not for you!

Oh I wish you were here!

Your one and only
Beano.

(b)

265 Rue St Michelle
Versailles 2659

30 July 20--

Dear Fiona,

How goes it? We are very well. Maman has bought me a new dress for summer. It is blue with white spots, and has a white lace collar. I wear white shoes and blue socks with it, and also a white hat, sometimes, if it is sunny. I am very pleased with it.

I have also new shorts, yellow, and two new T-shirts, in black and blue. These I will bring with me when we go to the beach in the Midi next week. I am looking forward to it. It is very hot in Paris now, and you cannot breathe. We will drive down, Maman and I, and Papa will come later in August when he is free from his work.

My report from school came last week, it is not so good and Maman is unhappy about it, I am supposed to do the Bac next year. I do not care. School is so awful and college will be awful too. I want to work in a dress shop and become a great designer.

I hope you are having a nice time in Ireland this summer. I would like to visit you and your family again but we do not have enough money, Maman says. And of course it is nice in the south here, I will get very brown which will show off my white dress with the blue spots nicely.

Do you still go with Paul? Give him my regards. Also your mother and father. My mother and father say to say hello to you too.

Best wishes,
Francoise.

Chapter Fourteen

Dining-room

The documents found in the dining room, which appeared to have been used as a living room, at least occasionally, by the family, consisted of newspapers and magazines. The majority of those found dated from the week preceding the Accident, but a few were earlier publications, which had been left in the newspaper basket for some unknown reason, possibly simply as a result of inefficient housekeeping, which was evident in other areas of the home as well.

The newspapers numbered eleven in all, and have been packed in sealed plastic envelopes and stored in ideal conditions at the Swedish Newspaper Archive. Below are reprinted items deemed to be of particular significance, as illustrations of the state of Ireland in the period prior to its final extinction:

The Irish Eagle, September 28
ONE HALF OF POPULATION IS NOW LIVING IN POVERTY

One half of the population was found to be living below the poverty line by a new study conducted by the Economic and Social Research Institute. The principal poverty groups are families headed by an unemployed person, families with two or more children, and urban households, according to some results of the survey. The president of the Combat Poverty Association, Ms Brona McKeown, found the results "horrifying, frightening, startling and alarming. It is clear that terrible poverty persists in Ireland, and we must now try to eliminate it," she said, in a speech at the Berkeley Court Hotel, where the report was launched at a champagne and caviare reception.

"We have indicated this problem of poverty in the farming community many times," the head of the IFA, Mr Fiach Lynch, said in a statement to the press. "This is no surprise to us."

The Minister for Social Welfare, Ms Samantha Burke, said she welcomed the report but pointed out that in it poverty was defined as being the state endured by those whose income fell below £50 a week, ie less than one quarter of the minimum standard income in other European countries. If it were defined as being people living on less than £30 a week, only ten percent would be labelled 'poor'. "And if" she added, smiling triumphantly, "it were realistically defined as people having no income at all, Ireland could be said to be completely free of poverty! It's purely a question of definition, after all. A hundred years ago only those who were utterly destitute were described as 'poor'. Now it's people getting sizeable handouts from the government in return for doing absolutely nothing."

Mr Sean Sweeney, of the Progressive Workers Party, pointed out that people living on less than £30 a week did not enter into the statistics, because they were either dead from starvation or had emigrated.

"When I was a girl," Minister Burke added "I had less than £30 a week pocket money. I survived: I invested it, it grew. I was thrifty and shrewd and hardworking, and I throve. That, if you ask my opinion, is what it's all about. It's simple really, you just have to be a good girl and work hard and invest wisely, and then you'll be rich. Look at me now! I'm a minister! I earn £1000 a week, more than four times the standard minimum wage in France and Germany and all those places. Why can't everyone be like me?"

The Irish Eagle, 3 September
NEW TERM BRINGS CRISIS FOR PARENTS
The Welfare system is failing completely to help parents who are so poor that they cannot afford school books, uniforms, busfares and fees. Many parents are turning to moneylenders in order to keep their children at school. Even more, however, are making the decision, which is supported by government policy, to take their children out of school after the compulsory five years have been completed. It is estimated by the Combat Poverty Association that one third of Irish children are no longer receiving education after the age of nine. Many of them, whose school-days are spent in overcrowded classes, are illiterate.

"This is a national scandal," Ms McKeown, the chairwoman of the Association said in a press release yesterday. "From being the country with the best educated population, in the 1980s, we have sunk to the lowest standards in Europe. Our children are being betrayed by a system which educates only the rich, who get richer, while the poor remain uneducated, illiterate, and get even poorer."

Replying to this statement, the Minister for Education, Ms Nora Walsh, said: "Free education for all was a phenomenon of the sixties. Until then, education was a commodity to be bought, like any other. The fact that we have returned to that way of thinking should not be seen as a failure of the system, but as one of its successes. Our economy is healthier than it has been since the foundation of the state. Our national debt is reduced to zero. Our universities are flourishing, and research in Ireland is at last making strides which allow us to take our rightful place among the national financial research units of the world. No longer is an entire population, many of whom are not even married, do not even have children, burdened with the cost of educating other peoples' brats. Excuse the language. But really, this kind of thing makes me sick. It's so wet, it's so unprogressive. People who deserve education will always get it. Look at Patrick Bronte, a penniless farm labourer's boy from Antrim. He got to Cambridge, on the strength of his own intelligence and ambition. Free education has merely hindered the bright from working and provided the stupid, whom we should be striving to eliminate, not encourage, for heaven's sake, with a bed of feathers in which to hide from reality."

This is the longest statement from the minister on record.

The Irish Eagle, 3 April
IRISH IMMIGRANTS RECRUITED TO IRANIAN ARMY
The army of the Republic of Iran today launched a recruitment drive to attract young Irish men and women into its ranks.

"We are offering specially attractive conditions to Irish recruits who enlist for the minimum period of ten years," General Khallid Khameni, the initiator of the drive, explained at a reception in Dublin Castle. "We realise that Irish men and women make exceptional soldiers, given the correct training. We hope that this scheme will benefit both Ireland and Iran, and strengthen relations between the two countries."

The Taoiseach Mr De Vere Montgomery said that he wished the drive every success. "Ireland has had a long and happy relationship with Iran," he went on "and, and we have been exporting beef to its markets for many years."

Over the past five years Irish schoolchildren have been encouraged to learn Arabic, in order to improve their employment opportunities in Middle Eastern countries. Arabic is now taught in most schools, having almost completely ousted Irish as a Leaving Certificate subject.

The Irish Eagle, 13 April
KATHERINE A
Britain yesterday ordered the Northern Irish port of Larne to accept the *Katherine A,* a container ship carrying toxic waste which has plied the seas from Nigeria to Britain in search of a taker for its noxious cargo.
op. cit., p. 4.

WORLD POLLUTION WORSENING
A devastating picture of an increasingly polluted world has emerged from the United Nations studies monitoring air, water and food contaminants in rich and poor countries.

The studies suggest that while conditions in a small number of countries are improving slightly, in most, and particularly in Third World countries, a process of rapid deterioration is in train. Less than a tenth of the world's 1.8 billion city dwellers live in air conditions that pose no risk to health. Eight in ten of the world's population breathe air that contains disturbingly high levels of sulphur dioxide and dust.

Around fifty percent of all rivers are polluted, and fifteen to sixteen million infants in developing countries die each year from diarrhoea and other water-related diseases. Untreated sewage in water supplies is a crucial problem.

Food contamination is no longer under control, even in the industrialised world: everywhere, pesticides and cancer-causing aflatoxins are causing problems. Food poisoning is an increasingly prevalent disease, causing more fatalities than ever before.

The greatest killer is, of course, cancer, with skin cancer still the most common cause of death in adults and various leukaemias the major area of concern among children.

AIDS is no longer a serious health problem, except in a few countries (including Ireland), where prevention programmes have been largely ineffective.

These are some results of a study sponsored by the United Nations Health Programme and the World Health Organisation.

The Irish Eagle, 16 April
RADIOACTIVE WASTE "SAFE"
The Department of the Environment in Belfast dismissed a claim that radioactive waste dumped into Belfast sewers was a health hazard.

Mr McAllister, the department's director, admitted that waste was and continued to be dumped, but was completely harmless. He stressed that it was low-level radioactive waste which would not "hurt a fly".

The Irish Eagle, 17 April
DEADLY HERRING VIRUS COMES TO IRELAND
The epidemic which has destroyed the North Sea herring population has spread to Ireland. Results issued last night by the Veterinary Research Laboratory show that the virus has infected herring in the Irish Sea, and will soon spread to other fish.

"It means we had better watch out for the west coast immediately!" a spokesman said. Most herring shoals are found on the West Coast.

Already several thousand dead herrings have been washed up on beaches on the coastal strip between Dundalk and Bray. These will quickly become hazardous to health as they rot. A side effect of the herring virus is a disease affecting sea-birds who feed on the dead fish. Many of our sea-bird species have already become extinct, and now it is virtually certain that the few which remain on Irish coasts, such as the cormorant (or shag) and sandpiper, will soon vanish.

The Irish Eagle, 18 April
NUCLEAR MATERIAL SINKS OFF WALES
Department of Energy officials were seeking information from British officials yesterday about a container carrying radioactive material which was on board a ship that sank in the Irish Sea off Wales last week.

The material was on its way from Liverpool to Belfast in one of 91 containers on board the 998-ton Minerva which sank in heavy seas 30 miles from Llandudno. The 10-member crew were rescued.

Mr Mersy Brian, the Liverpool pollution officer, said the material was in canisters inside the container and that there was no way they could break open at sea. "Even if they did," he said, "I am assured there would be no significant threat to the food chain."

A spokesman for Liverpool Packing, the company which had dispatched the containers to Belfast, said it was not known if the container with the radioactive material was still with the sunken vessel or had broken free. "The material is low-level radioactive," he said. "It is not really dangerous."

The Nuclear Energy Board in Dublin said it had not been informed of the incident. It could not possibly have any impact on Ireland, a spokesman said.

The Irish Eagle, 23 April
NUCLEAR PREPAREDNESS AT ITS WORST
Dublin Corporation has criticised government assumptions that a Chernobyl-type disaster could not occur in Ireland, and has asked for an improved nuclear emergency plan.

It demanded a suitable plan which would help minimise the effects of a crisis on the public. This followed an emergency planning exercise held last week.

"The main thing to come out of the exercise was that preparedness is at rock bottom," said the chairman of the Dublin Corporation Emergency Planning committee.

"There is no emergency plan at local level to deal with a nuclear incident. All we have is the government's assurance that it can't happen here."

Ireland's national nuclear emergency plan was drawn up ten years ago but has yet to be published. There are no local authority emergency plans in Ireland.

The Irish Eagle, 24 April
HIGH RADIATION LEVELS FOUND IN DONEGAL SHEEP
Restrictions on the slaughter of sheep may be forced on Donegal farms, in an attempt to protect the lamb export business.

A report released yesterday by the Nuclear Energy Board reveals that between 68 and 98 per cent of Donegal farms have been contaminated by fall-out from the Sellafield disaster.

A survey of 1300 sheep on 130 farms showed that 70 per cent of the sheep tested had radiation levels of 1000 bequerels per kilo. The 1000 bequerel limit, however, is that applied in Britain. In the rest of Europe, 600 bequerels is the danger limit. And on this basis, all of the 130 farms examined would be regarded as "contaminated".

It has been learned also that 40 tonnes of powdered milk exported to Mexico from Ireland have been destroyed owing to its high levels of radioactivity.

"We are very surprised" said a spokesman for Bord Bainne. "It is well known that Irish milk is perfectly safe." When asked if it was intended to take any precautions vis à vis the sale of milk on the home market, Mr Lynch said: "Of course not."

The Irish Eagle, 3 March
POLLUTION IN POULAPHOUCA RESERVOIR
Poulaphouca Reservoir, the main reservoir for the Dublin West region, has been heavily polluted by radioactive material for the past five years, a report released by Professor Ian Jordan of Trinity College revealed yesterday.

"The contamination has been caused by the dumping of canisters of radioactive waste into the reservoir," Professor Jordan explained. "It is not known yet who has been responsible for the dumping, but we suspect that the material originated in the North of Ireland. The canisters were perhaps not intended to leak, but one of them has done so, with the result that this water is toxic and contains levels of radioactivity in excess of 500 bequerels per gallon. It is extremely dangerous and, since the water has been drunk by people in such places as Tallaght and Clondalkin over an extended period, the outcome of the disaster for them must certainly be tragic."

Professor Jordan went on to suggest that the population served by the polluted reservoir should be immediately offered emergency medical services. It is unlikely, however, given the current state of health services in the country that this suggestion will or can be acted upon.

The Irish Eagle, 26 April
DEATHS FROM CANCER INCREASE AGAIN
Deaths from cancer in Ireland last year reached an all time high of 700 000.

The majority of deaths resulted from various malign skin cancers, caused by the Greenhouse Effect. Leukemia, however, is also on the increase, and 100 000 deaths were of children affected by this form of cancer.

Attempts to link the huge rise in leukemia fatalities with the proliferation of nuclear power stations in the British Isles have been described by a Department of Health spokesman as "completely unverifiable" and "alarmist".
op. cit., p.5

PLAGUE OF MICE AFFECTS PROPERTY VALUES
Residents of Dublin's most exclusive suburb, Foxrock, are experiencing difficulty in selling their homes because of the infestation of the area by mice.

"They've been here since Christmas," Mrs Sally Anderson, of Kill Lane, told us. "Nothing seems to get rid of them, they're making life impossible. Sometimes I wake up at night to find them crawling over my face. I'm scared to let the children sleep without mosquito nets, but they can chew through them anyway. It's sheer hell!"

The mice, which swarm over roads, gardens, and houses, can be numbered in millions, and belong to a new strain which resists all normal poisons. The Eastern Health Board is attempting to blast them away, but this extermination technique has obvious limitations in a residential area.

Life in Foxrock has become unbearable, and many homeowners have put their properties on the market. It is impossible to sell a home in Foxrock, however, except at rock-bottom prices. The average going rate is £10 000, one thirtieth of usual values in this area.

op. cit., p. 13

TROUT SIGHTED IN LOUGH CORRIB

A County Galway schoolboy on his way home from school sighted a trout in Lough Corrib yesterday afternoon.

"It jumped into the air, about a foot out of the water," the boy, Michael Bourke, reported. "It was a silvery colour. I'm sure it was a trout."

Marine biologists have been called in to verify the report.

No trout have been seen in Lough Corrib since 1995, and they are believed to be almost extinct in Ireland.

The Irish Eagle, 29 April

CEGB GOES AHEAD WITH TEST

The Central Electricity Generating Board in Northern Ireland has no plans to postpone the test scheduled for 30 April at Ballylumford.

During the test, the number 1 reactor's cooling system will be turned off.

The Republic's minister for energy has speculated on the possibility of legal proceedings against Northern Ireland.

Greenpeace stated that it has been calling for legal proceedings against Britain and Northern Ireland since last June. The British nuclear industry is "clandestine and willing to risk thousands of lives on both sides of the Irish Sea" a spokeswoman said in a report released yesterday.

A CEGB spokesman said that "there was absolutely no danger, and those who used the media to express their fears were scaremongers, doing much more harm than the test possibly could."

Chapter Fifteen

Analysis of Report

Having presented a description of the artefactual and documentary evidence which came to light in the excavation of the Bray House, I would now like to offer an interpretation of that material. Although I am certain that some of the theories in my analysis will be questioned, I would like to point out that, apart from being the person best acquainted with the material in question, I am also in possession of contextual and background information which is not common knowledge among Swedish or world archaeologists/anthropologists (insofar as they exist, apart from myself) on account of my long-standing, in-depth knowledge of Ireland. I feel, therefore, that I am in a strong position as far as the examination of the Bray House finds are concerned.

The survey of the Bray House yields fascinating insights into not only the family which inhabited it, but also into the social, cultural, and economic state of Ireland immediately prior to Ballylumford.

I will initiate my analysis by discussing the family, their characters and relationships, and go on to examine the wider issues.

Residents of the Bray House

It is obvious that the house belonged to Murphy and Elinor MacHugh, and was generally occupied by them and their daughter Fiona. It is possible that Murphy MacHugh was not resident in the house for some months preceding the disaster, and it is also possible that at that time a guest was staying with the MacHughs, since a room which appeared to be a guest room bore traces of recent habitation - clothes, rosary beads etc.

Murphy MacHugh was a solicitor, a man of culture and refinement, as is evident from his collection of books, his theatre-going habits, and the general aura of intellectualism which pervaded his home. Photographs and video films (in Swedish Royal Archive) reveal him to have been tall, thin, grey haired, with the type of physiognomy sometimes termed "distinguished". He wore spectacles and appears on one video smoking a pipe. His favoured dress appeared to be a leather casual jacket, brown in colour, a pale green checked shirt, and corduroy pants.

The quality of the Bray House, of its furnishings and various other effects, and particularly the decidedly upmarket tone of the rooms particularly apportioned to him, indicate that Murphy was successful in his career. Notes in his diary, letters and other documents found in the study suggest that he had a wide variety of contacts, within the legal world and in other circles. When it is taken into account that Murphy MacHugh had apparently been living somewhere other than the Bray House during the period prior to the Incident, and would presumably have removed some of his personal property from the said residence, this seems even more likely.

Of Mr MacHugh's personal life we know a great deal. Indeed, it is true to say that the Bray House provides us with more concrete facts concerning him than any other of its inhabitants, although this is not what one would have anticipated. Of his relationships with his mother, wife and daughter we learn much from his letters and pocket-diary: it is apparent that he enjoyed a close bond with the former, Annie MacHugh. Her letter to her son indicates that she was a woman of strong and domineering character, who enjoyed a great deal of influence over Murphy, and who was bitterly hostile towards his wife. The fact that Murphy had allowed this type of situation to be perpetuated throughout his entire married life is proof that he was, from start to finish, tied to his mother's apron strings: not only did he maintain contact with her, he continued to send her money, to invite her to visit his home, and listened to her complaints about his wife. This type of mother-fixation - for such it must have been - although it seems unusual to us, was quite common in Ireland, and I have seen many examples of it in the past.

Murphy MacHugh also had a close relationship with his daughter, Fiona. Presumably he met her at home from time to time, but he also made a practice of accompanying her to the theatre and cinema at regular, more or less fortnightly, intervals. Although this may indicate nothing more than a shared interest in those particular art forms, both of which were highly developed in Ireland, it certainly strikes one as odd that his partner in his interest was his daughter rather than his wife. My suggestion is that Fiona had become for him a surrogate wife, since his marriage to Elinor was a dismal failure. Perhaps it would be even more accurate to say that Fiona was a surrogate mistress, being of the age usually most attractive to middle-aged men who are tired of their marriages ie about eighteen.

Of his relationship with his wife, the documents speak for themselves: not only can we see that Elinor and Murphy MacHugh never went out or holidayed together, and had very few interests in common, we know that a short time before the Incident the marriage had broken up: the barring order, found in Murphy's study, indicates fairly conclusively that violence had been a factor in causing the rupture, since usually such edicts are issued only in cases of domestic violence. The barring order explains too, of course, why Murphy was living away from the family home at this time. But it makes it difficult to comprehend the reason for Murphy's initiation of proceedings for a legal separation (divorce having remained illegal in Ireland) without informing Elinor of his intention. Perhaps this move simply resulted from the rift between Murphy and his wife: clearly all communication had broken down. Although one can speculate as to the precise causes of this, and although some reasons are plain enough - incompatibility, Murphy's egotism, violence, etc - we are, unfortunately, not in a position to say exactly why the relationship had become so hopeless, any more than we can guess what brought it about in the first place, since it is difficult to understand why Elinor and Murphy ever married. It can hardly have been a rational decision on either part.

Murphy MacHugh, embroiled in relationships of one kind and another with his three closest female relations, also seems to have had many friends outside the domestic sphere. The principal of these was BOB, presumably Brian O'Brien, also, it would seem, a married man with family responsibilities, and also, it seems likely, a solicitor, perhaps even a colleague or partner.

With Brian O'Brien, Murphy MacHugh had a friendship based on a mutual interest in alcohol: they met at frequent intervals in pubs in the centre of Dublin. It is reasonable to deduce from this that Murphy was an alcoholic, probably the kind of man referred to in Ireland by the quaint euphemism, "serious drinker". However, all possibilities can be borne in mind. We do not, in fact, have conclusive evidence that Murphy drank alcohol while visiting pubs, but it seems likely.

Neither is it necessary to suggest that Murphy enjoyed a homosexual relationship with Brian O'Brien. However, the nature of their friendship - regular meetings seem to have been of great importance to them, as Brian's letter of apology testifies - does not rule out this eventuality. And Murphy's inability to relate successfully to women as equals, and probably not as sexual partners, adds weight to the hypothesis. It can also be pointed out that, apart from his mother, wife and daughter, there is no evidence of any other woman in Murphy MacHugh's life. Women, for him, were part of the household, like the furniture, perhaps, or the garden plants. He does not seem to have learned to form friendships with them in a normal healthy way, outside the sphere of family and home.

Although the greatest quantity of documentary and other evidence relates directly to Elinor MacHugh, she remains a shadowy and elusive personality. In the final analysis, we know less about her than about her husband. This undoubtedly is owing to the fact that she was a less straightforward character, possibly very complex or perhaps simply very confused.

As far as appearances are concerned, Elinor was not especially beautiful in the conventional sense, being small, dark-haired and with a dark complexion, and having rather sharp features. In photographs, she looks quite plain. In the one video film in which she appears, however, she is, on the contrary, attractive in a lively, energetic way, and dressed in rather pleasing clothes. All her clothes, as evidenced by the content of her wardrobe, were very beautiful. Her favourite colours were yellow and blue, closely followed by black, and she seems to have worn heavy costume jewellery of a quite spectacular nature on all possible occasions. In short, Elinor had dramatic looks, largely affected but partly natural since, as the video shows, her colouring could be quite striking, especially in summer.

This general type of physique and apparel could be described as artistic, and there is ample evidence to indicate that Elinor was indeed an artist, and in more than one field. It would appear that she was primarily a painter, as entries in her Filocomputer and pictures signed EMacH in the house indicate. The lists of flowers, made in Kerry, where Elinor seems to have spent her holidays - as far away from Murphy's birthplace and his mother's home, Donegal, as is possible within the Irish island - would perhaps have been made with a view to drawing or painting them, although of course they might simply evidence some interest in flora on her part: obviously she was concerned enough to note that over an unspecified period, probably a few years, many varieties of flowers disappeared from the Irish countryside, in common with flora in most parts of Europe.

All the MacHughs appear to have had vague, sporadic interests in nature studies (vide Fiona's letter to Murphy). Such uncommitted interests were common in Ireland, as everywhere, in recent years.

Elinor also made films, or was involved in their creation, perhaps as a designer, and finally she seems to have had aspirations to be a writer. There is not much to indicate that she took this final occupation very seriously, and indeed the only proof that she dabbled, or intended to dabble, in literature is her writer's notebook, which is almost empty. Were there other notebooks in Elinor's life, no longer extant? Did she ever, in fact, achieve anything as a writer? The answers to these questions are lost, and will never now be found.

Nor do we have any example of her film work, but her paintings are good, and she enjoyed some success and popularity, as is evidenced by her preparations for exhibitions and her attendance at openings.

Apart from art, her most significant interest was in women's affairs: she belonged to a women's group in Bray, attended lectures at the women's group in the university, and all her friends, with a single exception, seem to have been female. It is logical to deduce from these facts that she was a feminist.

It appears too, however, and somewhat paradoxically, that she was obsessed with some of the occupations of traditional women: her filocomputer is full of shopping lists; she attended a slimming club, which, of course, exists in order to exploit women and to force them into a male-designed mould. She held mixed parties which caused her a great deal of anguish and took much time to prepare. She did not have a full time job, indeed, she had no paid job, because we can take it that her work in the artistic area was more in the nature of a hobby than a profession. It is also probable that she had an affair with someone named Billie, male or female: the name is, of course, androgynous, and it is possible that the affair was lesbian. Elinor's feminism and interest in women's groups, as well as her exclusively female list of friends, suggests that this is highly likely. Whether or not it was the case - and there is, of course, much in Elinor's make-up, insofar as it is known to us, to suggest that it was not - we can state with some certainty that from 28 February, when she attended a dinner party, she was involved in some sort of affair, since from then all other social engagements seem to have stopped. It is interesting to note that this period concurs with that of the final breakup of her marriage, and a connection between the fatal party and that event must be conjectured. Perhaps Murphy, after all, was the spurned partner, perhaps he left Elinor in a fit of jealousy? This seems most unlikely, in view of his very strong personality and Elinor's weak dependent one, but we must consider every contingency.

To conclude my analysis of Elinor's character, she was confused and lacking in a single-minded approach to life. She was a feminist, but with many conservative, non-feminist habits and traits. She was an artist, but a dilettantish one. She was a housewife, who probably did not want to regard herself as such. She was totally incompatible with her husband, as any feminist, even a weak one, would be, but she probably did not wish to separate finally from him: this seems to be the only reasonable explanation of his failure to inform her of his plans to seek a legal separation. It is not improbable that economic considerations would have obliged Elinor to remain in a marriage which was not only meaningless, but which was actually violent as well: as far as we know, she had no income apart from that derived from her husband, and was basically a dependant. She had made some attempts to find employment, as is evidenced in letters of application to various schools (not included in the Appendix, apparently lost or destroyed. Ed) but none of them were successful. (In Ireland, where a high unemployment rate had been a permanent feature of life since the 1970s, it has always been virtually impossible for a married woman in her forties to find work. So it is not surprising that Elinor's applications failed.) Possibly the explanation for her inconsistent behaviour in relation to her marriage is as simple as this. Alternatively, we can impute that she was either a masochist or a would-be martyr, or both, and remained in a difficult marriage in order to indulge these personality defects. There may, of course, be some other explanation for her strange and illogical behaviour, but I am quite unable to suggest what it might be.

Fiona MacHugh, the daughter and only child of the MacHughs, was, it appears from the few traces of evidence we possess, an adolescent girl with problems. Divided in her loyalty to her parents, as was inevitable in the situation she found herself in, she tried to play to both parties, and exploited both. Although obviously, and again naturally, according to most psychological thinking on filial relationships, closer to her father than to her mother, she pretended to be equally attached to the latter, and used her as a source of money, clothes, free labour, etc. On the other hand, she accompanied her father around to the cinema, theatre, etc, and usurped her mother's place in his life. We know this was going on in the months prior to the Incident. The question is, for how long had this situation obtained? My hypothesis is: since she was born, probably, and, I would not hesitate to say, that Fiona added to the pressures which finally contributed to the break-up of her parents' marriage. My own experience in this area tends to confirm the likelihood of this hypothesis.

Fiona was the type of child who uses her parents: she demanded money from her father and mother, spent holidays at her aunt's house etc. She was extremely lazy, doing no work at home or at school: her bedroom was disgracefully untidy, and her school reports were appalling.

The letter addressed to her from "Beano", who was probably some sort of boyfriend, suggests that she was, moreover, criminal: it is clear from certain references in this missive that she and Beano were not averse to shop-lifting, and had stolen books from shops and public libraries on more than one occasion.

She was, in short, an undesirable human being, typical of that wave of middle-class juvenile delinquents produced by the economic depression in Ireland, Scotland Wales and other less fortunate countries in western Europe. Although we have no concrete evidence of it, we can be sure that she drank cider on the beach at Bray at weekends, probably experimented with drugs, and would most likely have died of AIDS or some similar malady had the Incident not occurred.

The final member of the MacHugh family who has left some traces of her existence in the Bray House is Annie, Murphy's mother. Annie MacHugh was a Donegal woman, in this different from the other MacHughs, who were probably city people. She had a rough and vulgar peasant attitude to life, of a nature quite rare in Europe now. Indeed, although all the MacHughs are of interest as human beings, it is alas true to say that the three younger ones, while having some specifically Irish, and thus rare, traits, were on the whole part of the global society. Their lifestyles, their ideas, their customs, were not essentially different from those of anyone in Sweden, France, Germany or any other developed European country. Annie MacHugh, however, belonged to what has been called "the little community": she was almost medieval in her habits (ie use of rosary beads, icons) and in her attitudes (traditional son-worship and daughter-in-law antipathy). Annie MacHugh was a living representation of the evil stepmothers, and again the helpful hags, that we encounter again and again and again in the folktales of Europe, in the works of the Grimms, of the Moes, of Anderson, of Patrick Kennedy. As such, she was a type extremely rare and valuable to the anthropologist, and it is her and her counterparts, few enough in Ireland even in 20--, that the world must really mourn.

Before leaving the MacHugh family to contemplate wider issues relating to the state of Ireland as a whole, we can take a brief look at the economy of the family, as evidenced by the state of their home. This is a feature which is, of course, of great relevance to our understanding of the Irish economy in general.

As has been pointed out previously, the MacHugh home showed many signs of affluence: the house is old, spacious, and gracious. Its rooms are tastefully and in some instances beautifully furnished and decorated. It contains equipment which could not have belonged to a poor family: video camera and machine, modern kitchen conveniences, etc. Nevertheless, the overall effect of the house, to a Swede or to anyone from a truly affluent society, is of great shabbiness. The carpets, although originally of high quality, are almost all too well worn. There are unrepaired cracks in one of the walls, cracks which were not caused by the blast. The bathrooms are fitted and plumbed in an antique fashion, but it is clear that this is not a deliberate effect, and it is in no way picturesque. Similarly, although Elinor's clothes are lovely, none of them is very new, and most are of a vintage of several years, if not decades, ago. And as far as diet is concerned, the MacHughs had a low, almost subsistence standard. Although the collection of recipe books suggests that one of the MacHughs, Elinor or, as is less likely, Murphy or Fiona, was interested in cookery, they actually ate a round of monotonous basics such as potatoes and eggs. This was due in part to food shortages, and in part to the poverty of the family.

The result of my observations in the house is that, although it is certain that the MacHughs belonged to the middle class of Irish society, probably, indeed, to its upper echelons, they were nevertheless not very well off. Their standard of living fell far short of that of a similarly situated family in Sweden.

Ireland before Ballylumford

In one sense, simply understanding the MacHugh family gives us more than a glimpse of the state of Ireland immediately before the Incident, because they can be seen as a microcosmic example of the country. And, just as they were falling apart at the seams, torn by internal strife and beset by lack of self-knowledge, so, it would seem, was their country, Ireland.

Using the evidence of materials found in the Bray House alone, what sort of picture emerges? The documents, exact copies of reports taken from a small selection of newspapers published over a three-week period, tells us that Ireland was a country of poverty, violence and ignorance: the most obvious examples of this are the numerous reports we have of violence to animals and to people, on the streets of Belfast and Dublin (not all of which we have included in this report, due to lack of space). Less obvious, perhaps, is the violence to the environment: dangerous chemical plants, nuclear power stations, leaked their lethal waste into the Irish countryside, A dreadful, deadly state of apathy, on the part of the authorities and the people seems to have existed. Ireland was not always directly responsible for the pollution, the environmental hazards, which were destroying her. She suffered, for instance, much more from radioactive waste leaking from English container vessels and from English power stations and pipelines than from anything situated in Ireland itself. Similarly, the violence in northern Ireland could be, and must be, to some extent, blamed on Britain, whose rulers have mishandled the Ulster situation so badly over a period of at least a hundred years, if not more. Attempts seem to have been made to alleviate the various problems. What all have in common is that they failed. There seems to have been a lack of will to succeed in making Ireland a safe civilised place to live. Or else some strange lack of ability to do so.

Besides these internal factors, Ireland was, in the pre-Ballylumford period, suffering from severe emigration problems. No longer seen as a problem by politicians, educators, or even by the common people, it is nevertheless obvious that a country which constantly exports its youth will have difficulties, eventually. It is, really, a country on the wane, a dying country.

Ireland did not die a natural death. As a country, she was murdered. And who was the murderer? The usual one, it seems to me. But the writing was on the wall. In the papers, and no doubt on the TV and radio and everywhere else as well. If Ireland failed to pay adequate attention to the warnings, who is really to blame, in the final analysis, for her demise?

Chapter Sixteen

My report and analysis have now been presented. It would be easy to assume on account of their neat logic and easy flow that the excavation they describe followed a similarly systematic and untwisting path. But unfortunately this was not so.

I could have anticipated hazards: after all my crew had been difficult and unruly from the word go, if not before. But I am nothing if not optimistic, and I had hoped, fondly, as it turned out, that once we reached Ireland and began to work that the problems would lessen. I couldn't have been more mistaken. From the start, the dig was blighted by disharmony, petty jealousy and discord. In short, it proceeded in the manner of most enterprises involving the co-operation of workers who are human beings and not robots. The friction was, therefore, a necessary evil, in my opinion, since I always prefer human beings to robots. The latter I can never get to work at all, I must confess, since I am not gifted mechanically.

Although my attitude to the various problems which arose was one of forbearance and understanding, it would have been simpler for everyone if they had not taken place. Their main instigators were, and this surprised me, Jenny and Karl: Karen, although cantankerous as ever, was generally fairly sensible when it came to doing some real work. She was a professional, Karen, she enjoyed digging, and besides, she was used to working with me on excavations. Jenny and Karl, however, were sadly lacking in that and I suspected in all work experience. They had no idea of their own limitations and were quite incapable of following my command.

Karl and Jenny had been hired for a dual purpose: to guide the boat safely from Sweden to Ireland, and back again, and to excavate, in the roughest sense of the word. It had never been intended that they would participate in the more delicate and demanding parts of the excavation. Sifting, sorting, cataloguing and analysing were tasks for archaeologists of long standing, like Karen, or of exceptional ability, like me. Jenny and Karl had simply not been trained for such operations. This was the simple fact of the matter, and one which I imagined any intelligent person would accept and understand.

Such being the situation, after the initial two weeks digging, when the Bray House had been released entirely from its coat of ash and rubble and stood, pristine, demanding exploration, I advised Karl and Jenny to take a holiday, until Karen and I should complete our part of the job: the tricky and challenging part.

This advice I proffered to them one morning, while we sat on deck and breakfasted: it was a perfect summer's day. The sunlight danced on the waves, sprinkling them with a million flashing silver swords. Our spirits were high, as we drank coffee and basked, or allowed our faces to bask, in the lovely heat: Karen was already brown and wrinkled as a walnut, and this cheered her up enormously.

"Well," I pronounced, looking up from my plate, "we've done very well so far, haven't we?"

Karl was staring at the sea, enjoying, I assumed, its sparkling brilliance. He did not respond. Jenny continued to carve her slice of toast into ten small squares, to butter one at a time, eat it, and butter again. Only Karen shrugged, put down her coffee, and said coldly:

"Yes we have, haven't we?"

This pique I understood immediately. I am not a complete fool. It was caused by the perfectly comprehensible fact that I had taken no active part in the physical digging. Naturally I had had the role of supervisor, and could not be expected to work manually as well. The rest of the team resented this, as I well knew: it proved their immaturity, their complete lack of professionalism.

"What I should say, of course, is that you've worked very well. You and Karl and Jenny." I needed to humour them: it is easier to control people who are gratified in their small whims, as every manager worth his or her salt knows. "And as a matter of fact I think some congratulations are in order. You've been efficient and thorough. I can frankly say that I do not think I could have found a better team anywhere."

Jenny smiled enigmatically at nobody in particular, although for a second, catching my breath at the gleam of her hair in the sunlight, I rather hoped it was at me. Karl, oblivious of the smile, the hair, and my reaction to both, continued to look out to sea, his brow thunderously dark. And Karen swallowed coffee, cup after cup: she was now on a diet, and did not eat certain meals, such as breakfast.

I continued:

"It's only fair to admit that I had my doubts, initially."

Karen's face puckered. The wrinkles turned black.

"About you, Karl and Jenny, I mean, naturally. I knew, of course, that you had the necessary qualifications, technical skills and so on, to carry out the excavation. But of course I worried about your ability to cope with the psychological strains involved. No excavation is easy, and this one imposes many more demands than most. A high degree of stamina, mental and physical, is required. I am glad, I'm delighted, to have learned that both of you possess it, and in no small degree."

Jenny looked up from her toast, and smiled. Karl took out his pipe and began to fill it with slices of ersatz tobacco. Karen glanced at Jenny and raised her eyebrows, in the traditional gesture of disbelief.

"This may sound like a lot of silly rhetoric," I said, noting the look. "But it's no more than the truth. Let us be honest with ourselves, and fair. We've not only begun to carry out research such as has never before been undertaken by humankind, we've also undergone psychological experiences that have not been known for hundreds of years. We've taken a voyage across the seas, into the unknown. Who has done that, since, let us say, Christopher Columbus? Nobody. Even the space voyagers have plotted every move in advance, have rehearsed their trips thousands of times, and have usually made them tied down like babies in perambulators. But we, what have we done? Something truly dangerous, exploratory, something brand new! And it is the new which is also psychologically the most taxing."

"You're saying that we've endured a greater strain than anyone ever has before ? Is that what you're saying? That nobody has ever suffered what we have, psychologically? Is that it?" Karen smirked as she asked this question.

"Well no, that's not precisely what I'm getting at. I suppose others have suffered greater strain, as you put it..."

"For instance, Jesus Christ," interrupted Jenny, rather abruptly.

"Well..."

Jesus Christ. A name guaranteed to embarrass. We all looked suitably uneasy. The more so because we knew Jenny was not being facetious: of late she had become more and more vocal, and simultaneously more and more "religious": it was not the first time she'd mentioned an embarrassing name, and we had all observed her praying and meditating in the evenings, after work. Indeed, it would have been impossible not to observe her, since her religious practices were unctuous, to say the least. And, although she had not begun to proselytise directly, she had made it clear that she wanted us all to become aware of her religion, and of its significance in her life. I have observed before that women who are accomplishing little in the real world and who have, consequently, a low sense of self-esteem, often become fanatically Christian, or Buddhist, or something or other, in an attempt, I feel, to make their mark on the other world, since they haven't made it here. Jenny possibly had higher motivations, but I could not for the life of me imagine what they might be.

"Well," I said again, and decided to ignore the interruption. "For Karen the strain has been worse than for any of us, we all know that. She doesn't show it, of course, but we all know, at least I know, that she misses her dear little boy a great deal, and we all know, I think, what a tortuous feeling that must be. It is hard to cope, isn't it, Karen, dear?"

Karen's eyes filled to their painted brims with tears. She tried to fight them, but failed. They spilled, swollen shining drops, down the dark runnels of her cheeks, and then fell onto the table where they began to form a little sad pool. We all looked at it, watching it expand, until, with a high-pitched cry, Karen jumped up and ran into the galley.

Jenny prepared to follow, but I restrained her.

"Don't! It's better for her to be alone."

"Why did you do that to her? Why are you so cruel?" she shouted angrily at me.

" You're beautiful when you're angry!" I smiled, and she looked as if she might wring my neck. " And I'm not cruel at all. Merely sensible, in a subtle way, of course. Look at it this way: Karen is bottling up her anxiety and worry about Thomas, until she becomes impossible, for herself and everyone else. It's much better that she should get it all out of her system like this. Much healthier."

Not looking as if she agreed, Jenny sat down again.

"Well, let me continue from where I broke off," I said in a more business-like tone. "I was just saying that you and Karl had all the qualities I need in my team-mates. You're efficient, you're strong, you're mature. And what I really want to do is thank you for the work you've done so far, and congratulate you on doing it well. And I know I will be able to rely on you to help out again, if you're needed, over the next month or so, but for the moment, you've earned a holiday. Take it and enjoy it!"

Karl, who had been leaning over the railing as I delivered this speech, gazing into the water, probably in the somewhat futile hope he had long been nurturing of spotting a fish, turned around very quickly and stared at me in blank amazement. Jenny jumped up and grabbed the corners of her chair: I hoped she would not throw it at me.

"And what the hell do you mean by that?" Karl snapped. "Are we supposed to take it that we're not needed to work any more, now that the shit stuff is finished?"

"No no no," I attempted to sound unruffled. But I was nervous: I had anticipated some over-reaction to my suggestion, but was not prepared for melodrama. I loathe melodrama. "As I mentioned, I want you to be available for work, if your skills are needed. But the simple fact is that you've completed your main task now. Karen and I will take over from you at this point, and finish the investigation."

"I see," said Karl. "We were here to do the digging. We don't get to sift material, to write reports, anything that requires a slight bit of intelligence?"

"That is not your job."

"Like hell it isn't. That's the first I've heard of it, if it's not. For Christ's sake, I'm an archaeologist..."

"So am I," piped in Jenny. Karl looked at her as one might observe a fly on a stalk one was mowing down, and went on.

"If all you wanted was a digger, you might as well have employed a couple of navvies. Horses for courses!"

"You were employed to drive the *Saint Patrick* and to excavate. Those are the terms of your contract. "

"Contract? We're not even paid!"

"You signed a contract, nevertheless, to work under my supervision, and perform the tasks I've just described. And let me ask you to take a more respectful attitude to your own work. You do not dig as common labourers dig. You are archaeologists. You excavate. There is a difference."

"Bullshit!" Karl kicked a chair, close to my foot: he had by now walked across to the table, and, standing beside Jenny, confronted me from one side of it.

"It's not just," said Jenny, who was always rather touchingly and childishly concerned about that particular quality. She took Karl's hand and seemed to squeeze it, hoping, perhaps, to draw inspiration from its solid flesh: by now his hands were calloused and swollen with digging, and so were hers. She had also, like Karen, become suntanned, and had a high colour in her cheeks. And, unlike Karen, she was getting fat, or at least fatter than she had been. She looked a more suitable match for Karl now than she had done before. She was beginning to develop the same sort of trollish looks: they could have been a cowherd and milkmaid.

"Well, I'm sorry you're taking this attitude. I'd expected you to be much more positive, and enjoy the chance of a rest. You certainly could do with a holiday!"

"Oh yes," snarled Karl. "A holiday in the sun! On Paradise Island. Whoopee, Jenny, got your bikini? Let's go, on our summer holiday. Bloody marvellous, exactly what we need. Doctor's orders!"

They went ashore in the dinghy, and I watched them stride along the strand, his long shaggy mane of hair tossing, her long thick plait slapping, in anger, pique, resentment.

Ah, youth!

But such are the snags which attach to youthful employees, or volunteers. They are strong, physically, and occasionally they combine their physical toughness with a certain amount of infantile enthusiasm. But they have no moral stamina, usually they are semi-skilled, they are bursting with vanity and self-importance, and they can see nobody's point of view but their own. This is especially true if they happen to be postgraduate students.

Dismissing them from my thoughts, as I customarily banish all uncomfortable negative associations, I began to clear away the breakfast dishes. In so doing, I intruded on Karen, who was lying on the galley berth, her head buried in the pillow. She was not crying now, however, and, as soon as I had stacked the dishes in the machine and turned it on, I walked over to her and said cheerily:

"I'm off to work now!"

She looked up at me. Her eyes were red-rimmed, and there were smudges of black mascara on her cheeks.

"Hold on a minute," she said, in a brave little voice. "I'll be with you."

She washed her face at the kitchen sink - I forbore to lecture her on the importance of hygiene - gathered up her toolbag, and accompanied me, on the second and very small dinghy, ashore.

Then began the huge job of sorting out the entire contents of the house: we had to enumerate and describe them, decide what should be taken home to Sweden and what should be left behind, catalogue and pack. It was a many-faceted and highly demanding brief, and really Karl and Jenny had been most unrealistic, in believing themselves capable of carrying it out.

We began work in the kitchen of the house, since this was the most challenging room, in that it contained the most artefacts, and since I had also judged it initially to be the most interesting of the house's apartments. Later I revised my opinion, as my report, I think, indicates.

On this first day, we were highly excited by the sheer range, quantity and condition of the materials, and we tackled our tasks with energy and enthusiasm. Karen quickly became absorbed in her work and forgot about her depression, as one does. Indeed, she seemed even more excited than I was by the matter in hand.

"Goodness!" she would cry, "just look at this cup! Did you ever see a more delicious cup in your life!"

or

"I never have seen such a perfect pot, this is a really lovely little pot! Isn't it a really lovely pot?"

And she would wave aloft a willow pattern cup, made in Staffordshire, or a saucepan from Le Creuset, items which she, and I, had met with thousands of times in contemporary kitchens, but which for her seemed thrillingly interesting in this context.

Of course, we made genuine "finds" as well: crockery manufactured in Arklow, cutlery from Newbridge, some handthrown pottery from Louis Mulcahy and Nicky Mosse, and various other artefacts made in Ireland, which are by now exceedingly rare, and worth their weight in gold.

So we beavered on, turning out cupboards, upending drawers, lifting jars and cups and dishes from shelves. There is, after all, very little to beat an investigation of the contents of someone else's kitchen as a diversion, and we both enjoyed the job thoroughly, and did not notice the passage of time. Before we knew it, an evening shadow was falling across the tiled floor, and suddenly Karl and Jenny appeared in the doorway.

"Hello there!" Karl greeted us, in his customary grunting style. His expression was amicable enough, however, and I returned the salute.

"Did you enjoy your walk?" I enquired, politely.

"Yes, thank you," Jenny replied.

Karl went over to the table and sat down, to my discomfiture: the furniture of the Bray House was not there to be sat upon.

"We'd an interesting walk," he said slowly, picking up a saucer and examining it in detail. "We saw a lot of interesting things. Quite a lot!"

"Yes," Jenny nodded eagerly, from her position in the doorway. "We did!"

"Good," I said, and continued to look at knives and forks.

"Yeah," drawled Karl, his accent becoming more American, as it did, I noticed, when he was feeling some stress. "Yeah, you never would believe it, but there's a heap more interesting sites around Bray. This isn't the only one!"

"I never implied that it was," my tones were even, and almost warm. Secure in my triumph - what could yield better results than the Bray House? - I had no wish to provoke argument. And I had learned in life to anticipate censure whenever I was above it, and successful beyond most people's capabilities. "So what is it you've seen?"

Karl laughed, and took out his pipe.

"Sorry," I said, "no smoking in here, I'm afraid. It's too risky."

With a smile he put it back in his pocket.

"We feel it's better not to say anything about it as yet," Jenny spoke in apologetic tones. Really, she was a very enigmatic person: sometimes she seemed full of confidence, and at other times, she fell over herself to please.

Karl spoke quickly, and gave her a sharpish look.

"Sure, we want to surprise you two! How are you doing here, anyway?"

"Very well, thank you," I answered. Karen had stopped work, and was sitting on the kitchen table, close to Karl. She smiled at him, but was not talking.

"Then you won't be needing us for the moment, will you?"

"Well, no, not at the moment."

"Great stuff! In that case, we'll just amuse ourselves investigating another site. I guess that's OK with you?"

Karen laughed outright, somewhat gleefully.

"What a good idea!" I said calmly, having decided already on my strategy: I have always been able to think on my feet, an essential attribute for anyone in management.

Karl and Jenny looked at one another, obviously mystified and taken aback: naturally they had expected me to oppose their plan.

"We'll be off then," Jenny said. "Goodbye."

I waited until they were both just in the doorway. Then I called:

"Just a minute!"

"I just wanted to ask, is it really possible to excavate this new site with your bare hands?"

Jenny looked bemused, and Karl disgusted.

"We'll use the Volvo, of course," he snarled, "just like before."

It was difficult for me to utter the next sentence. It pained me more than I care to admit. But, in the interests of science, it had to be said.

"I'm afraid I can't authorise the use of the machine for work not carried out under my supervision."

Jenny sighed: "We might have known."

"You bitch!" Karl screamed. "You're doing this out of sheer bloody-mindedness. Why shouldn't we use the digger? Who knows what we'd find?"

"Precisely," I said coolly. "That is just why you must not be permitted to go ahead. And secondly, I am head of this excavation. I have a responsibility to you, to the sponsors of the project, and to the world, to supervise everything that goes on here. Moreover, I have an obligation to leave Ireland as unspoiled as possible, for future generations of archaeologists to explore, for the children of the future to enjoy."

"Pshaw! The children of the future to enjoy! What bloody awful double think! You're always saying that unless we excavate the place as fast as we can, there'll be nothing left at all!"

I ignored this remark, and all subsequent ones, and returned to my work. Jenny and Karl hung around for a few minutes, making insulting comments, cursing, swearing and blaspheming, encouraged in all this by Karen, who joined it from time to time, even though the matter did not really concern her. Then all three vacated the house, and the chorus of angry ejaculations faded to a cackle, and then to a faint hum, as of distant hornets.

Youth must have its fling, they say. How trying that is, for youth's keepers!

Chapter Seventeen

During the evenings which followed this event, the atmosphere aboard our little craft was neither relaxed nor industrious. Boats, especially those of modest capacity, are demanding environments at the best of times. They are like dolls' houses, where everything is on a reduced scale, except the dolls. The physical constraints caused by this anomaly, the lack of privacy, and the relative impossibility of escape, engender tension, and had done so in the past on board the *Saint Patrick*. The crew has to have much self-knowledge, coupled with an almost superhuman capacity for self-control, gifts which no one is born with, and which few acquire without a great deal of painful experience. It is true that old sailors, like old soldiers, are creatures of remarkable wisdom and stoicism. The same may be said of old archaeologists. But there was only one of them on board our vessel and one out of four is not sufficient to control an difficult situation.

The earlier part of our days passed pleasantly enough. Karen and I continued to work at the Bray House, while Jenny and Karl amused themselves. How I do not know, but they appeared to spend their time going for long walks along the coastline, or into the interior, and Karen and I usually did not lay eyes upon them from morning till evening. Which was just as well.

But we could not avoid them altogether, and it was when work was over and we were obliged to return to the boat, at about six o clock in the evening, that my troubles would begin.

The boat would be deserted, and in a state of utter chaos: dirty dishes scattered everywhere, the floor littered with scraps of food, torn packages, even ripped-up books: a disconcerting element of violence crept into Karl's behaviour - I assumed he was responsible for this; Jenny, whatever her faults, continued gentle as a lamb. Or as a sheep at one of those intermediate stages: a hogget or some such thing, since she was becoming sturdier by the day.

My first task, after the day's work, would be to set about tidying up the abominable mess on board. Meanwhile Karen would cook an evening meal. We both carried out these tasks in tired and resentful silence. Nobody wants to face kitchen chores after a hard day's employment. And, most fascinatingly, while we both found our job at the Bray House stimulating and exciting, although in many respects it involved the procedures we used in housecleaning the boat, we found the latter utterly boring. This must have been due to some more profound cause than tiredness. In my case, I blamed my mother's early conditioning which encouraged me to despise and scorn all housework. And I do not know what gave rise to Karen's discomfiture, unless it were simply irritation at Karl and Jenny. But if this indeed were so, she never gave voice to it, and was stubbornly and maddeningly loyal to the degenerate pair. Her obstinate streak knew no limits.

It normally took us about an hour, at least, to do all that had to be done, and then we would sit down gratefully to our repast, hungry, because, as I have pointed out previously, we did not eat in the field. Invariably, before we'd had time to swallow a single mouthful, Jenny and Karl would arrive on the scene, laughing and joking lightly with one another, in a fashion designed to exclude us. Or me, it is perhaps nearer the truth to say.

"How wonderful! Supper is served!" Karl would try to adopt his superior accent, and did it very badly. His natural accent was anything but refined, and his appearance, although obviously attractive enough, was not of the noble variety. As I may have had occasion to indicate, he looked a bit like a wild pig, the kind with lots of hair on. Although incidentally I believe that until the eighteenth century or so all pigs were much hairier than they are today. The fat babysoft porker is a modern development.

"Super!" Jenny, a better actress than one might have imagined, given her, let me be frank for once, quiet and dull personality, would cry, in a similar but much more successful accent. "And what have we tonight? Ah, lobster thermidor, my favourite! Goody goody!"

"And you'll never guess what we have for pudding! Do guess! Do try, I'll give you three guesses!"

"Mm. Let me see: is it pavlova?"

"No."

"Mm. Can it be, oh, can it be, Gateau Saint Honoré, the way Robin makes it?"

"Wrong. Try again."

"One last chance. Oh, I know, it must be strawberry shortcake! How too scrumptious!"

"You're right!"

"Three cheers for cookie! Hip hip!"

"Hurrah!"

"Hurrah! Hurrah! Hurrah!"

I ignored this side-show to the best of my ability, while Karen served their helpings of stew, or baked beans, or whatever banal and utterly tasteless dish we might have: Karen could not cook at all, and anyway only the most talented chef could have rendered the available ingredients palatable. Being on a diet herself, she tended to be more careless than ever in the preparation of our meals: people on diets make dangerous chefs. She insisted on ruling the roost in culinary affairs, only because she hated housecleaning more than cooking. Or because she was a sadist.

Jenny would sample the mess on her plate, then grimace horribly and put down her fork.

"Oh dearie me!"

"What is it, my heart's delight?"

"She's done it again. Oh, how could she? It's too too bad!"

"Done what again, my dearest love?"

"She's forgotten the brandy!"

"Unforgivable!" Karl would put a forkful of mashed potato gingerly to his lips. "You're right! There's not a single drop in this sauce. I shall write to Papa and complain, I most definitely shall. The food in this rotten old school is inedible. I shall write and demand to be removed immediately."

"And I will too, oh yes I shall!" Jenny, slightly less inventive once her initial burst of steam had run out, would follow his lead.

"Do you have a father, Jen?"

"Oh dear! I've gone and forgotten again. My incorrigible Papa. Eloping with the nursery maid when I was at such an impressionable age, how could he do it to me! The rotter, the rotter! I meant, I'll write to Mamma, she'll take me away, she knows how vile this place is. Papa sent me only because it's so cheap."

"So abominably cheap. That's the very worst thing about it. I can't think why they put me in such a horrid cheapie school. It must be because it's the only one left."

"In the world, you mean, Karlie?"

"That I haven't been expelled from."

"Maybe they'll expel you from here too. Oh, Karl, just imagine, if we're bad enough they'll expel us and we can go right home!"

"Naw, nobody gets expelled from schools like this, too mean, they need all the fees they can get. And nobody wants to come, that's the problem. We're stuck, Jen."

Karen was an appreciative audience to these farces, staged for her amusement and my mortification. I ignored them as best I could, busying myself about the boat, going for a walk on shore, and then retiring to my cabin to write the notes for the day. Lying in the small pool of yellow light supplied by my lamp, I would contemplate, and write, all the time hearing from the deck the clink of glasses and the fluting sounds of laughter, music, cheerful conversation. Because every night now a small party was held, by my colleagues, a party to which I was not invited. Although I held nothing but scorn for those involved in these convivialities, I was, in spite of myself, hurt: but I put the experience to good use. It has been my habit, for many many years, to waste nothing, however trivial. I took note of my feelings and the causes giving rise to them, with the intention of writing an article for publication when we should return to Sweden and these events would be but a distant memory: *Parties and Celebrations: the Trauma of the Uninvited*.

About a week after my misunderstanding with Karl and Jenny, I returned from my solitary ramble along Bray Strand later than usual, and my approach was unobserved, even though the boat was moored very close to the shore, and under normal, less noisy circumstances even my footsteps on stones would have been heard by anyone on deck. The usual festivities were well underway as I returned, and it was owing to the furore they engendered, and perhaps also to the almost inebriated condition of the participants, that I was not noticed. From the shore I could see my companions on the lighted deck, drinking and making merry. The sound of music, Handel's *Water Music*, obvious, perhaps, in this setting and this place, but delightful nevertheless, and deriving from the sea even more beauty than it possessed inately: music on water is indescribably lovely, as Handel, composing for and about water, no doubt understood.

The stars were large in a Prussian blue sky, and the moon was full, creating a great silver lake across the dark sea. It was a romantic scene. I wished I was a part of it.

Voices, like music, float on water. And as I drew near to the *Saint Patrick*, I heard every syllable, clear as glass, crystalised by the stillness of the night and the calm of the sea.

"... so incredible. This insatiable lust for power. I mean, I lust for power myself, who doesn't?"

"Not me." Jenny's quiet voice blended harmoniously with the strains of the pianoforte. She had what is called a musical voice, that I had always realised, but at this precise moment I understood that it had the tinkling quality of keys, rather than the more profound tone of a stringed instrument. The latter quality is rarer in the human voice, but I have known it. Actually my own voice resembles a well-seasoned violin in tone, and has been compared to a Stradivarius by objective listeners.

"Aw, sure. Even you do, Jenny, or if you don't, it's because you've already got it, or as much of it as you want. But Robin! God, the terrible hunger for it, the ruthlessness. A person like that should be locked up, not set loose upon the world."

"I couldn't agree with you more, really, I couldn't!" Karen was speaking in her highest pitched, most excited tones, as she did when drinking. Alcohol brought out the worst in her. It transformed her from a mild pain in the neck to a raving harridan. "You're so right, absolutely right. But if you know something about Robin's background, as I do, you understand how it came about. It does help to understand, it doesn't make it right, it doesn't make it good, but it helps."

"We know all that shit about the parents splitting up and abandoning the vulnerable little girl to some sort of ghastly stepmother or whatever. But let's face it, that sort of thing has happened to lots of people. Let's face it, it's happened to me. But that didn't turn me into a megalomaniac, did it? Not quite, anyway. That's just not a good enough reason, there must have been a streak of it in Robin from the start. Baby Robin must have been a tyrannical little girl, just like grown up Robin."

"Except..."

"Except. And why that? Why go so far?"

"Well, there were good reasons. Listen, I hate Robin as much as you do. More. I've known the beast so much longer. I've known Robin for sixteen years, can you imagine that, sixteen whole years! How can I have survived knowing someone like that for sixteen years? I really can't understand it, I really can't! I just can't understand it! But it helps to know the background, it really does."

At this point, I sat down on the beach, with my back to a rock, and made myself as comfortable as I could. It's not easy, getting comfortable on a radioactive rock, while you overhear calumny about yourself. But I did it.

"So what are they? What are the circumstances? It'd help us to know too, wouldn't it? It'd help us to take a more forgiving, Christian attitude to everything. It's hard to forgive a complete lack of any kind of morality, human or Christian. But I would like to do it."

"Help to handle Robin too. I thought I could a while back. I believed I'd got it all sewn up. Boy was I wrong!"

"Well, you know all the basic facts already, you know those. They're so bizarre, who doesn't know them? And basically all that stuff about the parents' divorce and Robin's breakdown and so on is true. But I think what was much more significant in her life, as a girl, was her connection with Per Bishop."

Ah yes. This was becoming enjoyable!

"The archaeologist?"

"Of course, yes. Robin came to Uppsala soon after the business in Lulea, totally fed up with life, presumably. And there she suddenly found her niche, in Per Bishop's classes, which were terribly exclusive and difficult to get into and hard to keep up with when you did get in, if you managed to get in at all there was still no guarantee that you'd keep your place, none whatever. So of course everyone was dying to be on that course, it was the most sought after one in the whole of Uppsala University, it's hard to believe because who wants to do archaeology really? But it really was. And Robin managed to get a place on it. Not only that, she managed to worm her way into Per Bishop's favour, don't ask me how, and she became the star pupil, the brightest star on that course, then or ever. Which was very nice in a way for her, naturally, after all the disappointments in Lulea and all that, but difficult as well. It made everyone admire her, of course, but it made them hate her too."

"Well, there isn't a logical connection, necessarily. Could it have had something to do with Robin's personality?"

"Well, who knows? I didn't know Robin then, I didn't come to Uppsala until later. I was there when the crisis came, that was much later, after Robin's marriage to Michael, and all that. It wasn't such a big thing, it mightn't seem important to us. Or to any normal person, but maybe to an academic, and especially to one like her, a really competitive, throat-cutting academic, who'd devoted her whole life to her work. Bishop had always seemed to dote on Robin. She'd had everything, prizes, scholarships, a job as soon as her doctorate was finished. Then Bishop was retiring, they were appointing a new professor, and of course Robin was tipped for the job by everyone. But she didn't get it. Bishop let her down, he turned against her at the eleventh hour, and gave his support, which is crucial for one of those appointments, it seems, to someone else. A much younger person, a young man who had just finished his PhD and had no experience, and was, apparently, not half as brilliant as Robin. She took it that her sex was against her, although that cannot really have been it. I don't think. But she could think of no other reason."

"What bullshit," said Karl. "Who cares about anyone's sex in Sweden nowadays? Actually my feeling is that it's to your advantage to be a woman, boards are still afraid of discriminating so they go for one."

"That's not my feeling," Karen retorted. "Although in Robin's case I think it might have been that Bishop had seen how strange, crazy she was getting. He'd have known Michael, and how she treated him, and all that. I mean, anyone who'd seen her and Michael together would have wondered about her. She treated him like a bit of dirt, it was awful, it was really awful, when I remember what went on..."

I left my seat by the rock, and walked quietly back along the beach in the direction of Killiney. The tide was low, so I continued on the strand for a few miles, until I reached a crevice in the rocks that I could not cross. I stood there, gazing into the black depths of the small canyon, for a long time. My mind was filled with memories which made me doubt if life were worth the expenditure of energy and other resources I had to lavish upon it, simply to survive. Only my sense of responsibility to my project, to the people of Ireland, and to my colleagues, prevented me from ending it all there and then. In the small hours of the morning I returned to the boat. It was silent and dark, and I slid into bed, in my cabin which was bathed in strong, pale moonlight, without disturbing the sleeping party.

Chapter Eighteen

My father was a silent man. Not taciturn, which suggests an element of wilful sullenness, far from being sullen, he was one of the happiest people you could imagine, his happiness amounting to something more than complacency, although it was of a passive ilk. But he did not talk, not more than was essential, and he enjoyed being. Being, alone, or with a companion, such as me. In a room, or, preferably, in a garden. His own garden, our garden, the lawn which sloped from our dining room window to a clump of birch trees on the lane behind our house in Lulea. There he spent all his free moments, digging, weeding, thinning, pruning, tying up with wires, tying down with string, spraying, watering. Or sitting on the rustic seat he had made himself, looking at the prettiness - I hesitate to call it beauty, although I am not sure what the distinction here is - he had helped create. It was a charming garden, in the cottage style, with herbaceous borders in glowing shades of pink, lavender, gold and blue, banks of silvery shrubs, and even a round stone-edged pond in which a solitary goldfish swam round and round, during the summer months (in winter it lived in a heated bowl in the den).

I liked that goldfish. I liked to think of it, living within the confines of its small stone pond, with some pebbles on the bottom and two water lilies always on its surface, swimming round and round, or back and forth in straight lines, from June until the end of August. I liked to think of it then being transferred from the pond to the bowl, to that tiny space, from which, however, it could observe with its round stupid eyes the life going on that room, all around it. The goldfish I admired and envied, and likened to my father.

He too lived, wished to live, a circumscribed life. Work - at a paper-mill, where he was a computer programmer - and garden. House and Me. That was all he needed. Because from the beginning he and I enjoyed a specially close relationship. I loved him more than I loved Mother, and he, I knew, from the earliest age, loved me more than he loved Mother. (What she loved I never guessed. Her job, perhaps? Travelling? Perhaps). Apart from the garden, his great pleasure was in taking me to the zoo, to the swimming pool, to the skating rink, to ski, to the cinema, to everything Lulea had to offer in the way of amusement for a child. He seemed to have no desire other than to see me pleased, and every Saturday of my life during my childhood was spent in his company, doing exactly what I wanted to do. Sundays he devoted to the garden, leaving me to my own devices, or to Mother.

What Papa clearly did not enjoy were our holidays abroad, which were very numerous, owing to Mother's great interest in travel. He always made it painfully obvious, while we trotted across the Sahara or gazed at refugees in Kampuchea, or at maimed toddlers at the Calcutta bazaar, for our holidays were exotic, mother did not baulk at expense or adventure, that he would much rather be at home, on the wide dusty streets of Lulea, or, probably, in the green haven behind our perfect house on a hill to the south of that strange, rather bleak little town. Hence, probably, my image of him as goldfish. Besides, he had somewhat fishy eyes: protruding, and yellowish in colour. As are my own, when I remove my hyacinth-tinted contact lenses.

I did not, as a child, ask myself if there were a reason for my father's quietness. It was a fact I took for granted, as any child would, just as I accepted that my mother was attractive and fairly loquacious. And initially his refusal, or inability, to express himself verbally did not concern me in any way, or create any obstacle to the perfect relationship which I believed I enjoyed with him. We communed, I believed, without of course being conscious of this thought, on a level which was higher than the merely verbal. Our hearts conversed, even if our tongues did not.

Anyway I had plenty of alternative gossips: most of my life was spent, not at home, but with my beloved Lena. Lena who was everything that Mother was not: kind, playful, imaginative, tolerant. She was fun. And she was what Father was not, too. She could communicate perfectly well, with a child of six months, six years, or with an adult of sixty. In short she was a thoroughly, marvellously, perhaps - I can understand now, in retrospect - exceptionally normal person. I adored her. And, since she was a gifted human being, endowed with very rich emotional and artistic talents. I was not unique in this. What distinguished me from other children in her care, however, was my total dependence on her. If Lena considered this a burden, she did not let me know it. I always felt welcome at her home. I thought of the day care centre, which was in fact a government-run institution, as her only sphere, although of course I must have known that she had her own personal abode as well (actually, she lived in an apartment somewhere near the old Russian settlement, which I never visited). I could not envisage Lena, who looked and dressed for her role as a childminder - bright colours, dungarees, gaily spotted socks - away from the nursery environment. She seemed to belong with slides and swings, and big plastic boxes full of educational blocks. I suppose I considered her to be some bright, cheery doll, dispensing love and advice with glasses of orange juice and digestive biscuits during the day, switched off, in her box, when I or other children were not there. Comforting, to think of that, of Lena always there, always in the nursery, ready to succour and comfort. While Mother rushed about, here, there and everywhere, elusive, uncontrollable. With Lena, as with Father, but even more so, I knew where I stood, and felt safe.

It is impossible to enumerate her gifts: she sang to us, nursery songs, carols, old folk songs. From her I first heard *Egil Gammalson*, *Elvira Madigan*, and other songs which I still sing with pleasure myself. These Lena taught us, by the simple method of singing them over and over again, strumming along on her guitar as she sang, by the fire in the nursery den, on dark winter evenings. Just at that darkest and cosiest hour, before our parents would come to bring us home, we would gather there, on the rug or on the sofa, and sing happily or sadly until the day was over, and we were carried off into the cold winter night, walking through the snow to our empty, bright houses. Besides, she taught me to cook. In the neat kitchen of the centre, on the orange table, I learned to make rolls and buns, quiche and lasagne, the kind of things Mother would never bother about, as being far too much trouble and bad for the figure anyway (Mother ate, for preference, tabouleh, and beansprouts, and thin slices of raw ham, followed by a small peach).

Lena also taught me to draw and to paint, skills which I developed at school, of course, but which I first learned from her, in the important formative years, and which have been extremely useful to me in my career.

More important than any of these talents, however, was Lena's ability of talk with me. I had no confidante, other than her, and no adult to whom I could look for advice. My Mother was too aloof and too wrapped up in her own life to care about mine. And Father, as I have said before, did not talk: he too was aloof, perhaps, in his own way. Although I felt close to him, I could not express this closeness, nor could I tell him about any of my feelings. But to Lena I could bare my soul, and I frequently did so. She understood my interest in the emotional life of germs, or the favourite desserts of

Tyrannosaurus Rex. She discussed with me my teachers, my classmates, my friendships, my lack of friendships ... anything that needed to be talked about. Our relationship was, therefore, very intimate. Indeed, it was Lena who told me the facts of life. It was Lena who told me everything worth knowing, and in return I confided all my secrets, or nearly all, to her.

She was the most important adult in my life, slightly more significant, as time went on, than Papa. Him I continued to love deeply, but, as I grew older and required more in the way of companionship, my relationship with him cooled. Some exchange of ideas and thoughts is essential, in any friendship. It is not, in fact, enough, simply to exist contentedly side by side. And Papa, it seemed to me, considered this to be so.

Mother was not, of course, totally absent from my life. Although, as I have indicated, she travelled a great deal, on her own on business as well as *en famille* during the holidays, she was nevertheless at home more often than not, and her presence in the house was much more apparent than Father's. It was her house, as it was his garden. Its decorative effects were hers entirely, so that even in her absence one had a sense of her personality. However, she was physically there, often enough, and one heard her, one listened to her, bustling busily about, listening to classical music, writing letters, telephoning her wide circle of "friends", who were all also business contacts. It was not so easy, to escape from Mother. She had a knack of trapping one, unconsciously or otherwise. Hers was an insidious character.

Indeed, it was due to her ability to scoop me up in the net of her wishes that the great crisis of my early life occurred. It all happened quite simply, quite by accident, as great events, great tragedies, often do, so that one can ask oneself a thousand times, in their long sad aftermaths, "what would have happened if only ... the train had been five minutes earlier, that telephone had not been broken, the woman had been in when I called." Accident, that can be the tragedy, as well as the blessing, of life. Accident it is, not fate, that governs our destinies, and it was as a result of a stupid mischance that my little tragedy came about.

It all happened because of Mother's fanatical interest in sailing. It is, of course, an up-market sport, and as such likely to suit Mother's tastes and ambitions. Also Lulea's situation is such as to make it almost foolish to live in it, and suffer its many inconveniences ... and not make use of the one great amenity it possesses, the amenity which, after all, is the *raison d'être* of the place, because were it not for its position by the sea there would be no reason for Lulea's existence. It is only a port. But an excellent one, and few parts of Sweden can match its archipelago in beauty. So Mother was sensible, in using the sea, and sailing. And this she did every Saturday afternoon, always had done as long as I could remember. When I was small, I spent Saturdays with Papa, and Mother went off sailing alone or with some of her clubmates. But as I became older, and gradually grew out of Papa, Mother prevailed upon me to accompany her on her sailing outings. This I did initially with some enthusiasm, but, having learned the rudiments of the skill, I found that it did not interest me in the least, and I tried as often as I could to escape from the Saturday afternoon voyages. Escape was not easy, however, and I frequently found myself a reluctant mate to Mother's very commandeering captain.

One Saturday, when I was sixteen, I planned to participate in one of these adventures. It was June, late June, and the day was heavenly, so I was almost looking forward to it: I loved the hazy, white light which floated like shrouds on the sandy, marram grass-covered islands at that time of the year,, and I loved the islands themselves. They too seemed to float like some light swathes of cloth on the misty waters. The quality of the scenery out in the archipelago was unique, and I loved it more than any beauty spot I had ever encountered on my by then extensive travels. The best way to experience it was - is - by sailing boat.

I found, however, when we were down at the harbour, preparing to embark, that I was suffering from a migraine headache, which I used to get frequently at that period in my life. It was blinding and debilitatingly painful, as even Mother recognised, and I had to drop out of the expedition. Mother set off alone, and I walked slowly home. (Our house was not far from the harbour, it overlooked it from a fairly gentle hill on the south side of the town.) My plan was to go to the garden, and spend the rest of the afternoon lying in the hammock which Papa had strung between two fir trees there. To lie and listen to the gentle soughing of the firs, while seeing the lovely arrangements of blooms and catching their scents was a very soothing experience, and one which I had found useful in dispelling my headaches before. It was an experience of deep peace, and that is what I always sought and found in the garden.

But today I found instead Papa and Lena, lying together in the hammock, laughing like adolescents and making noisy love.

Somehow I escaped without being seen or heard. And somehow, although I cannot now remember how, I survived that day.

Soon afterwards, I moved out of home and took a flat in town. A year later I moved away from Lulea anyway, and became a student at Uppsala, and after that I went "home" once a year, at the very most, to visit Mother. "Home"? After that, I ceased to have a home, is perhaps closer to the truth. (Did I ever have one again?) Mother occasionally came to see me in Uppsala, too. She seemed to have more time on her hands than I remembered her having in the past, and to have more interest in me than I would have imagined possible. I understood this, and gradually I came to understand it even more. Indeed, my awareness of her new need for me became a burden. But our relationship never prospered: it seemed to me that Mother felt she needed me only from some sense of guilt. She did not like me. She had never liked me. And I could not bring myself to like her. It was as much as I could do to maintain rudimentary courtesy, when she was with me, and I discouraged her visits because they were occasions of profound stress for me and, I suspect, for her.

Lena I never spoke to again. I caught sight of her, once or twice, or more often, in Lulea, as was inevitable in a town so small. But I always avoided meeting her. And since she lived with my father, it was not possible for me to meet him either.

Chapter Nineteen

The conversation to which I had accidentally been audience proved to be a turning point in our fortunes at Bray, and not, I believe, entirely by coincidence. Although my companions were not aware that I was listening to their backbiting session, the fact that they had indulged in it effected an alteration in their attitude towards me, and towards one another. They felt guilty and, as a result, their behaviour towards me became even more intolerant than before. Indeed, it became positively cruel. This might seem paradoxical, but it is quite normal, as anyone who has investigated the witch-hunting process - I have - will tell you. Guilt caused by mistreatment of the witch is transformed to hatred of her, and even further ill-treatment. Blame is transferred from the community to the individual who has been victim all along.

In our little community, the witch was me.

For a few days, nobody spoke to me, and all three cast filthy dagger looks at me at regular intervals.

Karen worked sluggishly and inefficiently on purpose to annoy me. Of course, I had too much self control to rise to the bait, and indeed I almost feared for my safety if any crisis should occur: I had taken to arming myself, with my tiny revolver, at all times. It was strictly against my own code of practice to carry a gun, but I had smuggled one aboard the *Saint Patrick* before I left Sweden, in case of emergencies and in the atmosphere which prevailed during these days, I was very glad of my prescience. The gun was the only factor which stood between me and complete paranoia.

On the third day, after "the party", I was busily excavating Fiona's room, while Karen put in time somewhere else in the house, when Karl and Jenny trundled in. I continued to do my work - I was examining scraps of letters, copy books, and other documents, in Fiona's desk - and pretended not to notice the intrusion. My hand closed comfortingly on my gun, which was concealed in the inner pocket of my pants.

Karl and Jenny sauntered heavily around the room, picking up one object after another, scrutinising them with great care and then depositing them, with deliberate sloppiness, in the wrong place.

"That's an interesting looking drawing!" Karl said, after a long few minutes. He held in his hand a scrap of lined paper, upon which was sketched a quite unremarkable cat. "Real interesting! What are you going to do with that?"

I replied in carefully measured tones:

"My intention is to catalogue it along with all the other art work, and then file it away in a portfolio lined with acid-free paper."

"Is that a fact?" he drawled in his most provoking tones. "Interesting, real interesting." He raised the paper to the light and examined it even more closely. "Now, please forgive my impertinence, Robin, in daring to express a thought. But if I may be so bold as to make a suggestion, Robin, just one tiny little suggestion, it's this: I think this is an object of great importance and significance, and I really don't think it ought to be consigned to the depths of an acid-free portfolio, never to be seen again. This, Robin, is a work of art. Primitive art maybe, but art nevertheless. And it is my firm belief that it should be treated just as such. This here drawing, Robin, should be displayed where the whole wide world can see and enjoy it, it shouldn't be allowed to rot in some mouldy old archive, no siree!"

Jenny nodded her head vigorously in agreement. She was seated, cross-legged, on the floor, trying on Fiona's clothes. At the moment of speaking, she was attired in a yellow T-shirt, a pink skirt and a pair of black silk knickers, the latter being tied around her head in a sort of turban arrangement. When she nodded they fell to her shoulders, and she presented an amusing spectacle, no doubt, to Karl, who laughed very loudly and long at her. On me the humour of the scene was lost.

"Look at these clothes now!" Karl removed the pants from Jenny's shoulders. "These clothes are real interesting too." He held them up to the light. They were a common pair of polyester knickers, edged with factory lace, designed to look titillating and utterly useless otherwise. I have seen millions of such garments in my life. They are part of the stock-in-trade of every department store in the world. "What are your plans for these clothes, Robin?" his voice suddenly became menacing.

"My intention is to catalogue them," I said, "with our other clothes, and then to store them in a plastic bag."

"Really! I am surprised. You see, I must admit, Robin, that I have grave reservations about the validity of that approach. That is antiquarian, it is also antiquated. What good will this 'garment' do, locked away in a plastic bag, in some mouldy old archive? The public should have access to it! It should be forced upon them! This garment has a unique cultural value. From it, we can learn a great deal about a society which has vanished, we can learn much more about Ireland from this single garment than we can from dozens of books. Isn't that so, Robin, isn't that what archaeology, and ethnology, is all about? This garment, in my humble opinion, should be displayed in a museum, where the public can examine it, enjoy it, taste from it a culture which is no more. Just imagine how much it would mean to millions of Swedish teenagers to see a garment like this, properly displayed, of course, with proper contextual information, in a nice, accessible, friendly folk museum! To put it away in a plastic bag ... For shame, Robin, for shame!"

Jenny nodded again. She had now wrapped a spotted nightgown around her waist, as a kind of avant-garde belt. It held up wide striped pyjamas, and she danced slowly around the room, wearing this silly looking outfit, and looking amazingly graceful in it, like a prima ballerina playing the part of a clown.

I did not reply to Karl's remarks, which I considered, incidentally, to contain a certain amount of sense as well as a great deal of idiocy. I continued to sort out the materials in Fiona's desk. Behind me, Karl and Jenny muttered to one another, as they picked things out of drawers, or from the floor, held them to the light, exclaimed about how interesting they all were. Since their activities meant that the window was blocked most of the time, I found myself experiencing difficulty in deciphering Fiona's spidery handwriting, and decided to vacate the premises.

"I'm taking a walk," I said. "I need some fresh air."

I strolled slowly down to the boat, drank a cup of coffee, and listened to some music for a quarter of an hour. Soothed, I fashioned myself a small cardboard notice, bearing the legend: DO NOT DISTURB! This I carried back to the house, which the others had by this time left. I hung it on the door of Fiona's room, and worked there, in peace and quiet, for the remainder of the afternoon.

At about five o'clock, I heard Karl's and Jenny's footsteps on the stairs. They went into the main bedroom, then out onto the corridor and towards Fiona's room. Outside the door they halted. Karl expostulated: "What the hell!" From Jenny, there was no sound, until her footsteps, along with Karl's moved away again, along the landing and downstairs. They slammed the kitchen door as they left the house.

I went back to the boat at dinner time or thereabouts. Karen was already on board, preparing the evening meal, more frugal than ever, now, since our best food was used up, and since her dieting had become more intense. She laid the table on deck for four. But at nine Jenny and Karl had still not shown up. I ate my meal at that point, and Karen waited. As I worked at my notes in my cabin, I could hear her in the galley, watching a video. Two videos.

At midnight, the couple had not returned, and Karen had not eaten her dinner. I scraped the pots and put all the dishes in the machine, and went to bed. When I got up, early next morning, I found Karen asleep in her chair. Karl and Jenny were not on board.

I went to the house alone, after breakfast. Karen joined me there at noon or so, and we worked in silence, rather nervously. Karl and Jenny did not turn up that day, or the following, and, after about a week, I assumed they had perished. But I did not venture to tell Karen my opinion.

Chapter Twenty

Some two weeks after the disappearance of our colleagues, Karen and I completed our excavation of the Bray House. All that remained for us to do then, in Ireland, was to pack all documents and artefacts which we wished to take home to Sweden onto the *Saint Patrick*, to check our notes, lists and catalogues, and to ensure that no important item was left unaccounted for. This final, tidying-up stage of the dig is always the most difficult, but it is essential that it is carried out properly before the field is vacated, even if the dig is incomplete, and one plans to return to it again. I realised that much more work needed to be done, not only in Ireland, or Bray, but on the Bray House itself, and I hoped that an opportunity to come back would present itself. Indeed I had no doubt but that it would, since I was fully confident of the reception my findings would receive in Sweden. Nevertheless I carried out my final days' work in the spirit of one who regarded it as an ultimate, final task. This meant that it took more time than would always be the case on excavations of like magnitude but more commonplace circumstances.

In spite of this, however, a week saw the completion of the packing and stowing, and I then suggested to Karen that we should begin the voyage home. Predictably, she objected violently. In the first place, she doubted our ability to reach home without the assistance of Karl and Jenny. Secondly, and much more importantly, she claimed, we could not yet abandon them: it would be tantamount to murder.

"Hardly, Karen," I said gently, "and we must face facts. You know what they are."

No. She did not know. She did not want to know, she refused to accept what seemed to me to be glaringly obvious. Instead, she spent a lot of time scanning Bray and the Wicklow hills with her binoculars perched on her sharp little nose, she took long, long walks daily, into the interior, in spite of my genuinely concerned warnings: if I lost Karen, I, too, in all probability, would die, since without one other person I did not feel capable of making it home, although with her help, I thought I could do it now. So much had I succeeded in learning about the art of navigation, my old *bête noire*!

"It's important that we get the report on the excavation back to Sweden," I explained. "The world is waiting for it, Karen, our report, our most important piece of work. Our magnum opus, Karen. If we don't deliver the goods everything is lost. The enterprise will have been a failure."

"We owe such a lot to Science, and to Posterity, don't we?" she asked, ironically, sneering at me.

"Well yes, we do. You may not want to believe that, but we do."

"We owe something to Karl and Jenny too, don't we owe them something? Nothing important, of course, nothing that matters, but something?"

Did we? Certainly I did not feel very indebted to them, although perhaps she did.

"Two human beings? This report illumines the lives of millions. It documents a really important, lost culture. A great civilisation. It's quite likely that nothing of its kind will ever come out of Ireland again. And probably not from anywhere else, either."

Karen yawned, and sat down. She had become tired of late, and her face had grown extremely, almost grotesquely, haggard, as her body seemed to waste away.

"I don't care," she said wearily. "I'm not going without them. You go, if you want to. But I'm staying here."

Finally, we checked our food supplies, maintaining the fiction that Karen still ate food. It seemed that we had sufficient to last two people for at least a month, four for two weeks, so we made a decision to remain in Ireland for a further ten days. If at the end of that time Karl and Jenny had not been found, we would sail home without them.

This decided, I settled in to write this report, and Karen to scour the landscape for any sign of the vanished pair.

I worked with enthusiasm and energy, and, since this is the type of activity I enjoy more than any other, I became totally absorbed in it. The hours and the days flew by without my being aware of their passage. I spent whole days and nights secreted in my cabin, tapping away at my keyboard, oblivious of time, Karen, the boat, the world. I was divinely content, as I am only when engaged on some important scholarly activity, the most creative, the most intellectually stimulating, of all the works of humankind.

My absorption and my happiness did not prevent me from sleeping at night, but my dreams were peopled by those whom I had not thought of since my student days, and I dwelt especially on my first professor and mentor, Per Bishop, to whom I owe so much. Both joy and pain. At first the dreams were rather calm, peaceful dreams. I saw Per Bishop, his lined, bony face, his rimless glasses perched half way down his aquiline nose. He was sitting at a table, a breakfast table, holding in his two hands a quite ordinary mug, white with some blue harebells on it, the type of mug one will buy very cheaply in a supermarket, or receive as a free gift with a purchase of petrol. Someone at the table - some old friend, perhaps Selma, a girl I had shared a room with in Uppsala - said: "What a wonderful mug that is!" I felt surprised, because it was so terribly ordinary and unimpressive. And then I noticed that Per was moulding the mug. Or rather that it changed shape in his hands, as he held it: it grew long and round, it sprung a spout, it was a coffee-pot, it became slender like a vase for tulips, it widened into a fat flowerpot, it became tiny as a delicate china cup. Per did this with a mischievous smile on his face, and glanced knowingly across at me. With his little goatee beard, his expression, for once, was demonic. As he stared, my eyes lost sight of the mug in his hands, and now his face itself changed, not quickly, magically, as the mug had, but gradually. Its contours softened, its thin cheeks filled out, its beard grew fuzzy and fluffy, a great brown mop. He became my father.

What did it mean? The popular Freudian interpretation is too boring, all popular Freudian interpretations are so similar, that is the problem with them. Every dream is not, in my opinion, about sex. No more than life itself is, contrary, perhaps, to Freud's view. Sex is important, it infiltrates everything, but it's not the only thing. And dreams are about life in all its aspects.

Anyway, for Per Bishop I had never felt the faintest sexual desire. Perhaps, of course, my dream was telling me that I had suppressed my feelings for him. Perhaps. But it is my experience that my dreams often tell me facts which are perfectly well known to my conscious mind already. The dreams simply confirm that knowledge, often using another set of images. Per Bishop had moulded me. I was the mug. The vase. The china cup. And that was not news to me.

I had arrived at college when I was nineteen years of age, having spent two years living alone in a flat in Lulea, and so rather mature, for one so young in years. I mean simply that I was independent in all practical matters: I could fend for myself on a purely domestic level. My experiences in Lulea, however, had made me wary of human relationships, and I was less than adept at forming friendships, assessing people's characters, and generally getting on in society, than was normal for a person of my age. Once bitten twice shy. It took me many years to learn to trust humanity again, and then indeed I was bitten once more, since, as I realise by now, humanity, while it can be suffered, tolerated or loved, should never be trusted. Only children and idiots believe that it can be. At nineteen, I was not an idiot. But I was still a child, although I did not know it at that time.

I had come to college full of expectation, as, I suppose, is usual among students who have had no contact with a university town or any kind of intellectual community until they finish school and arrive, as they believe, on the brink of life, in some kind of third-level establishment. Since Uppsala was not just any modern polytechnic, but the oldest university in Sweden, the Oxford of Scandinavia, I think I could be forgiven for having imagined that simply being there would change my life, and for the better.

I was doomed, of course, to disappointment. Universities, even venerable, traditional ones, are what one makes them. One will not simply dive into the pool of college life, and find oneself steeped in a stimulating intellectual atmosphere. Soul searching dialogues will not happen, unless one initiates them oneself. Brilliant wit and repartee will not assail one's ears: one will have to be a brilliant wit, in order to find others of like gifts. The intelligentsia are not to be found in a particular cafe, pub or dormitory. The only way to find the intelligentsia is to be intelligent and not to be afraid to show it. The only way to join it is to start it.

But how was I, raw and wounded, from a town like Lulea, a town which is, I think it may be objectively stated, the sticks, in every sense of the term, to know all this? How is any student expected to know it? None of them do. The lucky few act as if informed, probably because they permit themselves to be guided purely by instinct, or because they are brash and harebrained. So it was they who quickly perched their perky bottoms on little antique chairs in the fashionable coffee shops and restaurants, opened their cheeky mouths and became the new student elite. While such as I paced the autumnal streets, or mooned dejectedly on the banks of the wide, bleak river, or sat in our new, bare, boring little college rooms, and wondered why it was all so flat.

Oh, the flatness of Uppsala in those first weeks! The emptiness of my stomach, which developed a pit of despondency as gaping and empty as the wide plain which surrounded the low, grey town. Even its light, that cold clear light which I now think of as a symbol of the intellectual honesty which the city stands for, I hated. It seemed so cruel, revealing, as it did, all flaws and blemishes, totally without mercy.

I thought I would die. I thought I would take the train down to Stockholm - only an hour away, but who could feel so close, there? - and get a job as a waitress, plunge into the hot rawness of working-class life, live in an ethnic ghetto, perhaps, marry a Turk and have six babies. Or I would emigrate to Australia, and learn perfect English and ride a surf-board at weekends. I would do anything to escape.

The lectures were dull, the courses seemed silly, everywhere was thronged with great crowds of giggling students, every space was filled with fatuous laughter. Whenever I saw someone who, like me, seemed to be lost and alone, they were people I would have died sooner than become acquainted with. They were the dregs of society, ugly or stupid or dowdy or weak. I began to believe that I, too, must be the dregs.

Then I met Per Bishop. Or rather, he met me. A month after I had come, and, perhaps, just before I was about to abandon the whole thing. He had given his entire class, on Course 4a, Introduction to Archaeology, an essay to write. "The Archaeology of the Modern Urban Settlement". What a stupid topic, had been my reaction, but I did the essay mainly because I had so much time on my hands. Three weeks later he called me to his office, he told me it was the best he had received (only one third of the group had actually handed work in), he said he hoped I would continue as I had started.

And I did. I fell for him, in love, not in any normal way, but as a dog loves a master, as a soldier worships some brilliant general. I hero-worshipped him. And he was a good general, he rewarded me for my adulation. He made me a star.

And this was where the ancient scholarly traditions of Uppsala helped me. In another environment, my scholarly success would have ensured that I remained unpopular and cut off from my fellow students. At Lulea Gymnasium, I had been regarded as a leper, simply because I was good at lessons: academic success was not tolerated by the teenagers of that town, although achievement in any other sphere, for instance, sport, was rewarded with adoration. In Uppsala, I am happy to say, being a good scholar brought me the popularity I had never before enjoyed. Because I came first in my year every year, I was invited to all the most prestigious parties, my company was welcomed, or at least tolerated, in the brightest artistic and literary circles, to which I had absolutely nothing to contribute except my taciturn and somewhat practical genius. I never became a skilled socialiser. But it didn't matter. It was enough that everyone knew how clever I was: they didn't worry about my persistent silence and apparent stupidity with regard to any popular matter.

For all this, I had Per Bishop to thank. It was he who had spotted my talent, it was he who continued to encourage it, it was he who saved me from the fate which would have certainly awaited me, if I had not found a meaning in life precisely when I did.

He continued to help and boost me throughout my undergraduate and then my postgraduate career. He gave me more help than was necessary with my doctoral thesis, spending many weeks revising it with me. He ensured that I was offered a fellowship as soon as I had been promoted to the grade of doctor. He seemed to believe that I was his best student, ever, a true follower in his footsteps. I was sure I would be his successor, when he retired from the chair of archaeology at Uppsala, and so was everyone else. He was my intellectual father.

There was a barrier, a sexual one. As I have said, I was not attracted to Per Bishop, and I am sure this was mutual. But he, rather than I, felt that our different sexes stood in the way of a true marriage of minds. "What good friends we would have been, Robin," he would sometimes sigh, "if you had been a man!"

And I would smile and breathe, "yes" although I revolted against the point of view contained in this utterance. I did not give too much thought to it, I did not want to know if it was true or not. Because in my opinion we were the best of friends. Indeed, I considered him to be the only true friend I had.

Then he retired. His chair fell vacant, and the position was advertised. I wondered that he did not ask me to apply. When I finally mentioned to him that I was about to, and asked for his reference, he refused it.

"I do not think this is a job for a woman," he said. "You are a great scholar, Robin, and, believe me, you will find greater fulfilment, as a scholar and as a human being, if you do not have this chair. It is too demanding a role, it requires someone of perhaps lesser ability than you, as a researcher, and more as a leader of men."

I applied anyway, and failed to secure the post, which was given to a man from Lund who had barely finished his PhD, and who had never been on a dig further from home than Jutland.

It was not only because of that that I changed. When outsiders look at somebody's life, and note its more dramatic events, they will attribute causes and motives as a detective might, supposing that every act has one cause. But reality can be different. And in this instance, a conglomeration of motivations and causes lead to the result. Nevertheless, I have become what I am owing to Per Bishop's influence. And had he not betrayed me, it is possible that the changes would not have occurred at all. An accident of judgement, on his part, and I became a brilliant student. Another accident, and I became what I now am. My control over either event was nil.

I did not forgive him. I do not. I will not.

Chapter Twenty-one

My report was progressing favourably: I had written it to this point, and felt that the time had come to pack away my floppy disc and wait until I was home in my own room, at my desk which overlooks the botanical gardens - there is a lovely clump of coconut palms just below the window, it was for them that I chose the apartment - before writing any more. The ten days which we had agreed on as a waiting period were almost over. I was certain that Karl and Jenny could not turn up at this stage.

I did put away my disc, and locked my computer into its waterproof box, but not for long, as will soon be learned. However, I decided that I would use my last few days in Ireland in relaxation. I was surprised to find that it was quite easy for me to switch to a holiday mood. Normally I hate vacations or any break from my normal working routine, I consider them an unnecessary luxury and a boring waste of time. Now, to my amazement, I found that for the first time in many years, if not in my life, I was perfectly content to do absolutely nothing. My days were spent stretched on a deckchair in the sun, listening to my beloved Sibelius and allowing Thomas Mann's novel to dangle from my knees. From time to time I would read a snatch of his immortal prose, a page or two at most. I found it most soporific.

There was, unfortunately, nothing else to read. I'd got through about half of *Robinson Crusoe*, but didn't feel like finishing it. It drags, really, after a while. Karen had a heap of popular thrillers, Le Carre, Jeffrey Archer, that sort of thing. I cannot read them. I cannot read Mann either, or even more accessible novelists, with ease. but still less can I lose myself in adult fantasy literature. In any case, at this point I found that I really did not want to amuse myself with any external agency apart from music and sunshine. I lay and dozed, and the greyish landscape seemed to borrow colour and texture from my own memories and ideas. I found that I drifted from it to other, richer regions: I moved from gardens of paradisal loveliness, brimful of spiky dark green foliage, of brilliant crimson blooms, yellow fruits, to the pale watery gardens of Ireland. Delicate in colour as apple blossom, the sunsets, the sunrises, the pale green meadows, the little yellow wildflowers. The primroses, the cowslips, the early purple orchids. Lilac time. From one garden to another I floated, carried on the waves of music, which was to me now more harmonious than ever, of a sweetness almost unbearable. But not unbearable, ultimately acceptable, delightful to the ear and the soul.

This was, for me, a time of the most intense happiness I have ever known.

Karen and I did not enjoy much social intercourse during these days. She did not seem to require my companionship and I was possessed of an unusually intense desire for solitude. I was wary lest any unnecessary commerce with another person destroy the sense of peace which I was fortunate enough to bask in just then. I recognised this sense of serenity, utter contentment, as a feeling which was my birthright as a human being. Although I had never, in my conscious memory, experienced it before, I knew it was mine. I knew it belonged to me, as a most precious possession, an inheritance buried deep in earth, never seen but still owned, and known. This happiness, I suddenly knew, had been there, under the surface of my life, like soft green fronds deep in the sea, always. But I had never been able to get at it before. Not once. Not until now. And I was wary, because I knew too that I could lose it at any moment. I was not worried: worry had no part in that sense of well-being and joy. But I realised that any external influence could spoil everything for me. I was perfectly happy, but I knew that at any moment the geese would start cackling, the gulls screeching, the ducks squabbling, the boats roaring, and that the glassy calm of the lake would be shattered.

I did give some thought to my mate, however. We shared meals, that is to say, I ate and Karen fasted simultaneously. In her favour, I must say that she never referred to her diet, she never bored me with details of her weight, in fact, she did not seem particularly interested in it as a topic of thought or conversation. Since I have had the experience of being the confidante of women on diets in the past, and had been nauseated by their obsessive harping on calories and milligrams, their insatiable lust for praise, and their remarkable proselytising attitude - for some reason they wanted everyone else to be just as thin as they themselves had become - I was most grateful for this. But in a way it made Karen's continued weight loss much more worrying. Initially I had assumed that she dieted from the common motivations: simple physical vanity, or concern with health. And I had assumed that it must have had some connection with her missing Thomas. Was she dieting in order to be attractive for him, her six year old pig of a son? Or was it some sort of atonement for the guilt she obviously continued to feel for her leaving him? Then it struck me that Karl might have something to do with it. But in that case, she should have given up when Karl disappeared. On the other hand, she did not believe yet that he had finally gone, and continuing to behave as if he were around, or likely to reappear at any minute, might have strengthened her pathetic faith in the continuing survival of the hapless couple. Perhaps her dieting belonged to the type of behaviour pattern which makes bereaved spouses keep their dead partner's effects exactly as they were when he or she was alive: slippers by the door, pyjamas on the bed, clothes in the wardrobe. By pretending that nothing has changed, these people hope to change reality. Karen, I thought, was just the type of individual to carry on in this ridiculous fashion. But eventually I came to the conclusion that she must be starving herself from guilt: about Jenny and Karl, or about the abandoned Thomas, or about all three.

Whatever the reason for it, however, I heartily wished that she would give up her dieting, snap out of her anorexia, or whatever: I needed an able-bodied partner if we were to sail home alone, and Karen, although she had manifested no symptoms of ill health, oddly enough, by now looked so frail that I had no faith in her stamina. Unfortunately, my gentle hints to her regarding nourishment fell on deaf ears. I soon realised that any attempt I made to remedy the situation would have the opposite effect, and had to reconcile myself to optimistic non-interference. Her condition, however, made me more anxious than I otherwise might have been to begin the homebound voyage as soon as possible.

On what was to have been our penultimate morning in Bray, we were sitting at the breakfast table on deck. The coffee cups were empty, their little brown dregs were stiffening into stains before our eyes, and crumbs from my toast littered the table. But we both seemed to feel too lazy to move. Anyway we were earlier than usual, and the sun was rising over the sea, setting the sky ablaze.

"Ah, " I said, "the cold glory of the dawn!"

Because it was, naturally, at seven o'clock on a September morning, chilly.

"What's that?" Karen asked sharply. If ever I referred to something which was not immediately familiar to her, she seemed to suspect me of some sort of foul motive.

"A line from a poem," I said, nonconsequentially.

"Do you know more of it?"

"Something about a house..

A naked house, a naked moor

A shivering pool before the door
A garden bare of flowers and fruit
And poplars at the garden foot.
Bleak without and bare within
Such is the house that I live in.
Yet shall your ragged moor receive
The incomparable pomp of eve
The cold glory of the dawn
Behind your miserable trees be drawn..."

"It's nice. Who wrote it? Yeats?"

"No. Somebody else. I can't remember. It's something I learned at school, you know I never read poetry normally. Ugh!"

"It's good. Bleak, that's what this all is, isn't it? There are no ragged trees, even. Or poplars at the garden foot. Isn't it awful?"

"Mm. I wonder. No, I believe I think it beautiful, in its own way. And it's got the light, the dawn, the sunset, in a way, they're better here than in the kind of places we're used to."

"You're ..."

Karen stopped. She had been about to say I was mad, or something to that effect, I'm sure. But I was not. It was just that I had come to appreciate this barren place. To tell the truth, I had come to love it. Perfect design. Contours clearly outlined against a pure sky. The shape of the earth, plain at last. Uncluttered by the frippery of flora and fauna which masquerades under the name of nature. Unfussed by the work of human hands, which always tend to overdo things, to leave the parts of the world they touch as gaudy and messy as a Victorian drawing room. So had Bray been, before. And I'd missed that when I first saw this new place. But now, this had grown on me, and I saw that it was right. I saw its perfection. The pure and simple perfection of form and light. There is nothing else. Nothing else that I want.

I stared at the sky, pondering: now, with no work, no demands on my time, I allowed my mind to wander away, I allowed myself the luxury of gazing and not thinking at all.

"Look!"

Karen screamed.

"Look, look, look!"

Reluctantly, I turned.

But even before I did so, my heart sank. And I knew.

Far off, specks on the sand, moving slowly towards us.

A day, and we would have missed them. We would have sailed off, unburdened.

Home.

Home, which I have never had. Mother, mother! I cried, as I watched the specks. Mother, take me home! Mother, say it, Mother, just once. Say, say you love me!

I almost wept.

But sighed instead and, in one sad second, relinquished my tranquillity. Then I dashed into my cabin and fetched my binoculars.

Jenny, Karl, and one other, between them, supported by them. They looked as if they had been sleeping in their clothes for three weeks, which of course they had been doing. But otherwise they were unaltered. They did not appear injured or particularly unhealthy, insofar as I could tell. Their companion, on the other hand, had the appearance of one of those survivors of Belsen or Auschwitz that one sees on old black and white newsreels: emaciated, apparently bald, with wide crazed eyes staring from greenish skin. The clothes were ordinary clothes, of course, not prison garb. But they were in terrible condition, they looked like an assortment of rags clinging to the body by some miraculous means, and were probably quite dangerous in the circumstances.

I felt exhausted and passed my hands over my face, in a gesture quite exceptional for me.

I sat down on the boards, and handed the glasses to Karen, who gazed, spellbound and silent, for many minutes.

In less than half an hour, the trio had reached the shore, and Karen rowed them out to the boat, since the tide was high. I helped Karl and Jenny aboard first. Karen jumped, laughing, crying, childishly overjoyed to see her friends again. She embraced them, kissed them, drooled over them, and entirely ignored the stranger, as, indeed, did Karl and Jenny. Her I helped aboard. Rather, I took her in my arms and lifted her onto the *Saint Patrick*: she was featherlight, and appeared to be very ill. I took good care that no part of my skin came in contact with hers.

"Welcome to the *Saint Patrick*," I said in my very warmest tones. "You're quite safe now, don't worry about a thing. We'll help you to get better."

She made no response whatsoever. Her bright, wild eyes remained curiously expressionless. Her mouth did not smile, indeed, the muscles of her face seemed atrophied. And so did her tongue.

I looked inquiringly at Karl.

He looked away.

"She doesn't talk," Jenny said. Her voice had changed. It wasn't as tinkly as before, but, rather, husky. "She seems to be dumb."

"Ah!"

I took "her" in my arms again, and carried her down to the galley, where I laid her on the berth and covered her with a blanket. She was light but whatever weight she possessed was dead: she was as easy, or difficult, to manipulate as a rubber doll. It was as if she had lost all use of herself. But I had seen her, walking, albeit supported. She was not paralysed.

"I know you've had lots of terrible experiences," I crooned over her. "But now they're all over. You're safe, you're in good hands, you don't have to worry about a thing!"

I smiled at her but she did not smile back.

"In a few minutes I'll bring you something to drink!" I said. "Now try to get some rest."

I returned to deck, and shook hands heartily with Karl and Jenny.

"So wonderful to see you again!" I made my voice as enthusiastic as possible. "So wonderful, and so unbelievable. Frankly I'd given you up as lost."

"Not me! I didn't! I knew you'd come back!" Karen jigged up and down by the rail.

"Well, we'd given ourselves up too, I reckon," Karl laughed heavily. "I never thought we'd make it!"

"No." I paused. It is not easy to find the right words in dramatic situations. I was too tired now, by the idea of their new presence and of the new creature, to feel any emotion other than a slight disappointment that they had shown up and shattered my brief experience of contentment.

Jenny and Karen sat together, heads nodding, chatting away in whispering voices.

"Who is she?" I asked, finally. "That creature. Where did she come from?"

"From the bowels of the earth," Jenny raised her head, smiling sweetly at me. "Literally. "

"Is that a fact?" I smiled in return.

"Yes, it is," Jenny's tone did not change. She sat on deck, hugging her knees, her long plait draped over her shoulder: it had grown, naturally, since we'd come to Ireland, and seemed to reach almost to her feet.

"Would you tell us the whole story? We're both dying to know everything that's happened."

"I'll bet!" Karl grinned wryly. He was stretched out in a deckchair, smoking his pipe as if his life depended on it.

"Well, for once she is speaking for both of us," Karen interjected. "I mean, you will have to tell us what happened, eventually, so you might as well save time and energy and do it now. I mean to say, you probably want to, anyway."

"I do, actually," Jenny spoke matter of factly. "So I will." She stood up, walked out to the centre of the deck space, and sat on the edge of the table.

"Once upon a time," she said, in a low intense tone, a story-teller's voice. "Two people called Karl and Jenny were feeling very sad and dejected. Rejected, dejected, worn out, useless. Fed up with life. They did not know what to do with themselves."

I interrupted her:

"Must you use this style? It's irritating, frankly, in my opinion."

"Too bad," said Jenny. "It's this or nothing."

I sighed and she continued, a small smile playing across her pale face.

"A spell had been cast upon them by a wicked old witch. And wizard. A witchlike wizard. She had banished them from her kingdom, and condemned them to wander forever in the desert. Dressed only in bikinis."

"This is intolerable," I protested. "I only did what was right. Admittedly," I added, noticing that her face turned stubborn, "I may have mishandled the situation. I may have been tactless. But my basic judgment was perfectly sound, anyone would have had to make the same decisions."

"Oh yes indeed. The wicked witch was cunning and wise, and she sent Karl and Jenny over hill and down dale. They wandered, not knowing where they were going, for a night and a day and another night and a day. And in and out of months and up and over years. Up and down, up and down. The desert was very bleak and bare, they saw nothing, no animal and no human, no tree and no flower. The desert had not been touched by the hand of the creator.

Still, in Jenny's mind there was a picture. The picture was simple, a very simple oil painting of a twig, a bone and a broken pot, in shades of brown and yellow. These things were painted on a plain grey background, and framed in an old-fashioned, heavy gilt frame. And that picture remained in her mind all the time. She knew it meant something. It was light at the end of the tunnel. It was promise. It was her gift, that picture, the gift a good fairy might have given her, if there had been one. Instead of a beautiful dress, or a coach and four, Jenny had been given this image, to guide her through the desert."

"Fascinating," I murmured politely, wishing she would get to the point. Karen glared angrily at me. But Jenny was lost in her ridiculous tale, and did not pay any attention to my remark or to anything. Her eyes had a spaced-out, drugged look. Which made me wonder.

"Ah yes, fascinating!"

So she'd heard.

"And how did Jenny receive that gift? Her little picture? She received it from God. He put it there. Oh yes, he was her donor, her helper and friend. As he is everyone's."

Oh God! I thought, but did not say.

Even Karl passed his hands over his eyes in embarrassment.

"And where did Karl and Jenny actually go?" I prodded gently.

"Over hill and over dale."

She'd said that already.

"Towards the mountain that is known as the Sugar Loaf. That is a fine mountain, and it's easy to pick out from all the others, because of its special shape. So they walked towards that, thinking of it as a landmark, and then they walked past it, and deep, deep into the forest."

"Forest?"

"I speak metaphorically. South they went and west and south again. Down in the direction of Ashford, Wicklow and the Sally Gap. The garden of Ireland, it is known as. They walked for two or three days, and then, in a flat field in the middle of nowhere, they saw a hill."

"Astonishing!"

"Yes, absolutely. Because this was not a great mountain, like the Sugar Loaf, but a small, perfectly circular, mound. It was covered with grey dust, as everything was in this land, but there was one narrow gap in the dust, just a few inches wide. And in that gap was a piece of grey rock."

"Hm."

"When Karl and Jenny arrived at this mound, Jenny had a strange sensation: the picture she carried in her mind, which was always there, night and day, changed. It began to glow. She tried to suppress it, because it glowed too brightly, it hurt her mind as a brilliant light hurts the eyes. But it would not be quenched, the more she tried to turn it out the brighter it shone. It was like a vision. It was a vision, but an internal one."

"Like all visions," I said.

"Perhaps. Jenny knew what it was: a sign from God. "We have arrived at a good place," she said to Karl."

"And what did Karl say?"

"Karl was sceptical."

He smoked his pipe, increasing the tempo slightly, so that rings of blue smoke rose in rapid succession above his head. His hair had grown, like Jenny's, and he had tied it back behind the nape of his neck in a pony tail. It looked rather silly, I thought.

"Nevertheless, they stayed close to the rock, because they arrived there just as a thick fog was sweeping across the countryside. It was so thick that it became impossible to see anything, so Karl and Jenny sat down, in the shadow of the mound, and waited for it to lift. Time passed, however, and it seemed to get worse, not better, and finally night fell.

"We will sleep here in this good place," Jenny said. "It's safe here." Karl was worried about the danger of sleeping in the open, but they had no choice. And since they were very tired, they fell fast asleep."

Jenny paused and smiled distantly.

"I woke up first. The sky was clear, and I could see that the fog had lifted. There was an almost full moon, and it was very bright: the landscape looked like a moonscape, the way it does, sometimes, here. I got up carefully, so as not to waken Karl, and walked all around the mound. Really, it was exactly the same all around, but it had such a regular shape, it was shaped like an igloo, that I knew it must have been built by human hands. So ... another house, I thought. So what, the country seems to be full of them. It took me about ten minutes to get right around the hillock, and when I came back to where Karl was sleeping still, I got the most terrible shock: the rock we had noticed before had parted slightly, and a light was shining through the crack!"

Karen and I gasped.

"I was frightened, suddenly: I knew it must portend something good, I knew that. But it was so abrupt, and so unexpected, that I felt more scared than I ever have been in my whole life. I shook Karl violently and woke him up. He was shocked, too, but less so than I was, maybe just because I had seen the light first.

"What shall we do?" I asked, clinging to him.

"Well, I guess we should investigate it," was what he said. But he continued to sit still, staring, and we both stayed rigid for ages. It seemed. Afraid, really, to move.

And then, the rocks parted, slowly, before our eyes. And Elinor emerged."

"Elinor?"

"Elinor MacHugh. That is what we call her. I'll come to that in a minute. She looked - well, you've seen her. But she looked even worse then, she looked totally inhuman, I fully believed she was a ghost, or some kind of otherworld creature, the kind of thing you read about inhabiting fairy mounds in Ireland."

"Fairies."

"Fairies, the Tuatha De Danainn, you know, that sort of thing. A race of little people who have vanished into the mounds. I mean, she was so small, and thin, and green, and bald, she looked like one of the more horrible kinds of gnomes we have in Swedish tradition. Certainly not human. As soon as I said the word "fairy", though, Karl came to his senses. He just laughed, and said "Are you crazy?", or something like that. "It must be a human being. Let's follow it." Because she'd taken one look at us, and vanished, back into the mound. She was more frightened than we were, and there was only one of her. But she left the rock opened, so we could follow. I think we were meant to.

We could pass through the opening in the rocks quite easily, and then we walked along a narrow passage, which was - we found this out later - built with great blocks of granite. The passage was low, and we had to bend in order to move along it. It was about three yards long, and at the end of it was a circular room, also built of great blocks of stone. There were some big stones placed here and there around this room, and it was littered with various kinds of debris: tin cans, plastic bags, bones. There was a human skeleton lying on a folding bed in one corner, visible from every part of the room. And, hiding behind another folding bed, crouched down on the ground, was Elinor."

She paused, and stared at the distant mountains, and we all observed a moment's silence, while we pondered the fact of Elinor's existence: it was a fact not easy to grasp, to realise, even after the proof of it had been seen. And still more impossible was it to realise its significance, or to begin to speculate as to its cause.

"She was like some kind of wild animal?" I offered, encouragingly, remembering science fiction movies I had seen on this subject.

"Well," said Jenny, and did not elaborate immediately.

"She was more like a leper, I'd say," Karl interjected. "Sort of rotting."

"She still is," Karen almost screamed: her voice was so naturally high pitched that any excitement in it led to this effect.

"Well, she was much much worse then than she is now. That was one reason why we stayed away so long: we wanted to nurse her until she was strong enough to walk, or to be carried, to the boat."

"That was very noble of you," I said, not ironically: I would not have thought them capable of taking any great personal risks for the sake of another human being. I do not think many people are capable of this, actually.

"Why didn't one of you stay with her while the other came back for help?" Karen asked with unusual perspicacity. "Were you afraid of getting lost?"

"No," Jenny smiled, pleased, for some reason. "Oh, no. We didn't think we'd get lost, and we did think of doing that. I mean, that was the obvious thing to do, wasn't it? The problem was, neither of us wanted to stay with Elinor, alone."

"Buried alive," I said, trying to envisage the mound.

"No, it wasn't that either. We had no sense of claustrophobia in the tumulus, oddly enough, really. We both felt perfectly at home there, from the moment we emerged from the passage into the chamber. Don't ask me why, it was eerie enough, between the skeleton and the rubbish and the stones carved with old runes."

"What?" I could not keep my sharp excitement from my voice, to my subsequent annoyance. Noting my interest, perhaps, Karl became very irritated, and looked angrily at Jenny.

"Well, runes, I don't know what made me say that. There were some stones in the chamber with scratches on them, you know, made by Elinor, maybe, or whoever had been with her."

"The skeleton?" I said, not covering my irony this time.

Jenny elected to ignore it.

"Well, yes, I suppose so. Nothing interesting at all. But they did look weird, they certainly did. And of course it was all dark and pretty horrible looking, in a way. But it felt cosy. Right from the start. It felt, what it was, perfectly secure. Like the kitchen of your own home, sort of, that very peaceful warm feeling. Must have had something to do with the air, or something."

"Most interesting."

"Yes, oh yes. But Elinor - I mean, she's obviously totally harmless, and she's not got anything that's contagious or anything like that, as far as we know."

"You can't have known that from the start."

"Well no, we didn't. And also she looked so horrible, so really horrible, like the daughter of Lazarus or something like that. You could smell death off her. That was why, I think, we couldn't bear to be with her, we couldn't bear to separate. So we had to stay."

"How did you survive?"

"The way she survived. She'd got some food, still quite a lot of food, although she's obviously been there for a couple of years now. And she had a supply of water. That is the miraculous thing about the mound: it has its own spring, deep in rock, and obviously that water never got contaminated. So we had that, and she had that, and whoever was with her before had it too."

"Who was with her?"

Karl glanced across at Jenny again, and she looked down, slyly.

"We have no idea."

"Can't she talk?"

"No. Not at all. She seems to be completely dumb. Or else she can't talk because it's so long since she has had to. She wrote a few things in Karl's notebook ..."

Karl started again.

"Just saying who she was, you know, at first. That stopped then, she refused to do any more, so really we know nothing at all about her."

"Oh dear," I sighed, not believing a word of it. "Who knows, she may change as time goes on?"

"No doubt she will," Karen proffered this drily.

Karl and Jenny went to bed soon after this. And then we lifted anchor and set sail for home.

Chapter Twenty-two

It was October: we had spent four months on the bay which was now receding into romantic mists behind us, four months which had been filled with more adventure and trauma than many people experience in an entire lifetime. As Karen and I guided the *Saint Patrick* out of the cove where we had been moored all summer, I tried to allow the major events of our sojourn in Ireland to pass through my mind, but failed. They were too many and too various, perhaps, or, as seems more likely, they were too unfinished, to allow of any easy review. The expedition was winding up now. But we were beginning the final act, not letting the curtain fall: I had felt, during my few days' peaceful relaxation, that it was all over, that I had nothing more to do but make the homebound journey before releasing my startling report to the world. And it was that expectation, precisely, which had made me feel so relaxed. Now I was electrified by a new excitement, a sense of urgency. There was suddenly such a lot to do, and so little time in which to do it. Because it was, I intuitively realised, absolutely imperative that the mystery surrounding "Elinor" should be solved before we arrived in Gothenburg. It was of vital importance that the person to deal with "Elinor" and to interpret her story for the world should be I, and not some sensationalistic journalist, some conservative academic, some Freudian psychologist. I, and I alone, had the expertise, sensitivity and experience, to be capable of understanding Elinor and whatever it was she would have to say, properly. My strong wish to do this left me nervous and edgy, and already I was feeling that curious combination of exhaustion and restlessness which anyone engaged in a work of great moment must experience before it can be brought to completion.

My companions were not party to these sensations, as far as I could judge. They seemed to assume that our work was over, and to bask in a lazy complacency. Seemed. But I was uncertain of them now, as I had not been before: Karl and Jenny had taken me by surprise, I had never dreamed that they had it in them to do what they did, in walking off into the unknown. Clearly there were aspects of their characters, or of one of their characters, that I had not gauged correctly. They had hidden depths or strengths, streaks of ambition and ruthlessness the nature and extent of which were unknown quantities. They had shocked once and could do so again. They were no longer under my command, although they pretended to be now, as they had never done in the past: thus far had they developed, in guile, or manipulation, or maturity. They were no longer a couple of somewhat rebellious children, to be humoured and kept under control. It was they, now, who seemed to be in command of the situation, and I needed to wrest their power from them, if my project was to triumph completely. And I was filled with a new determination to ensure that it would.

Outwardly, they had both changed considerably. Jenny, who had been so shy and taciturn, was now extrovert and chatty. She laughed and talked all day long, running around the boat "making herself useful", as she put it, not entirely accurately, herself. She was constantly trotting in and out to Elinor, administering to the many needs of the latter with a

Florence Nightingale-like zeal. Once I gaily suggested to her that her true vocation lay in caring for the sick, rather than in an academic sphere. At this remark she frowned and said: "You would think that."

Karl had also changed as a result of his various goings on in Ireland. Originally he had been joky, talkative enough, but basically truculent. I had understood from very early on in the voyage that he regarded me as an enemy to his own ambition and to his male supremacy. His rather foolish, transparent behaviour and made this much clear. Now he seemed imbued with an inner calm. Perhaps that is not true: it was impossible to tell, rather, whether he was calm or not. But he was certainly quieter than he had been, and seemed to withdraw from our little society: he did not become silent, as Jenny had been before she had matured enough to be part of the group, and he occasionally made jokes and witty comments which were reminiscent of his old self. But he was not that old self. He possessed a control which he had never had before, and his every move was considered, his every comment monitored. He had taken command of his own personality. To what end? I asked myself.

And felt I knew the answer.

Karl had something to hide, something important. I was determined to find out what it was.

My ambition was to gain access to the notebook Jenny had inadvertently referred to in her account of her visit to "the otherworld" as she embarrassingly described it. Really, she talked more and more like an in-flight magazine of the more full-blown variety! If she did not want to be a nurse, I thought, she could have a very successful career as a writer of tourist literature: anything but an archaeologist! But I did not voice my opinion: it was important that I, even more than Karl, should be cautious in my every remark now. The time for naturalness - it had been short enough - was over: spontaneity is a luxury that a devoted scientist such as myself can ill afford.

I made a few attempts to take possession of Karl's notebook, or at least to find out where he had hidden it. A visit to his and Jenny's cabin early one morning, when they were both asleep, proved futile. I tried again later on during the same day, but was surprised in my searching by Karen, who looked at me with screwed-up eyes and, inclining her head on one side, in a most vulgar attitude, said:

"So what are you up to now, may I ask?"

"Oh nothing, nothing at all," I blustered conventionally, since I couldn't think of any reasonable pretext for my rummaging. I smiled confusedly at her. She continued to stare sardonically at me: with her strawlike hair tied in a bright pink bandanna around her bony, lined, dark brown face, she looked like some starved fishwife, cheeky, vulgar, loud. Fishwife? Don't I mean whore? Starved, tarty, fishy. But in fact Karen had progressed from the weak stage of starvation. She had begun to eat again - now that Karl was back? - and she looked glowingly healthy, I have to admit. Even rather attractive, if you like that sort of thing, which I most certainly do not.

"Clear out on the double or I'll call Karl, do you hear?" she spat out at me, playing, I suppose, the role of some third rate actress in a criminal romance. Unable to suppress my amusement at the little performance, I vacated the cabin.

Karen undoubtedly split on me to the others, because after that they were intensely vigilant all the time, and I did not get an early opportunity of revisiting the cabin.

I decided to concentrate my attention on Elinor, in the hope of eliciting information from her which would, in any case, be more useful than anything the notebook might contain.

I was sure that Elinor was not dumb. Moreover, I was convinced that she had already given quantities of information to Karl and Jenny. I knew that they had silenced her, by what threats, bribes, falsehoods, I did not know. But they had done it, to keep valuable data from me. They wanted my enterprise to fail, they wanted to steal the most important facts. Ruthless, selfish, blindly ambitious, is what they were. I would not succumb to their power.

But Elinor was obdurate in her pretence of dumbness, and I was forced to admire her stubborn will-power. Her health improved rapidly, as soon as we were out at sea. Her skin lost its horrible greenish pallor, her eyes grew clean and bright, and hair began to sprout on her head. Its colour was not black, as one had somehow expected - because of the association with Elinor MacHugh - but snow white. This, however, might have resulted from the pigmentation cells having been destroyed during her ordeal. Psychological endurance tests of any kind can result in white hair, so this seemed a likely enough explanation.

Of course, people can be shocked into dumbness, too. But this is, I believe, less common than the white-hair syndrome, and besides, what I had learnt of Elinor's character during the few days we had had her on board did not suggest that she was the kind of person who is easily shocked or disturbed. The rapidity with which she recovered from her "illness", her healthy appetite and fairly cheerful demeanour, as well, of course, as the fact of her survival, marked her out as an individual of unusual powers of endurance, physical and psychological. She was not a faint-hearted lady. She was, indeed, one in a million. One in four million. One in a hundred million.

When I thought of these matters, it seemed more urgent than ever to get her to talk.

With this aim uppermost in my mind, I spent all the time I had at my disposal seated at her bedside, holding her small shrivelled hand in mine, smiling gently at her ugly face, and offering her endless snacks and refreshments, in the form of chicken broth, chocolate, biscuits, coffee, and cups of tea, of which she could never have enough. She devoured almost everything offered, however, and thanked me with a glance, or, on very special occasions, such as after I had given her a cigarette (filthy habit, smoking, but I saw soon enough that she liked it), she would give me a slight squeeze of the hand. But never a word.

I tried to surprise her into speech by casually asking questions at times when she seemed off guard and totally relaxed, when she was falling asleep, for instance. But it never worked.

Jenny and Karen did not let my campaign to make Elinor speak go unnoticed or uncriticised.

"You are the limit!" Karen expostulated, coming upon me plying Elinor with a series of questions about Fiona, "her" daughter, on our third afternoon at sea: we were already passing the Mull of Kintyre, and I was getting more and more anxious. Our progress was rapid, and in no time at all we should reach home.

"Can't you ever give up? God, you make me feel sick, you really do!"

Jenny's complaints took a milder form, but were probably more virulently meant.

"Elinor is not well, Robin," she said sadly, twisting the end of her plait. "It's really too bad of you to bother her like this, and it won't look very well for you if you make her even more ill than she is."

Fortunately, there seemed to be little chance of that!

I calculated that we would be home in three days. Or less, if I were unlucky. I tried everything in my power to force words out of Elinor: bribery, threats, distraction. I offered her money, property, life-long protection. But to no avail. And really, I suppose such carrots meant very little to someone who had been through what she had endured.

"If you don't speak, Elinor MacHugh, or whoever you are, I'll throw you overboard!" I said finally. I was speaking with perfect spontaneity, for once, and really felt that I might do just that.

Her only response was a short dry chuckle.

But that was something! It was more than she had done before, it was a better response.

I plied her with drink. She liked whiskey, and would take three glasses of it in a row, but never any more. The only effect it had on her was to make her fall asleep: she would lie then, quite flat on her back with her mouth open, and snore. Once I spent the whole night watching her in this attitude, hoping that she might say something in her sleep. But the only sounds which emitted from her were long slow siren-like hisses.

I tried a technique I had learned from, of all unlikely places, an old Irish legend: the legend is about a mermaid who, like Elinor, refuses to speak to the human being who has captured her, and who has in fact married or raped her. In the end, by insulting her family, he manages to break her silence and, in order to protest against the calumny, she speaks. (Soon after she disappears into the ocean again, but I did not anticipate such a reaction from Elinor).

I used this method of primitive psychological torture on our fourth afternoon at sea. Jenny was in the cabin with Elinor, and I began to harass the latter.

"So how is the patient today?" I began, in a hearty, family doctor, manner. "Ah, putting on weight, I see, and growing more of that ugly white hair. Shall we see about some dye? A blue rinse, perhaps, would improve our appearance somewhat? What do you think?"

"Really, Robin, this is going too far!" Jenny was very annoyed. "It isn't good for her at all."

"No? I think the old dame is a lot stronger than you seem to think!"

From where I now stood, at the dressing table, I could observe Elinor's knees twitching angrily under the bedclothes.

"What on earth gives you that opinion?" asked Jenny, rather stupidly and much to my gratification.

"She's a tough old cookie," I said matter of factly. "She's survived what four million Irish people could not survive. That tells she's of rough stock. Rough and ready. And see how she eats! Like a horse, you can't satisfy her. Besides, there's something about her, the texture of her skin, for instance. It's blotchy and thick and rough, like goatskin, or something. She's obviously of peasant stock."

The knees twitched more than ever and Elinor's eyes contracted into two tiny black beads. Her complexion turned to a shade of deep damson. I walked over to her bed and stared hard at her.

"Yes, you can always tell, with the Irish. Their genes are not mixed very well, you see, they're inbred, because until very recently most Irish people stayed in one place, the place they were born in, the place their ancestors had lived for hundreds of years."

"Except for the Irish that went to America and England and Australia and Germany and Japan" said Jenny, with unusual irony.

"Except for those. I'm not talking about them, naturally, I'm talking about the ones who stayed at home. The survivors. Or, if you look at it in another way, the ones who were too weak and unadventurous to go away. People like Elinor here. Their genes are quite pure. Characteristics linked to the type of environment in which her people have always lived are very noticeable."

I pinched Elinor's nose. She hit me, quite hard.

"Elinor's nose is of the variety known as "snub", a type of nose usually found among the lowest social classes. Slaves, serfs. Trolls, you will remember, are depicted with such noses, in Scandinavia. And look at these legs..."

I hitched up the quilt, and Elinor immediately pulled it down again.

"Her legs are thick, stout at the ankles. The legs of a milkmaid, someone born to carry children and other burdens from the beginning to the end of her days."

At this point, one of the said legs was raised into the air quite abruptly, and its foot landed, very painfully, on my nose. I withdrew swiftly to a safer stand-point, and continued my tirade of insults and racist abuse. But I was losing heart, and ground: Elinor, relieved, no doubt, by her little display of physical violence, was lying back on her pillow, a tiny smile of amusement playing on her lips.

I tried a few more remarks of the kind quoted above. But to no avail. She would not speak.

We had been at sea for four full days and nights at this point. Time was no longer on my side, and, as I stood on deck, under a beautiful starlit sky, I reversed the decision I had made earlier, that is, to forget about Karl's notebook and to work on Elinor. The latter course seemed hopeless to me now, so I planned to spend the last days of the voyage seizing and studying Karl's notebook. I was unsure, but not too unsure, of the method I would employ in the pursuit of this goal, and, exhausted after twenty four hours of hard work with Elinor, whom I found enervating beyond belief, I went to bed.

Chapter Twenty-three

My one and only chance to snatch Karl's notebook arrived just three days before we reached the port of Gothenburg.

By one of those miraculous accidents which occasionally occur I found myself in an ideal situation in which to achieve my goal without having had to contrive in the least to bring it about. From the moment I caught sight of Karl on that fatal evening, all alone on deck while Jenny and Karen were both preoccupied with Elinor MacHugh, I knew I was about to be successful.

He was leaning over the rail, smoking his pipe and staring into the waves, as had been his habit throughout the voyage. His hope of spotting some form of life in the water was no longer as absurd, however, as it had once been: at some point in the journey, the sea would begin to live. We did not know exactly where, but Karl's ambition was to locate the border between the dead and the living world, and to mark it on the map. This was the least harmful of his ambitions, in my opinion.

Watching him, as he stood there with his bottom projecting into the air and his brownish reddish curls dangling, I remembered my erstwhile attraction for him, something which I had, in his long absence and in the excitement of his and the party's return, forgotten. But he was as attractive as ever, from any objective point of view, and so, let me admit it, was I. I have always been lucky with my looks, as in other respects, and have been able to preserve my neat and rather striking appearance with no great expenditure of effort. I remembered, moreover, that Karl had responded, albeit ambiguously, to my earlier advances. How long ago all that was! But - possibly that distance was itself an advantage - absence makes the heart grow fonder, and so, I have noticed, can passage of time.

The crucial moment was now. Now, three days before we would reach Gothenburg. Now, when Karl was alone on deck, staring at the ocean, while Karen and Jenny were busily occupied elsewhere. The dormant beast must be awakened now. There was not a moment to lose!

For it would, any fool could see, be very much to my professional advantage, and to the advantage of Science, and Scholarship, and Truth, to enjoy easy access to Karl's thoughts at this juncture in our adventure.

"What a delightful evening!" thus I announced my presence, and moved towards him fractionally. The sea was a mirror all around us, and to our leeward side the Scottish highlands could be seen as majestic black silhouettes against an apricot sky. Just the setting for a romantic seduction!

"Yeah, it's pretty!" he responded nonchalantly, and did not turn around.

"It's been a good trip so far, hasn't it?"

"Not bad," he said, taking his pipe out of his mouth and knocking it against the side of the boat, in a series of short swift raps. A shower of silver ashes fell into the silver sea.

"We've been lucky."

"How's that?" he turned towards me now, for the first time. His expression was not markedly friendly, but at least he did not seem to be entirely uninterested in what I had to say.

"Well ... we could have run into a real storm, in the straits of Jura, say. That passage is famous for them."

"It was rough enough for me."

"Yes. A little uncomfortable, all right. I'll certainly be glad to get home, we all will be, of course."

"Sure thing."

"When do you think we'll make it?"

I edged somewhat closer, partly in an attempt to hear him better: he addressed the water rather than me, and seemed to communicate with it in a series of barely audible mumbles and grunts.

"Oh, two, three days at most, wouldn't you say?"

He began to take his pipe out again, and I realised I had to act quickly.

"Karl!" I whispered, moving in swiftly for the kill, "have you really hated this trip? Do you believe I've mishandled it so badly?"

A cloud of discomfiture flitted across his visage, which was at last facing mine.

"Hell, no!" he said, shrugging. "Not now. I did think so at one stage, I guess. But not so much now. It's been a hell of an experience, though!"

I placed my hand, very very lightly, on his arm.

"I'm so glad," I said, and paused, and stared at the dimming water.

"You see," I said, after two or three minutes, during which time I allowed my hand to remain resting on his arm, "you see, Karl, I feel now - maybe I haven't always felt like this but I do now - I feel that you're the one kindred spirit I have, on board this boat. I don't want to be disrespectful to the others, but lets face it. Their - well, let me say it, what the hell! - their minds can't match mine. With you it's different, somehow."

I nuzzled his shoulder with my cheek.

"Mm," he said. I could not, of course, see his face from the angle mine was at but I sensed a softening in him. The air seemed to float more gently around us.

I nuzzled more enthusiastically.

He stooped, ah, so little resistance, the weakling, he stooped and kissed the crown of my head.

I slid my arms around his waist.

His lips moved over my hair to the nape of my neck, and rested there. "Rest" is not the word: they were extremely active, and, as that part of the body is a most erogenous zone for me, I was immediately seized with an overwhelming desire for him: my thighs trembled, my whole body lost its strength and in an instant was transformed to that delicious liquid essence of itself which, seeming vapid and without substance, is so insidiously - or delightfully - powerful. As Karl kissed me on my back, my breast, and began to explore more deeply with his hands, I was obliged to make a huge effort to regain my sense of purpose. Just in time I succeeded, although not without pain, in restoring my equanimity.

Karl was clearly making no such attempt at self-control. Like a boy in a school sex manual, he allowed himself to be completely carried away, and became the mere instrument of his passion. Realising it, I caressed him with seeming desire and tenderness. My hands roamed from his shoulders to his waist, and thence to his ample hips. And there it was, what I sought: something oblong and hard, under the thick cloth. Slowly I reached into his back- pocket and grabbed it: the notebook.

Immediately I sprang back.

"Your notebook!" I waved it aloft and smiled in joyous triumph. "And now, if you don't mind, I'll take a quick glance at it. There's nothing in it, of course, as you say, so no harm..."

I did not finish my sentence. Karl, whose face had assumed the expression of some ferocious animal's - a lion's, perhaps, or a wild boar's - pounced on me and pinned me to the deck in what can only be described as a vice-like grip.

I have heard that men interrupted during sexual intercourse can behave with great violence. It is sometimes said that Othello's chronicled murder of Desdemona arose largely from sexual frustration. But this was a bit much! We had not been having sex, after all - just a spot of mild flirting!

"You bloody bitch!" Karl snarled. "You bloody devil of a bitch!"

And then, instead of seizing his property, which I had expected him to do, he aimed a series of vicious blows at my face; then grabbed my nose and twisted it until I thought it must fall off.

His face seemed dark to me. Moorish.

His atavistic behaviour had unfortunate consequences for him: had he merely taken what rightfully belonged to him, I would have given in, and accepted that I was vanquished. But his arbitrary brutality aroused my anger, and gave me a strength I had not known I possessed, the sort of miraculous vigour granted to mothers rescuing their offspring from beneath the wheels of steam-rollers or kings' sons lifting rocks off swords. With just such an injection of divine power, I managed, somehow, to release one of my hands, and I tried to scratch his eyes out. Simultaneously I kicked him in the crotch, according to the best advice of all self-defence instructors. He fell back momentarily and I rose to my knees. Sensing, rather than seeing, that he was about to attack again, I resorted to the only course left to me: I shot him.

I did not, of course, intend to kill. Murder had never been part of my plan. But since I had never used a gun before, my aim was less than perfect. By sheer chance, I got him in the temple, and not in the knee, as I had planned. He cried out once, and fell. Seeing the blood seeping from the side of his head, and noting that he was not breathing, with one last burst of energy I pushed him under the rail of the boat and into the North Sea: surely the ocean he would have chosen for his final resting place, had he had a choice.

Not allowing myself the luxury of watching him disappear into the winey water, I moved swiftly to the control room and increased our speed by several knots.

Jenny and Karen, who had not heard my shot, since my gun has a very efficient silencer, now responded to the change in pace and the swelling noise of the engine. They came running to the control room.

"Hey, what's going on here? Why are we going so damned fast all of a sudden?" Karen shouted angrily.

Jenny looked closely at me and then ran out on deck, with a little squeal.

A minute passed in silence. Then Jenny returned to the engine room.

"Where is Karl?"

"I've no idea," I said, smoothing my dishevelled hair with my hand. I felt rather hot. "Isn't he up on deck? He was there ten minutes ago: I was speaking to him myself."

"He is not there now," she said grimly.

Then suddenly her face turned pale and she sat down.

"Look in our cabin, Karen, will you?"

"But..." Karen gave me a suspicious look, and went out. In a few minutes she returned.

"He's not on the boat," she said, in a shockingly calm voice. She sat down beside Jenny and put her arm around her.

"Where is he, Robin?" she asked, simply.

"I've no idea."

"Then he must be..."

"I've no idea," I repeated.

"Robin has no idea," Karen looked at Jenny, hopelessly. The latter seemed dazed. Shrugging, Karen helped her up and they moved to Jenny's cabin.

Later, some hours later, I went to Jenny and told her that Karl had shot himself.

I have difficulty now in understanding exactly why I did not made a clean breast of it. Because, of course, I had been in the right: I had killed Karl by accident, and in self-defence. Had I not shot him, he would certainly have murdered me. Under the circumstances, it was more important that I should be the survivor, that I should see the *Saint Patrick* safely back to port, that I should present "The Bray House" to the world. Besides which, I have an elementary and entirely understandable wish to survive.

Perhaps I realised instinctively that the shock would have been too much for Jenny. Perhaps I suspected that, had I told her the whole truth, she would have tried to kill me. And what would have been the point of causing further aggression?

Yes, I think I had hesitated because the truth seemed overly complicated. And also, of course, to give myself time to come to terms with the new situation.

Jenny did not in any event accept the news calmly. She immediately wept and screamed and protested, she wrung her hands and beat her head against the wall. Her reaction, in fact, was such that in the end I forced her to take a sedative, a strong dose which knocked her out for twenty-four hours.

In the meantime, I examined the notebook.

It included an inventory of the artefacts found in the tumulus - mostly empty baked bean cans and cereal packets, as well as one skeleton, some inscribed stones, a well, and the woman - who was here referred to as Maggie Byrne, not Elinor MacHugh. There were some elliptical descriptions of this individual, and notes on her background, which had been so hastily and haphazardly jotted down that I had difficulty in deciphering them. Much more care had been devoted to the transcription of the writings on the stones: these I immediately recognised as Ogham, but was unable to interpret since I am not an Old Irish scholar, as it happens. In any case, I found them much less interesting than the information about my passenger.

I went in to her.

"Ok, Maggie," I said. "No use pretending any more. The game's up: I know you can talk."

Maggie-Elinor smirked and did not, of course, say a thing.

"I've seen the notebook Karl kept while he was with you in the mound," I continued. "I understand from that that you can talk, and that you have spoken already, to Karl and Jenny."

Maggie-Elinor looked simply sad.

"Karl," I said then, "is dead. He killed himself and fell overboard earlier this evening. Unfortunate tragedy. Such a fine young man too."

I moved to the door.

"I thought you'd like to know, Maggie. And I wanted to be the one to tell you. Goodbye now. See you later."

Chapter Twenty-four

Maggie told her story.

She was not, of course, Elinor MacHugh, but one Margaret Byrne, a housewife from the small town of Rathdrum, near Wicklow Town. She was - had been - the wife of a carpenter, Eddie, who did odd jobs for people and made furniture for a shop that sold rustic reproductions in Bray. That, in fact, was her only link with Bray; she rarely even set foot in the place, apart from making an occasional visit to its bigger supermarkets to shop. But mostly Maggie shopped in Wicklow or Dublin, she told me. Her opinion of Bray as a marketplace was low: "hopeless, sure you'd never get a decent stitch in it, not what you'd need for an occasion, like." She had never heard of the MacHugh's, she said. She did not know if Murphy had been a solicitor in Bray or not, but she had never had any contact with the legal profession, so she really wouldn't be the one to ask.. MacHugh was not a common name in Rathdrum. She knew nobody of that name, at all, in Rathdrum or Wicklow or anywhere.

Her explanation as to how she had come to survive the Ballylumford disaster was the following: her husband, who had been a cautious and somewhat alarmist man, generally regarded as "a bundle of nerves", or "neurotic", had, as soon as the first news of the meltdown came through, insisted that they hide away immediately. He'd been studying a Civil Defence booklet on the subject of nuclear disasters and how to cope with them which had been issued by the government when he was a boy about fifty years previously, she said. He'd had been totally fascinated by its strategy for survival: "turn your back to the flash, wrap yourself in a warm garment, eg an overcoat. Hide under the stairs". For years he'd been storing up cans of beans and bottles of paracetomol, and his great secret hobby had been the fitting-out of an underground chamber he'd discovered not far from the village as a nuclear fall-out shelter. He was actually delighted with the news from Ballylumford: "he didn't admit as much but you could see it on him" Maggie said "he was like a cat with a bowl of cream, he really was. It's an awful thing to say but it's the plain truth." After all, he'd been waiting for a very long time for a chance to put his shelter to the test, and it had begun to look as if he wouldn't ever do it. Talk of denuclearisation and *Perestroika* had depressed him greatly in the recent past. After each summit in Reykjavik or Seoul or Mullingar, he'd been seriously worried lest the march of history be diverted and the nuclear disaster he'd anticipated all his life should finally be obviated. What had kept him going was the Greenhouse threat. He was delighted when he first heard that the only simple way of protecting the earth from this even more horrifying hazard would be rapid world-wide nuclearisation. Green talk about wind and ocean energy he had, like most people in Ireland, dismissed as so much well-meaning naïveté. Natural power was all very well, but... Sure we all needed our instant lights and cookers and washing machines and cars. Can you drive a car on wind power?

More and more nuclear stations, that's what the world needed, and that's what it got. And Eddie was happy. This threat was for him. He could cope with it. Sure he'd got the old Civil Defence Booklet to guide him. But nobody could have helped him to survive the rising sea-levels, the high temperatures, the famines, the plagues of insects, that the Greenhouse affect would bring about. Bombs and explosions any day, rather than a million rats invading your garden shed.

"It wasn't that he really hoped they'd push the button on us, but like it gave him something to plan for, a sort of reason for living, if you get my meaning. It was like he was looking forward to something that was never going to happen really, but he didn't know if it'd happen or not, and he didn't want to know for certain that it wasn't ever going to. Do you see what I mean?" What she meant was that he greeted the news of the imminent disaster seriously and with joy, whereas everyone else in Rathdrum - which we can take as representative of Ireland on the whole - reacted to it by worrying and shrugging their shoulders, if they paid any attention to it at all, and according to Maggie many of them did not.

"But with Eddie it was action stations straight away. Before you could say Jack Robinson he had a couple of old cases packed with clothes and crossword puzzles and cards and a few other odds and ends, and we were in the station wagon and on our way to the Cat's Hill, as we called it. And before the next news bulletin came on the radio we were safe inside the hill, me and Eddie and all our goods and chattels. He was quick, I'll give him that."

Which was just as well. Because they'd been in the tumulus for less than half a day when the news began to get much more grave. Before nightfall the explosions had started. Maggie had wanted to go out and take a look, but Eddie had insisted that she stay inside, facing south, away from the North where the first explosion had, of course, occurred. She did, and very soon there were no more radio messages, just them and their supplies and their crossword puzzles. She'd knitted herself, mostly, since she didn't like to read or to do crosswords: she was knitting a cardigan for her granddaughter: pink blackberry stitch.

"The awfullest part of it all was the boredom," she said. "I really and truly thought I'd go out of my tree with boredom, I really did, I'm not telling you a lie. To be perfectly honest with you, after about a week of it I wished to God I'd been killed like everyone else. I would have preferred that to being stuck in that awful place with nothing at all to do and nobody to have a chat with bar Eddie, who never was much of a one for the chat, I have to admit."

Eddie stuck it better than she did initially. He was after all psychologically as well as physically prepared for the event. He'd been looking forward to it for so long, and besides I gathered that he was more resourceful than she was, more able to amuse himself. He enjoyed working through his crosswords, and counting all his jars and cans and packages, and thinking up recipes for the food they had. He found plenty of work to do. Maggie, on the contrary, was not used to finding her own entertainment and had no inner resourcefulness. She was also too honest to pretend to herself that there was real work to be done, or that there was any point in doing it.

"Sure anyone can let on there's work to be done, no matter where they are. They can let on it's important and it's necessary and all the rest of it. But it isn't always, really. Really Eddie acted as if it was a matter of life or death that we washed up the plates after every meal and that we made our beds in the morning and all that. He planned out the days for himself: three hours work, two hours sleep, one hours exercise, three hours amusement, and so on. He said it was important to be organised, that survival was going to be hard work. But he was just letting on to himself that it was. He didn't know that, now, I'm not saying he did. But it was all just a game, just a way to put in time. And I couldn't be bothered. Putting in time till what? "

Eddie, however, was a believer in a cause. He maintained that they would be saved. The literature he had read had encouraged this credence: it had convinced him that after a reasonable period, which he assessed as a month, things would be getting back to some sort of normality, and "help" would be available. Red Cross, United Nations, International Relief Committees, something along those lines. Part of his programme was to leave the tumulus and assess the situation when a month had passed.

And this he did.

She broke down and cried, relating this part of the saga. Her account of the event was less than coherent. But obviously what had happened was that his spirit and health had broken, and soon after his outing he had died.

She assumed that she would die too, soon. But she didn't. There was ample food, and she continued to eat. She had an infinite supply of fresh water. Time passed, and she was really going mad, she said, by which she appeared to mean that she talked to herself and was very distressed. Eventually she decided to go outside herself, and take a look. She had nothing to lose, she would have been happy enough to die anyway.

So she went out, saw what there was to see, and survived.

"It was shocking, naturally, really shocking," she said. "But the funny thing was that after I seen it it wasn't so bad anymore. I don't know why, it's kind of funny. But I felt a bit better after that. And of course I could go for walks and things and that made it more interesting too."

"Did you ever see us, before we saw you?" I asked, curiously.

"No. No, I didn't. Not till Karl and Jenny came, and then I seen them, all right, before they saw me. I seen them soon after they came, and I was so frightened, isn't it funny? I went in and swore I'd never come out till they were gone. But then I sneaked out to have another look and they saw me and that was it, then. Thanks be to God. And now Karl is gone and me here. Isn't life funny, isn't it really?"

Apart from her story, which was of course fascinating in its way, I did not record very much from Maggie at this point. I was, frankly, disappointed that she was not a member of the MacHugh family. Although I had had my suspicions about her identity from the moment she came on board, I had clung to the hope that she was one of the MacHugh's, not Elinor, necessarily, but at least Annie. I had looked forward to reading my report to her, to having her comments on it. Her confirmation that my theories were correct. Ah, what an experience that would have been, what a dream come true! Ultimate proof that I was the world's most perceptive archaeo-anthropologist!

As Jenny was quick to point out, however, that would have been a bit too neat, it would have been too much to expect.

"So you really thought she was one of the MacHughs?" she asked with a venomous grin. Since Karl's accident, her personality had undergone a remarkable change. Not only was she suffused with grief, as one could have anticipated. She had also become quite bitter. Bitchy, in fact.

"You told me she was."

"Ah, what a pity, Robin! The dream didn't come true after all?"

"I never dream, least of all about professional matters."

"Wouldn't it be luverley! All I want is a real MacHugh, proving that everything I said is true!"

"Or the opposite."

"Opposite? You'd have made sure it wasn't, or I'm a monkey's aunt. Getting hold of a real live MacHugh before you've published a line, delivered a single lecture. Somehow I think your story, Robin, the story archaeologists are always trying so hard to tell with scraps of clay and broken bones, would have tallied with her's. I think that would have somehow happened, don't you?"

"Yes. Because of course my story is true. It doesn't need a MacHugh to prove it. It's true because my methodology is foolproof: positivistic and holistic. It has to work. Solid empirical research, rigid logical analysis, coupled with a vast knowledge of all circumstantial data. The story I'll write is the true story of the MacHughs. Even if a MacHugh came along and suggested otherwise, I would believe that. The MacHugh would be wrong."

Jenny frowned.

"Well, luckily one didn't."

"Yes. That is my good fortune. Because if one did, perhaps there would be no point in telling my story. Or doing my work."

"Is there anyway?" she laughed facetiously, but uncertainly.

"Yes. As long as there's no MacHugh around to tell it. If there were, she or he could do that, I would be redundant, obviously. It's only when there's nobody telling the story, nobody writing it, indeed, when nobody has ever written it, that archaeologists need to step in."

"That seems to mean that nobody ever knows whether what they discover is worth a fig or not."

"A fig?"

"True."

"True?"

"True!"

"It's always true, as long as they play by the rules."

"So it's all some sort of game."

"My dear, but of course!"

The truth was, I was disappointed, for the reasons she'd outlined. But there was nothing I could do about it, and in any event, Maggie was an important find, highly significant, and would have much of interest to relate concerning life in Rathdrum, its social customs, its beliefs and practices, its kinship systems, etc, which would be invaluable. But I felt it could wait for the future: there would be ample opportunity when we got to Sweden to interview her on these and many other topics.

In the meantime, there were other problems to be dealt with: when she wasn't quarrelling with me, Jenny was behaving with most inconvenient melodrama. She lay in her bunk for hours, days on end, and wept, refusing all comfort, food, drink. Even medication was flung in my face.

"She should be allowed to grieve naturally," Karen said. "We'll simply have to carry on without her. She can't do anything in the state she's in."

"It's not going to be easy, just the two of us."

"It's your own fault," she snapped. "Anyway it's only a matter of a day or two."

Jenny refused, even when she was in a relatively calm state of mind, to offer any assistance in the running of the boat. So for the final leg of the voyage, then, Karen and I worked ceaselessly, getting only a few hours' sleep. We managed, because we were obliged to. But by the time we reached port, we were almost dead with exhaustion.

I snatched an hour's sleep, however, just before we came to Gothenburg, and made sure to shower and groom myself for the reception which I anticipated. I assumed that the port would be thronged with journalists, media people, and members of the public generally.

Imagine my surprise, everyone's surprise, to find that there was nobody at all to greet us, not a single soul, even though I had radioed to Uppsala and to Swedish Radio to let them know that we were about to come home. Instead of enthusiastic crowds and avid reporters, a doctor, a customs official, and a representative of the State Detention centres met us, and told us that we were to be quarantined for fourteen days. I protested, of course, but to no avail. I, and the others, I assumed, although we were separated, were carried off to hospital in special ambulances and kept under strict medical supervision and the observation of some interested scientists for two weeks. I had no contact with Karen, Jenny or Maggie during that time, although I constantly demanded the right to see them. I was especially concerned about the latter, my most valuable discovery: I began to worry lest she fall into the wrong hands, again. But I was assured that she was being remanded in complete isolation, and would be kept in that state for at least six months.

"She'll go crazy," I protested to the doctor who told me this. He smiled ironically, and said in his quiet cool voice: "I do not think so."

At the end of a fortnight, just as I anticipated release, and return to Uppsala, I was moved from the Gothenburg

Hospital to the State Prison, where a police superintendent informed that I was under arrest, accused of the murder of Karl Larsson. I laughed and denied the accusation, but was remanded, nevertheless, and advised to contact an advocate. Luckily I remembered an old college friend, whom I telephoned. He agreed, somewhat reluctantly, to defend me, and came to Gothenburg to discuss the case with me. We were in agreement that the prosecuting counsel had not a chance, since there was not a shred of evidence against me. Although perfectly confident of the outcome of the trial, I was irritated by the time I was losing in prison, and by the attention which this aspect of my situation was getting, to the disadvantage of the voyage and my report on the Irish findings: I watched the media reportage of my case with interest, and was horrified to find that, apart from one or two brief interviews with Maggie Byrne, absolutely no coverage of the Ireland Excavation had occurred. Instead, half of every news bulletin seemed to be devoted to my so-called murder of Karl, and it was clear that the whole country awaited my trial with great glee. A month was to pass before it could take place, a month which I found trying in the extreme. I busied myself with this Report, and with other articles and features on the Bray House excavations, and I planned the exhibition of artefacts, photographs, etc which I wished to mount as soon as possible at the Archive in Uppsala.

At last the day of the trial arrived, and I had the pleasure of seeing, in the court-room and on the witness stand, Jenny - noticeably pregnant, to my great amazement - Karen, very svelte and louche, in a black leather suit, and Maggie, looking considerably older and sicker than she had on the *Saint Patrick*. I guessed that Swedish life was not agreeing with her: she had that glazed look I have noted before on the inmates of state institutions. A look of absolute capitulation. Gothenburg Old Folks' Home, incidentally regarded as one of the very best in the world, had done for her in six weeks what the combined experiences of Cats Hill, the *Saint Patrick*, *not* to speak of Rathdrum or Ireland, had failed to do over several years. She was finished. Killed by systematic institutional care at its most perfect. (I would not call it "kindness").

The case was heard, the witnesses called to give evidence, and the jury despatched to make its decision. It all passed off very calmly, although Jenny, looking pale and thin, in spite of the mound of her belly, gave an excellent and moving performance as the bereaved girlfriend. Not a dry eye in the court-room, and Lennart, my lawyer, whispered, "pity about that pregnancy!" I merely shrugged. Pregnancy or no pregnancy, I knew justice would be done.

It was: the Swedish system is nothing if not fair. Acquitted, I walked out of the court-room and caught the next train home. To my gratification, there was a large flurry of reporters and cameras outside the courthouse and a small band of them at the station. Their questions referred exclusively to the trial, but I managed to divert attention to the excavation and the exhibition which I was planning to hold at the earliest opportunity. Most of my comments regarding it and related matters were, predictably, cut from the actual news features, which concentrated only on the more scurrilous and sensational aspects of my story. But a few important messages succeeded in getting delivered.

Once in Uppsala, I deposited all the finds from the Bray House at the archive and discussed with the director the possibility of having them exhibited immediately. She was unfriendly but agreed that the sooner the exhibition was mounted the better: interest in it would fade, she nodded, if something were not done soon.

But she stalled.

She stalled.

There was another exhibition which had been booked in for years. It would have to be held first.

The exhibition hall was being rewired.

The artefacts were, perhaps, dangerous. A thorough investigation would have to take place, to ensure that they were no longer radioactive.

Such an examination was eventually carried out. Experts suggested that a period of five years be allowed to elapse, before an exhibition would be displayed. In the meantime, the material was to remain locked in its sealed boxes, and should not be touched by human hands.

I realised that there would be no exhibition.

There would be no television documentaries on the excavation. There would be no chatshows, with me and Maggie and Karen telling the world about our experiences.

There would be nothing, because there was no interest.

Even Karen and Jenny were not interested any more.

"No I will not meet you," Karen replied, when I rang her up and asked. "I don't care about the negative response to the expedition, I'm sick of it and you and I don't want to hear of either it or you ever again. I've got my life to live, you know."

Jenny would not speak to me at all. Whenever I phoned, she answered and then slammed down the receiver. Eventually she changed address. I lost any thread that linked me to her.

Maggie Byrne remained in Gothenburg, at the home. What surprised me more than anything else was the lack of popular interest in her. But, apart from one or two profiles in the national newspapers, and a longish interview on television, nobody paid any attention whatsoever to her. My worries that she would be lionised by the media, and assaulted on all sides by researchers and scientists, could not have been more futile.

Not an anthropologist, a sociologist, a psychologist, much less an historian, bothered to interview her. When I, on a rare visit to Gothenburg, asked her if she found her guests a nuisance, she said: "Sure I never see a soul. The only one who comes to see me at all is a priest, Father Olsen, his name is, God be good to him. All he does is ask me "Are you fighting fit, Mrs Byrne? That is good. Will you attend our Mass tomorrow then?" Then he's off like the hammers of hell. I don't think his English is up to scratch, to tell you the truth. That or he's not a talkative man."

I prepared a series of question lists for Maggie, and planned to do a number of interviews with her on various topics. But so far I have only succeeded in doing one. I am beginning to fear that my own interest in Ireland, like that of everyone else, is fading. There is so much else to think about: a new trip to space which is bringing back rocks and other materials which scientists will investigate with a view to finding new sources of energy for earth's needs; several teams of investigators have been to England, to southern Europe, examining the effects of Ballylumford on various locations. There is no longer anything new or startling about our finds, at least, that is what popular opinion holds. I, of course, know better. No other investigation has been so thorough, or had such exciting results as ours. This much will, I hope, be clear to anyone who has read my report on *The Bray House* and compared it to the others which have so far been produced.

Epilogue

Svenska Dagbladet, 3 December.

This morning the well known archaeologist Robin Lagerlof, who was recently involved in a murder trial, committed suicide at her home in Uppsala. It is thought that Dr Lagerlof shot herself in the early hours of the morning. A porter in the apartment building where she lives found her when he was on his rounds at six am.

Dr Lagerlof had a very distinguished career as an archaeologist and an anthropologist, and was renowned throughout the world. She published several books in her field, the best known of which is *The Whale Race: A study of the Faroe Islanders*. Recently, she has led a unique expedition to Ireland, to excavate sites there, and was responsible for rescuing from Ireland a survivor of the Ballylumford disaster, Mrs Maggie Byrne, who is now an inmate of St Birgitta's Old People's Home in Gothenburg.

An exhibition on the Ireland excavations will open early next year at the Archaeology Archive in Uppsala, and Dr Lagerlof's book on the expedition, which was completed before her death, will be published posthumously on the same occasion.

Commenting on her career and achievement, Dr Kurt Svensson, Professor of Archaeology at Uppsala University, said "She was the most remarkable archaeologist of her time in Sweden. Although I did not always agree with her point of view, I believe she will be remembered as one of the greatest thinkers in the world of Swedish scholarship. We have lost in her one of the truly original minds of the age."